Praise for the authors of
HAPPILY EVER AFTER IN THE WEST

DEBRA COWAN

Cowan's stories have the charm, tenderness and sensuality
that captivate and enchant."
—*RT Book Reviews*

"Merging the elements of homespun,
Americana romance with a strong western atmosphere,
Cowan succeeds at tackling big themes in a tender way."
—*RT Book Reviews* on *Whirlwind Secrets*

LYNNA BANNING

"Marc and Soraya's love story is touching, and the plot
will make you wonder until the last page how they will get together."
—*RT Book Reviews* on *C_____ _ady*

"…poignant tale of a w___ ___ ___ …"
—*RT Book R___ ___*

"A fine writer wi__ ___ ___ ___ ___ ___rming sensitivity."
___ ___Morsi

"The charac__ ___ ___ touching sentiments
have ___ ___ly warm appeal."
—*RT Book R___ ___s* on *The Hired Husband*

DEBRA COWAN

Like many writers, Debra Cowan made up stories in her head as a child. Her BA in English was obtained with the intention of following family tradition and becoming a schoolteacher, but after she wrote her first novel, there was no looking back. An avid history buff, Debra writes both historical and contemporary romances. Born in the foothills of the Kiamichi Mountains, Debra still lives in her native Oklahoma with her husband. Debra loves to hear from readers. You can contact her via her website at www.debracowan.net.

LYNNA BANNING

has combined a lifelong love of history and literature into a satisfying career as a writer. Born in Oregon, she has lived in Northern California most of her life. After graduating from Scripps College, she embarked on a career as an editor and technical writer, and later, as a high school English teacher.

An amateur pianist and harpsichordist, Lynna performs on psaltery and harp in a medieval music ensemble and coaches in her spare time. She enjoys hearing from her readers. You may write to her directly at P.O. Box 324, Felton, CA 95018, or at carolynw@cruzio.com. Visit Lynna's website at www.lynnabanning.com.

JUDITH STACY

fell in love with the West while watching TV Westerns as a child in her rural Virginia home—one of the first in the community to have a television. This wild-west setting, with its strong men and resourceful women, remains one of her favorites. Judith is married to her high school sweetheart. They have two daughters and live in Southern California. Look in on Judith's website at www.judithstacy.com She also writes contemporary novels under the name of Dorothy Howell.

HAPPILY EVER AFTER
in the West

WESTERN
WEDDINGS

DEBRA COWAN

LYNNA BANNING

JUDITH STACY

TORONTO NEW YORK LONDON
AMSTERDAM PARIS SYDNEY HAMBURG
STOCKHOLM ATHENS TOKYO MILAN MADRID
PRAGUE WARSAW BUDAPEST AUCKLAND

ISBN-13: 978-0-373-29639-2

HAPPILY EVER AFTER IN THE WEST
Copyright © 2011 by Harlequin Books S.A.

The publisher acknowledges the copyright
holders of the individual works as follows:

WHIRLWIND REDEMPTION
Copyright © 2011 by Debra S. Cowan

THE MAVERICK AND MISS PRIM
Copyright © 2011 by The Woolston Family Trust

TEXAS CINDERELLA
Copyright © 2011 by Dorothy Howell

Recycling programs
for this product may
not exist in your area.

Printed in U.S.A.

CONTENTS

WHIRLWIND REDEMPTION

Debra Cowan

Dear Reader,

From the time Quentin Prescott appeared in *Whirlwind Baby,* he elicited a strong reaction from readers. Half of my mail indicated people didn't like Quentin at all and the other half believed he could be redeemed by love. I wasn't sure.

Quentin lost his only family seven years ago when his sister and her unborn child died. He blamed their deaths on his brother-in-law. Mired in grief and rage, he tried to kill the man and the ensuing gunfight caused Quentin to lose the use of his legs. Embittered after being told he would never walk again, he pushed away the woman he had been quietly seeing and had fallen in love with, Zoe Keeler.

While I wrote other books, Quentin remained in the back of my mind and I realized he *could* be redeemed. Who better to understand this man than a woman who has had her own share of hard knocks, but has handled them in a completely different way?

Zoe was orphaned while still young and assumed responsibility for a deaf older sister, as well as a slow-thinking brother. She's never gotten over Quentin's abrupt ending of their relationship and she has no intention of letting him hurt her again. When she needs help, he's the last person she wants to ask, but he's the one person who can offer everything she needs if she will just give him a second chance. I hope you enjoy their story.

Happy trails,

Debra Cowan

To Keyren and Mike
Happiness Always

Chapter One

West Texas, 1886

Approaching the stage that would take her to Abilene, Zoe Keeler felt as if she were going to the woodshed. The very idea of having to ask her grandfather for anything irritated her so much that her entire body prickled with a heat that had nothing to do with the warm May morning.

The Whirlwind stagecoach waited in front of the stage stand between Pete Carter's saloon and the livery he also owned. She hung back as her younger brother, Zeke, clambered into the coach that would take them to the meeting that already had her stomach tied in knots. The urge to grab her brother and go back home was nearly overwhelming.

Instead, she opened her reticule and pulled out the telegram concerning her sister—worn from being read so many times. Dinah's tuition at the Connecticut Asylum for the Instruction of Deaf and Dumb Persons at Hartford was due in less than a month and it had been increased by fifty dollars.

It might as well be five thousand. Zoe sighed. She simply

didn't have the money. Or the means to get it, she admitted. Last year's drought had brought hard times to everyone. Many of her friends and acquaintances were having as hard a time as she was making ends meet.

Palms clammy, she smoothed down the skirt of her navy serge traveling dress trimmed in white then adjusted her matching navy felt bowler hat. Both had been a Christmas gift from Josie Holt, the seamstress who sometimes employed Zoe.

She didn't know why she bothered trying to look smart. Her mother had never measured up in Grandfather Upton's eyes; there was no reason to think Zoe would either. But knowing she wore her best clothes gave her a little bit of confidence.

Even so, she'd be a bundle of nerves by the time she faced her mother's father.

Zeke was settled. Pete had stowed their one valise and was waiting in the high seat. She moved around the back of the stage and toward the open door. A wooden step had been placed there for assistance in boarding.

As she slipped the telegram back into her reticule, a sun-darkened masculine hand appeared to help her inside.

"Thanks, Pete." She glanced over, her smile dying as her gaze collided with Quentin Prescott's.

His hand tightened on hers as if he could tell she wanted to pull away, which she did. He sat in the wheelchair he'd used for the past seven years, bronzed skin stretched taut over his sharp features. His black hair and mustache were neatly trimmed, his dark eyes sparking with a light she hadn't seen since his injury.

Zoe couldn't tear her gaze away. The broad shoulders and muscular arms gave testament to how active he was despite being chair-bound.

Neither of them went out of their way to avoid each other in the course of a day, but they kept their distance.

What was going on? His gaze held hers, softened. Lands! The last time he had looked at her that way was before his legs had become paralyzed and he had pushed her away as though she was diseased.

The flash of uncertainty on his face said he expected her to pull away at any moment. She tried again, but his hand tightened on hers. Taken aback at finding him so close, at his touching her, she could only stare.

Her brother leaned out the open window. "Hi, Quentin!"

"Zeke." The man's voice was deliciously low, causing a flutter in her stomach.

Realizing that the driver was staring as hard as her brother, Zoe quickly climbed inside and released Quentin's hand.

"Thank you," she murmured, arranging her skirts, cursing the heat crawling up her neck. As fair as she was, there was no chance Quentin would miss that. No one would.

"Going to Abilene?" he asked.

She nodded, her palms clammy now for a reason that had nothing to do with her grandfather.

He glanced at the driver. "Pete, you armed?"

The other man gave an indignant snort.

"Good." At Zoe's frown, Quentin said, "Matt Baldwin finally caught the rustlers who've been hitting this area."

"The Landis brothers?" she asked.

"Yes. They were all killed in a shoot-out yesterday except for one. Bram Ross is on his trail."

"That would be Cosgrove," Zoe said. Pete had mentioned that the man formerly believed to be a ranch manager was actually the head of a gang of rustlers.

She wondered if she should postpone her trip.

Quentin seemed to read her mind. "You should be safe. Pete's armed and if Cosgrove were anywhere nearby, Bram would've already caught him and hauled him back here."

The unmistakable look of concern in his eyes had resentment bubbling up. Since when did Quentin bother himself over her welfare?

She nodded. She might as well get this visit over and done.

Biting her lip, she looked away from the man who could still put a flutter in her belly. "Ready, Pete."

"Yes'm." The bowlegged man clucked to the team of four horses and snapped the reins.

The stage lurched into motion. Just before it reached the edge of town, Zoe eased toward the window, enough to peek out.

Quentin was still there in his wheelchair, watching.

He smiled, a slow warm smile that traveled right through her to the tips of her toes.

He lifted a hand in goodbye and she jerked her gaze away. She didn't know what he was up to, but she wasn't dancing that dance again. Seven years had passed since they had parted ways. Since they had kissed.

The memory of those kisses still sent a ripple across her nerves like a pebble over water. They were kisses she'd spent a lot of time trying to forget.

Humph. She didn't care how sweetly he smiled or how his voice did things to her insides. They were finished. He'd made sure of that.

Zeke settled back in his seat, humming with excitement. His blue eyes shone with his usual good humor. "Quentin said he would show me his bees sometime. He said I could come to his job at the newspaper, too, but I knew you wouldn't like me doing those things."

Zoe frowned. Though he was as big as any man, her brother was still a teenager.

"But you're friends again," he said excitedly. "So I can."

Zoe and Quentin weren't friends, but she didn't have the heart to correct her brother. Not for the first time, she wished things were as uncomplicated for her as they were for Zeke, whose mind worked a little more slowly than most people's did.

"He's really smart, huh?"

About most things, she thought grimly.

Zoe wished her brother would stop talking about Quentin Prescott. She had bigger things to worry about, like her upcoming meeting with Grandfather.

Four hours later, she and Zeke stood in Burl Upton's grand library on the first floor of his mansion just east of Abilene. The three-story stone house was fancy and modern. Grandfather had employed an engineer to build advanced mechanical systems for gas lighting, central heating and indoor plumbing with hot and cold running water.

Because her mother had been estranged from her grandfather, Zoe had never set foot in this house. She had learned all about it from the livery hand who had driven her and Zeke out here.

They'd been allowed to wash up in a bathing room that rivaled the fancy ones in Whirlwind's new hotel. And she'd been shocked to see a tintype of her mother on one wall in the foyer. Now, Zoe's eyes were as big as Zeke's as they stared around the spacious library with two walls of filled bookshelves, a massive oak desk and a hulking leather chair behind it.

Sunshine streamed in through a bank of windows along the opposite wall. The dark wood floor was polished to a sheen, covered by a large rug in muted reds and golds. A gold velvet-clothed settee and three matching chairs provided a separate area for sitting. The entire Keeler house would fit in this library with room to spare.

Zoe didn't care about that. Surely Grandfather could see his way to giving her the inheritance left by her mother so Dinah could stay at school. Once she began attending the special school, Zoe's older sister had rapidly learned sign language. She was now catching up on subjects she'd been forced to miss at regular school due to her deafness.

At the sound of heavy footsteps entering the room behind them, Zoe stiffened. Zeke pressed his man-size body closer to her. A tall—*very* tall—man walked behind the desk.

Blue eyes, the same shade as Zoe's and Zeke's, fixed on them. Apprehension skittered through her. Burl Upton lowered himself into the big leather chair that had probably been specially made for his size. He gestured to the pair of chairs in front of his desk, saying in a harsh, deep voice, "Have a seat."

Zoe's spine went to steel. "We'd like to stand, please."

"Stubborn, just like your mama." Beneath his slightly graying red hair, the older man's sharp gaze settled impassively on her face. "You look just like her."

Well, that wouldn't work in her favor.

She hoped that when Dinah's situation was explained, the man's heart would soften and he would just give Zoe the money or pay her sister's tuition.

Squirming under the hard gaze of the imposing figure in front of her, she told him about the telegram she'd received a month ago, ending with, "There just isn't enough work for me right now to earn the amount I need for her tuition."

"Work? What kind of work?" he asked sharply.

"Sometimes I help a seamstress. Other times, I fill in at Whirlwind's general store. I also have a steady part-time job at the Fontaine, our new hotel."

With each job she named, her grandfather's jaw clenched tighter.

By the time she finished, a vein was throbbing in his temple. "None of that is fit for a young lady. You should be married, tending to youngsters of your own."

Marriage and children were about as likely for her as flying to the moon. She had only ever considered marrying one man and any chance of that had ended years ago.

Upton looked her up and down critically. "You know the terms of your mother's inheritance so that must mean you're asking me for this money because you're about to be married."

Zoe couldn't bring herself to outright lie. "I want to keep Dinah in her special school back east."

"So, who's the lucky groom-to-be and when's the ceremony?"

Although she could later say the engagement hadn't worked out, she was loathe to name anyone. For one thing, most eligible men in Whirlwind were far too old or far too young for her.

Her friend, Mitchell Orr, would probably marry her for a satisfactory amount of time without expecting anything of her, but he was sweet on a young widow over in Merkel. Zoe knew he wouldn't risk losing what he had with her. If their roles were reversed, she wouldn't either.

"Well, girl," the older man prodded. "Who's this man you fancy?"

Zeke beamed at Grandfather. "Zoe loves Quentin."

She went completely stock-still, nearly swallowing her teeth. Had her brother really said that?

"Quentin who?" Burl demanded.

"Quentin Prescott," Zeke replied.

"Zeke," Zoe began.

Her brother continued, "He has bees and they make honey. He's going to show me how to take care of them."

The older man's eyes narrowed. "Is this true, girl?"

"Yes." She knew what her grandfather was asking, but she preferred to answer his question about Quentin's beekeeping.

She reached for Zeke's large hand and squeezed, hoping he

would understand not to volunteer any further information. He looked at her, his smile fading as if he picked up on the tension in the room.

"And the date of the wedding?" Upton asked.

It was ridiculous that she had to marry in order to get the money her mother had left her. "Um, we're not exactly sure. Soon."

The old man nodded, studying her through narrowed eyes. For the first time, Zoe noticed he had the same blunt jawline as her brother.

She held her breath. He had to give her the money. He just had to.

"I'll transfer the funds into your account at the bank."

"You will?" Her relief was so great her knees felt weak. Now Dinah could stay in school. "Thank you. Thank you so much."

"When I return from your wedding."

"What?" she choked out, panic welling up inside her.

He rose, his big shadow stretching across his desk. "I have no intention of missing the wedding of my one grandchild who's likely to marry."

"But—"

"Is there some reason you don't want me to attend?" His gaze, challenging and smug, pinned her to the spot.

Oooh, the mean old geezer knew she was lying. Well, she wouldn't give him the satisfaction of admitting it. "No. Of course not."

"You and Zeke will stay here tonight," he said. "We'll leave first thing in the morning on the stage."

"All right," she said shakily. Zoe felt sick to her stomach. She'd let her sister down.

Her mind raced for some other way to get the money, but she couldn't come up with anything. If she didn't have a plan by tomorrow morning, she would have to completely humiliate herself and ask Quentin to marry her.

Though she would rather tangle with a rattler, that wouldn't even be the worst of it.

Quentin would say no and she'd be right back where she'd started. No money for Dinah's tuition.

Quentin was sure he'd seen interest in Zoe's eyes. Well, pretty sure. The next day, impatience burned through him to find her, to determine if he was right.

That afternoon, he went out the back door of Dr. Annalise Fine's clinic, off the flat stoop and moved alongside her as they made their way to the front of the two-story building that also served as her home. Wagons rattled through the street and people called greetings to each other as they went about their business.

During his meeting with Annalise, he'd heard the stage-coach thunder into town and he wanted to know if Zoe was on board.

His gaze shifted to the opposite side of Main Street, to the Whirlwind Hotel directly across from Annalise's clinic, then it moved past the telegraph and post office, the Pearl restaurant and the jail. There was no sign of her.

As Zoe had gotten on the stage, she had looked worried. Of course, she hadn't volunteered any information.

Had she returned from Abilene yet? Why had she gone? He knew she had family there. A grandfather. But Zoe had never set eyes on the man, much less visited him.

After seeing her yesterday, Quentin hadn't been able to stop thinking about her. About *them*. He had been a prideful, stubborn fool to push her away after being crippled.

He had never stopped desiring her, and last night he had admitted what he had been thinking for a while now—he wanted another chance with her.

Maybe she was still gone, dammit.

Beside him, Annalise said, "You can think further about the surgery, Quentin. There's no rush."

Minutes earlier, they had discussed the operation that he hoped would allow him to walk again. Annalise had just performed a different back surgery on J. T. Baldwin. "J.T.'s doing all right, isn't he?"

"Yes, but it's only been a couple of days since I operated on him. It's not clear yet exactly what, if any, improvement he'll have. Besides, your injury is different. There's likely still a bullet next to your spine. I can't predict what will happen if I remove it."

Quentin nodded, still searching the town for Zoe. He'd been carrying this slug inside him since his brother-in-law, Jake Ross, had put it in him seven years ago. For a long time, Quentin had hated Jake, blamed him for Delia's death. He could admit now that his late sister's husband had had every reason to fire back when Quentin had ambushed him in a hail of bullets.

"I'm ready," he said to the doctor, one of his closest friends. "I've thought about it long enough."

His gaze traveled from the clinic to the stagecoach at the far end of the street. The coach was empty and he didn't see Zoe anywhere around. He fought back a surge of disappointment.

Annalise came to a halt in front of her clinic. "Plan to stay here until you're healed enough to fend for yourself."

"Okay." He glanced down the street and stilled. There was Zoe at the far end of the street coming out of the Fontaine. She wore exactly what she'd had on yesterday.

Annalise's green gaze swept the street. "Who are you looking for?"

"Found her," he murmured.

"Ah." His friend spotted Zoe. "Have the two of you patched things up?"

"No." With Delia gone, Annalise was the one person who knew that Quentin and Zoe had been seeing each other before he'd been injured. Before he'd ruined it. "Not yet."

"But there's hope?"

"If I didn't misread the look in her eyes yesterday." He smiled up at Annalise. "Maybe we'll work things out the way you and Matt have."

Annalise had recently moved back to Whirlwind after years away and had reunited with Matt Baldwin, the cowboy who had broken her heart so long ago. Two days ago, he had been in a shoot-out with a band of rustlers holding her hostage at a ranch outside of town. Now the cattle thieves were dead and Annalise was safe.

Zoe stepped off the Fontaine's wide sandstone porch, lifting a hand to shade her eyes from the mid-afternoon sun.

Annalise turned for the front steps of her clinic, touching Quentin's arm. "Good luck."

"Thanks." He would need it, he thought as he steered his chair away from the clinic, past Cal Doyle's law office then Haskell's General Store. More than likely Zoe would cross to the other side of the street when she saw him coming, but so far she seemed unaware of him.

He noticed that her attention went to the newspaper office then to the mercantile. Her gaze lit on him and she stopped cold.

So did Quentin. Her thick lustrous hair was hidden beneath the navy bowler hat. He was still too far away to see the expression on her face, but he had no trouble reading the rigid set of her shoulders. She was tall with lush curves, and though she walked gracefully, there was also purpose in her smooth gait.

"Quentin!" Picking up her skirts, she crossed to his side of the street and hurried toward him.

She had called his name. And…she was coming toward him. Trying to absorb these facts, he admired her clean-lined classic features.

There was nothing fragile about the determined set of her jaw and pretty mouth. Dark brows arched over sapphire-blue eyes, enhanced by her pert nose and high cheekbones.

Between the newspaper office and Haskell's, she stopped inches from him, frowning. As she spoke, she looked over her shoulder. "May I speak with you?"

"Of course. I wanted to have a word with you, too." He doubted she wanted to talk about the same thing he did, but his pulse thudded hard anyway.

When her attention returned to him, her eyes widened. "You shaved your mustache!"

Smiling, he touched the now-smooth skin above his lip. "This morning."

"It's nice." She tore her gaze away and smoothed a hand down her skirts. Courtesy of the hours she'd spent in the stage, her navy traveling dress was dusty and rumpled. "I need your help."

"You do?" That wasn't what he'd expected. "What's wrong?"

"Sister!"

Quentin peered around her to see Zeke. The boy's voice carried all the way from the porch of the hotel Zoe had just left.

"Oh, no!" She blanched. Even in the bright sunlight, her skin looked waxy.

Her brother hurried toward them. Along with a tall older gentleman.

"That's my grandfather," she explained urgently. "There's no time to explain. Please just say yes."

Yes to what?

That was all Zoe could relay before the pair were upon them. Quentin had no idea what was going on, but whatever it was had his former love desperate enough to come to him.

Zeke halted beside his sister and smiled broadly. "Hi, Quentin."

"Hi, Zeke." His gaze moved to the older man.

"This is Grandfather Upton," the boy said.

Panic flashed through Zoe's blue eyes. Quentin noted a definite resemblance in the family's blue eyes and red hair.

The big man looked Quentin over, features growing dark as he stared disapprovingly at Quentin's useless legs.

He stiffened.

"So, you're the man who's going to marry my grand-daughter?"

Marriage! By some stint of will, Quentin managed to keep his jaw from dropping.

Chapter Two

Quentin fought to stay focused on the older man. He didn't know what was going on, but there was no mistaking the plea in Zoe's blue eyes. *Please just say yes,* she had begged.

To marriage?

Holding the man's derisive gaze, Quentin extended his hand. "Hello, sir. Quentin Prescott."

The man shook and withdrew his hand quickly. "How do you propose to take care of my granddaughter when you're stuck in that wheelchair?"

Zoe made a small noise of protest.

Quentin gave her a reassuring smile. It wasn't the first time he'd met with a question like this. Or asked it of himself. "I may not be able to walk, Mr. Upton, but my brain and my hands work just fine."

"Can you provide for the girl *and* her brother?"

"Sir!" Her eyes sparked with anger.

Quentin glanced at her. "It's all right, Zoe. I'm sure your grandfather just wants the best for you." He had his doubts about that, but he saw no reason to fan the flame.

"And what about children?" Upton asked baldly. "Can you have them?"

"Grandfather!" The horror on Zoe's face matched that in her voice.

Quentin didn't flinch from the man's brutal question. "That's between your granddaughter and me."

Despite the flush of anger on Zoe's face, his words won a half smile from her and a look of respect.

"I want to know if you're marrying her for the money," the man rasped.

Quentin's hands tightened on his chair's armrests as he struggled to rein in his temper. "No, sir, I am not. I have my own business and I also work for the *Prairie Caller*."

"You raise honey?" Upton asked gruffly.

"And sell it. To everyone in Whirlwind and at Fort Greer. To the Texas & Pacific Railroad and several places in Abilene. I get by just fine. Besides, Zoe has more to recommend her than money."

For an instant, pleasure softened her features. He remembered a time when she had often looked at him that way.

Her brother moved closer to her, worry plain on his freckled face. "Why are you being mean, Grandfather? You know Zoe loves Quentin."

That was more than Quentin knew. Heart thudding hard, his gaze went straight to Zoe's. Even in the midday glare of the sun, he could see her flush. Interesting.

She shifted uneasily, looking everywhere except at him. "Um, I told Grandfather we didn't know for sure when we would marry."

He was slowly putting together what had happened yesterday in Abilene although that didn't explain why *his* name had come up.

Upton studied him. "I'd like you to have dinner with us tonight at the Fontaine so I can get to know you better."

More likely, the man wanted to dissect him verbally, but Quentin nodded. "Of course."

His newly intended looked wobbly and as if she might be sick. He maneuvered his chair closer to her and took her hand. "If you wouldn't mind, sir, may I have a moment alone with my fiancée? Seems as though she's been gone longer than a day."

The big man's gaze went from Quentin to Zoe. He gave a sharp nod. Releasing her hand, Quentin rolled his chair a few yards away and stopped just feet from Annalise's clinic. Zoe followed.

He situated them so that her back was to her family and he had a clear view of her grandfather. Keeping his voice low, he asked, "What's going on?"

"I know this is crazy," she said in a half whisper. "And there's absolutely no reason for you to say yes, but I didn't know what else to do."

"It's okay." He took her hand, brushing his thumb across her wrist. Her skin was so soft. "Why does your grandfather think we're getting married?"

"Because I told him so. Well, Zeke did," she clarified with a grimace.

Quentin wanted to know the reason for that. His gaze caught on a wisp of red hair blowing gently against her elegant neck. Beneath the grime of travel, he caught a whiff of her clean soap scent. "All right."

She tried to pull away, but he tightened his grip. She must've remembered they had an audience because she didn't fight it. She didn't relax either. "You remember my mother was estranged from my grandfather?"

When he nodded, she continued, "Her inheritance passed to me when she died. She never wanted the money and neither did I, but now I need it. My grandfather has control of everything and I can't get it unless I marry. Dinah's tuition has gone up. With the drought this last year, so many people have come upon hard times."

"You can't find enough work to pay for your sister's school in Connecticut and take care of Zeke."

"That's right. I thought if I went to Grandfather and explained, he might give me the money. But no. He doesn't think a woman should work outside the home at all. He refuses to deposit the money into my account until I marry. So when Zeke named you, I, um, went along with it. I said we were going to get hitched. Soon."

Quentin's gaze moved slowly over her face as he admired the straight nose, the pale pink lips, the petal-smooth peachy complexion that freckled easily. He found her tiny freckles charming; Zoe didn't and never had. He'd always wondered where else they were on her body.

"Zeke's the one who spouted off your name, not me." She tugged her hand away this time and folded her arms, drawing his attention to her full breasts.

When she realized he was staring at her chest, she stiffened. "After what happened between us, I would never mention you in a situation like that. Don't read too much into it."

"I won't." He ignored the stab of pain he felt at her blunt statement. After what he'd done, he could hardly blame her for feeling that way. "I'm aware of what you think about me."

She hesitated. "When Zeke said your name, Grandfather pounced on it. I didn't deny it. There's no one else in Whirlwind who can possibly marry me."

He nodded, his gaze fixed on her mouth. From past experience, he knew it fitted his perfectly. Seven years was a long time, but he remembered the sweet warm taste of her and wanted another one.

"If there was any other way— Quentin, stop looking at me like that!"

"Like what?"

"Like you want to…" She shifted uneasily. "You know."

"Maybe I do." He had missed her vibrancy, her energy.

She glared at him. "Our marriage doesn't have to be forever. In fact, I don't expect it to last very long after I pay Dinah's tuition. I imagine we'll have to stay together a short while in order to satisfy Grandfather that this is real."

If he had anything to say about it, it *would* be real, but he didn't say so. "Okay."

"I hate asking you for this. I *hate* it."

"You've been plain about that, Zoe," he said wryly. "And you haven't asked me anything yet."

He snagged her hand again, cradling it between both of his.

"This is pure-dee crazy," she muttered.

"What exactly do you want?"

"You know."

He did. And he wanted to hear the words.

Swallowing hard, she squeezed her eyes shut as if she couldn't bear to look at him. "Will you…marry me?"

This *was* crazy, but it was also the chance he'd been waiting for. For years, he'd stared stupid in the mirror and if he refused her, he'd be doing it again. He silently willed her to look at him.

When he said nothing, she opened one eye then the other. "Please?"

Exhilarated, he brushed his lips across her knuckles. "Yes, I'll marry you."

True, he hadn't been thinking about marriage yet, but if this was a way to get close to Zoe, he'd take it.

"Our minds must've been traveling along similar lines," he said. Why else would it have been his name that came up?

She stiffened. "What do you mean?"

"Over the last couple of months, I've thought a lot about us."

"There is no us." Her eyes narrowed.

He rubbed his thumb across her knuckles. "It was a mistake to push you away after I lost my sister and my ability to walk."

"Oh." Surprise flashed across her features. And pleasure.

Encouraged, he continued, "I want to try again."

She was shaking her head before he finished his sentence. "Why not?" he demanded.

"That's over."

He arched a brow. "In light of what we're discussing, I'd say it isn't."

"We're only marrying to satisfy Grandfather."

She was. Quentin wasn't. "Your grandfather isn't why I said yes."

She leveled a look on him. "This marriage is strictly a business arrangement."

"What if I want more?"

"You shouldn't. I don't."

Pain and anger gripped him. Winning her back wouldn't be easy, but that was okay. "When do you want to do this?"

"The sooner the better," she replied grimly, glancing at her grandfather. "Do you agree to my terms?"

"For now."

Her mouth tightened. "Quentin."

"I want more than a business arrangement."

"Stop it," she hissed, looking as panicked as she had when she'd first sought him out.

"I'm not going to lie about it."

"It's fine with me if you do," she muttered.

He smiled. He couldn't help it. "So, are we still getting married?"

Zoe looked over her shoulder and his gaze followed hers. The smug look on her grandfather's face said he knew Quentin and Zoe weren't a couple. He was probably just waiting for her to admit it, but Quentin knew she wouldn't.

She shifted her attention back to him. "Yes, we're still getting married."

"All right, then."

"I don't know the first thing about getting a wedding together."

"We can talk to Annalise," he suggested. "She'll be able to help."

"Okay." She looked slightly relieved.

"What about two days from now?"

"All right. I'll tell Grandfather."

She had to be the least happy-looking bride Quentin had ever seen. His admission about wanting more than a business arrangement was probably the main reason, but he wasn't taking it back.

She started to turn away then paused. "Thank you, Quentin. I really appreciate this."

"You're welcome."

That hadn't gone at all the way he'd expected, but he wanted a future with her. This marriage of convenience might be his only chance to convince her she wanted the same thing. He just hoped he could.

She was getting married.

Quentin had agreed, which relieved Zoe and made her wary at the same time. Even if she had wanted more than a business arrangement, she couldn't let herself get close to him again.

She knew how silly that sounded when she was fixin' to marry him. Still, she could resist the man who had once broken her heart. She'd spent seven years doing just that.

Keeping her guard up around her husband-to-be didn't concern her nearly as much as the possibility that Grandfather might see through the whole thing.

The next two days passed in a haze. Annalise and Josie helped with the preparations. Josie even altered one of her sample dresses for Zoe. That evening, as the sun dipped below the horizon, she walked toward the buggy where Quentin waited. Their friends stood around the carriage beneath the copse of trees at the northeast corner of the church.

The buggy wedding had seemed the perfect idea. Zoe knew how Quentin hated being in that wheelchair. This way, they could both remain seated in the buggy with their guests nearby.

As she walked with Grandfather from Annalise's clinic, where she had dressed, to the church a few yards away, Zoe smiled at their friends. Annalise was with her beau, Matt Baldwin. His brother, Russ, and wife, Lydia, were there, as were Ef and Naomi Gerard and Josie and Davis Lee Holt. Cora Wilkes, newly married to J. T. Baldwin, was alone due to her husband's convalescence from back surgery. Jericho and Catherine Blue were absent; they had taken a trip back east to visit the nuns who had raised her.

Of those in attendance, only Grandfather and Zeke believed this would be a real marriage. When Zoe had gone to Josie about a wedding dress, she had explained about her sudden nuptials to Quentin. Josie had expressed hope that the marriage-of-convenience would turn into a real and lasting union.

Zoe knew Quentin had told Annalise the truth about their marriage, too, and she wondered what the doctor had said. Zoe and Quentin had thought it better not to share the information with Zeke in order to reduce the risk of him telling Grandfather.

Reverend Scoggins stood to the side of the buggy with Zeke. Shade from the oaks' spreading branches and a slight breeze kept the day from being unbearably hot. Zoe reached the buggy and took the hand Quentin extended across the seat to help her up.

The black suit and white dress shirt made his eyes coffee-dark. The square line of his jaw looked freshly shaven. His sun-burnished features, though still sharp, weren't harsh as they had been in the past. Instead, they looked strong. Commanding.

Their eyes met. Though his hand didn't waver, the smile slid right off his face. He looked…poleaxed.

Heart sinking, her hand trembled as she let him help her up. It must have hit him exactly what he had agreed to do for her. Was he going to back out?

The thought disappeared when he squeezed her hand. Those dark eyes burned with hunger as his gaze moved from the intricate upsweep of her hair, down the length of her neck, over her breasts and down to the hem of her white silk alpaca skirts. "You're a vision," he said in a deep, low voice that shot sensation straight to her toes.

Zoe blinked, her cheeks burning. "Thank you."

Everything faded to a blur as the reverend began the ceremony. Rattled by the way Quentin had looked at her, she reminded herself he was putting on an act for Grandfather.

But it didn't feel like an act when Quentin slid a wedding ring on her finger. His mother's ring.

Zoe was suddenly, startlingly aware of exactly what they were doing. She didn't want the ring. It made things seem too permanent. Plus she hadn't gotten one for him. Still, she couldn't refuse it, not here.

"I now pronounce you husband and wife," the reverend boomed. "Quentin, you may kiss your bride."

Zoe leaned over to brush her lips against his cheek, but he slid an arm around her waist, pulling her close and cupping her cheek with his free hand. Pure panic shot through her.

"You don't have to do this," she whispered. "Our friends know this isn't a real marriage."

"It's real to me." His mouth covered hers and her heart kicked hard.

Her senses narrowed to only him. The unapologetic press of his lips to hers, the clean male scent of him, the solid wall of his chest against her breasts. Sensation whipped across her nerves and sent her pulse haywire. She'd forgotten how his kiss affected her, how her heart filled with warmth.

She kissed him back before she could stop herself. He finally drew away, the flush of arousal streaking his cheekbones. Heat burned her from the inside out.

She became aware of a smattering of applause and looked out at the crowd. Her gaze lit on Grandfather, who looked surprised. And pleased.

As people gathered around to congratulate them, Zoe got herself under control. She hadn't expected Quentin to kiss her like that, but it was over now.

They wouldn't be doing it again. Despite returning his kiss, Zoe didn't want a real marriage. She didn't think she needed to worry about him trying to seduce her. With the condition of his body, she didn't know if there would be any point.

They made their way to the Fontaine where Russ and Lydia had prepared a reception with cake and champagne punch.

They greeted their guests, Zoe standing beside Quentin in his wheelchair. After a few moments, she felt a sudden tension in him. Glancing away from her conversation with Josie and Davis Lee, she saw Jake Ross approach her husband.

Her husband. As odd as that sounded, Zoe was focused on the uneasiness between Quentin and the man whose bullet had cost him the ability to walk. Was Quentin still as bitter as he had been after his sister's death? Did he still blame his former brother-in-law?

Zoe realized she was holding her breath, waiting to see what happened between the two men.

Jake's blonde, petite wife, Emma, reached out to shake Quentin's hand. "Congratulations," she said quietly. "You, too, Zoe."

The women hugged as Jake and Quentin stared at each other. Jake cleared his throat. "Ike and Georgia would've been here, but they had to make a trip to Sweet Water. And Bram's chasing Cosgrove. They wish you the best. So do I."

"I appreciate you coming," Quentin said gruffly.

Zoe could see he was moved by his former brother-in-law's presence. He stuck out his hand and she knew she wasn't the only one waiting to see if Jake would take it. Long ago, before Quentin had blamed Jake for Delia's death, the men had been close.

After a moment, Jake shook the other man's hand. "Good luck to you both." Relief welled inside her as the rancher moved to her and offered his congratulations.

Zeke shook Quentin's hand and welcomed him to the family then stepped over to Zoe. He gathered her up in an exuberant hug. She hugged him back.

Burl Upton followed, his gaze searching her face. "I have to admit I didn't quite believe you would marry."

Quentin took her hand and she gave it a grateful squeeze.

"Your brother and I will stay at your house tonight," the older man said. "That will give you and your new husband some time alone."

No! Her hand jerked in Quentin's. After the way her toes had curled during that kiss, she didn't want to spend the night alone with him. Of course, she couldn't say so.

Quentin laced his fingers with hers. "Thank you, sir."

A couple of hours later, Zoe and Quentin were at his home. The modest white house was distinguished by a fancy arched window over the front door. By the light of the low-burning lamp, she took in the dining table and chairs across the large front room. A solidly built cupboard and glass-front cabinet holding his late sister's china were on the adjacent wall.

The kitchen and stove were visible through the door in the corner. Zoe hadn't been here since she had paid her respects following Delia's death. Except for the addition of the cupboard, things looked the same.

The excitement and anxiety of the wedding had taken its toll and Zoe was worn-out. Even though she was here alone with Quentin, she didn't think she would have trouble sleeping.

His gaze, dark in the soft light, fixed on her face. "You're tired."

"You must be, too."

Lines fanned out from his dark eyes. He dragged a hand down his face. "I made up the second bedroom for you."

"Thank you."

"I wish you'd stay in mine. We're married now and you'll be with me after Zeke moves in."

"I'd rather be alone tonight," she said quietly.

A muscle flexed in his jaw. "Very well."

"Good night, then."

"Good night. If you need anything, holler."

She nodded though she couldn't imagine she would need anything. In the bedroom he had prepared for her, she found a valise containing her nightdress, stockings, her brush and mirror. Her few dresses hung in the heavy wardrobe against the wall at the foot of the narrow bed. A small vase of blue-bonnets sat on the table next to the bed.

She tugged off her shoes and stockings then took the pins from her hair. She shook it out with a big sigh of relief. Fatigue made her movements and thoughts slow, a little clumsy. Able to reach only the top four buttons at the back of her dress, she realized that she would need help with the rest of them.

Staring down at the fall of her white silk skirts, she considered sleeping in the garment, but she didn't want to muss it. There was nothing to be done except ask for Quentin's help, and that seemed like trouble waiting to happen.

Still, she had no choice if she wanted the dress off. She walked across the hall and knocked on his door, opening it when he told her to come in.

He sat on the edge of his big bed, wheelchair to the side. A leather strap attached to the wall at the head of the bed provided assistance for getting in and out of bed. Stacks of books drew her attention to a small desk on the wall behind him.

He grasped the strap as she stepped inside the room.

"No, Quentin, stay there."

"Change your mind about sleeping in here?"

His teasing tone actually made her smile. "No."

Now without his coat, he wore only trousers and his dress shirt, no boots or socks. Something about seeing his bare feet on the pine floor sent a flush of warmth through her.

"What is it?" Fatigue drew his features tight.

"I'm sorry to bother you."

"It's no bother, Zoe. Whatever you need."

She touched her bodice, giving him a small smile. "I need some help getting out of my dress."

His eyes flashed hotly. "Maybe my luck is changing," he drawled.

"Quentin."

"Okay." He motioned her closer.

Turning away from him, she eased back between his legs and pulled her hair to one side. Being this close to him made her pulse race and when he laid a warm, broad palm at her waist, she nearly jumped a foot in the air.

His other hand moved to her spine, undoing one button then another. Air brushed her skin. Through the fabric of her dress, she could feel the warmth of his body, the occasional tease of his breath against her skin. She flattened a palm against her suddenly jumpy stomach.

His fingers flexed at her waist and a breath shuddered out of her. How many stupid buttons were there? How long had it taken Josie to fasten the dress before the ceremony?

To cover her nervousness, she asked, "Who did you tell about our wedding?"

"You mean, the real reason we got hitched?"

She nodded.

"Just Annalise," he said. "I don't have a lot of friends these days."

No, he didn't, but Zoe knew he was working on rectifying that.

"I told her the truth."

"What did she say?"

"She said good, and that she hoped it would work out."

"That's what Josie said, too," Zoe murmured.

Quentin's hand paused on her back. "I owe you an apology."

The deep baritone of his voice set her blood to humming. Relaxing in spite of herself, she shook her head. "You just married me so that I could help my family. I hardly think you owe me anything."

"I'm sorry for hurting you."

She went still, keenly aware of the burn of his knuckles through her chemise.

"After Delia died, all I cared about was making Jake pay."

"And me," she said flatly.

"That was wrong, but I couldn't see it for myself until the hate began to fade."

"Well…thank you." How much longer before he came to a button she could reach so she could finish for herself? "You could've told me this back then instead of just shutting me out."

"You're right. And that's what I should've done, but anger wasn't the only reason I pushed you away."

"Quentin, get on with my buttons. Please." She shifted uneasily. "I know your other reason was because you lost your ability to walk. That never mattered to me. Never."

"I know it didn't." Instead of continuing to unfasten her dress, he toyed with a lock of her hair. "But it mattered to me. I felt like half a man."

And did he still? She shouldn't want to know. She didn't want to care. He had hurt her deeply.

"I didn't want you having to care for me in addition to your siblings."

She looked over her shoulder. "That isn't how I saw it. It's not how I saw *you*."

"I'm glad." The smile he gave her had her facing front again. "Will you accept my apology?"

"Yes." There was a deep, sudden longing to try again with him. Because of their enforced distance over the years, she hadn't realized how much she'd missed him.

But wanting another chance and doing something about it were two different things. She couldn't reconcile with him. Surely he wasn't working his way around to asking her to consider it.

Shifting against the edge of the bed, she asked, "How are you coming with those buttons?"

"Almost finished." His fingers threaded through her hair.

The motion was soothing, enough so that Zoe inched back into him a little more. No one had taken care of her, had paid any attention to her like this since her parents' deaths.

Time slowed, moving like warm honey, making her limbs

feel weightless. He smelled of light sandalwood and the outdoors.

She involuntarily arched beneath his touch. She wanted to curl up and let him stroke her hair all night. Stroke her.

She stood between his legs and she realized she was pressed right up against him. The strength in his chest and arms gave her a sense of safety.

"That feels heavenly."

"Good." He lifted her hair up and brushed his lips across her nape.

She froze, knowing she should move, but she couldn't make herself do it.

"Your hair is gorgeous." He buried his face in the thick mass.

Against the small of her back, she felt something hard. Hot. Him. He was *aroused*.

She jumped away, whirling toward him. Her face flamed. "Was that—are you—can you feel me?"

"Yeah."

"Well, don't!"

He didn't look as stunned as she felt. In fact, he was smiling in a way that made her feel half-naked.

"I didn't think you could…" She drew a deep breath. "You know."

"I wasn't sure." There was no mistaking the excitement in his voice. "I've had sensation on and off, but nothing like this until earlier. When I kissed you at the wedding, I felt something although it was too quick for me to be sure. I definitely felt you just now. And you felt me, too."

No. No, no, no. Zoe didn't want to feel him. "What does Annalise say? Does she think the surgery might, um, fix that?"

"She isn't sure, but she's hopeful."

Not Zoe. She was leery and grew even more so when he said quietly, "We might be able to make this a real marriage."

Zoe didn't want that. She had only been able to make herself marry Quentin because she knew it wouldn't be forever. Knowing there was a possibility that he could regain feeling in his lower half had Zoe's stomach knotting up because she wasn't sure she would be able to resist him if he tried to change her mind.

If she slept with him, Zoe knew she would never be able to walk away. And she had to walk away.

Chapter Three

Last night had been the closest thing to a whole man that Quentin had felt in seven years. And he wanted to keep feeling that way.

Zoe was imprinted on his brain. He could still smell the clean soap scent of her, feel the thick silkiness of her fiery hair. Since his body had gone hard against hers, she hadn't let him close enough to even touch, let alone hold her again.

The feel of him had spooked her. Not that he was anywhere near an expert on women, but Quentin was pretty sure it wouldn't have bothered her so much if she didn't still care for him.

In the enclosed shed where he was overseeing Zeke's first extraction of honey, Quentin watched his wife through the lone small window beside the door.

She stood at the corner of his house. Her eyes met his and even from here he could see her flush. She was remembering last night. He knew it.

Ever since then, all he'd been able to think about was making love to her. She would probably run faster than a six-legged jackrabbit if she knew how badly he wanted to make that happen. If he didn't want to spook her, he would have to court her, move slowly so she would gradually accept the idea.

"I put the hive box on the table with the other three, Quentin." Zeke turned toward him, lifting the protective netting on his hat to look at him. "Now what?"

Quentin pulled his attention from Zeke's sister and moved closer to the table now covered with hive boxes, a knife, a small paintbrush, a smoker and a prying tool.

Before bringing in the hive boxes, Zeke had pumped smoke over the bees using a small fire cup attached to a miniature bellows. The smoke came from burlap burning in the cup and kept the bees calm while Zeke worked around them. Most of them stayed outside when he carried in the hive box, but there were always a few that remained.

"Remove one of the frames in the box."

The boy lifted off the top cover then took out a frame. Dipping the paintbrush in a cup of water, he brushed away the few remaining insects.

Quentin knew how much easier the process was than his grandfather's. He had explained to Zeke that a reverend in Pennsylvania had invented a hive box that used interchangeable parts and individual frames. These could be checked for honey or disease without having to kill or drive off the bees or destroy the hive as had been done in the early days.

Zeke flashed a satisfied grin. "The bees make honey and honeycomb in the frames."

Quentin nodded.

"And when the comb is filled with honey, they make a wax cap to cover the cells."

"Yes." So far, Zeke remembered everything Quentin had told him. "What you do now is cut off those caps on both sides of the frame."

Taking the nearby knife, Zeke did as instructed, carefully cutting the capping into a large tub on the table.

"Honey can be collected later from the tub, too," Quentin said. Under his watchful eye, the boy readied two frames. "Put the frames into the extractor so they remain upright. After you clamp them in, turn the crank to spin the cylinder."

"And I should go slow at first so the honey's weight won't cause the comb to bulge out to one side."

"That's right." Quentin smiled.

Earlier, Zeke had watched Quentin go through the process. He had agreed to check the hives and gather honey again, if necessary, while Quentin recovered from surgery.

"Spin the drum for two or three minutes. After the extractor slows to a stop, turn the frames on their other end and spin again. Once you finish those two, put them in the empty hive box at the end of the table and start with another two frames."

Zeke nodded, serious and focused as he cranked the extraction cylinder. The extractor emptied into a large pail beneath that was draped with cheesecloth to filter out wax and impurities.

"And I should always leave some honey in the combs for the bees to eat instead of sugar water."

"That's right." Keeping one eye on his apprentice, Quentin looked back at Zoe just as Burl Upton walked up to her. It reminded Quentin of a question he had wanted to ask her brother.

"Zeke, why did you tell your grandfather that your sister and I were getting married?"

Carefully watching the slowing extractor, the boy answered, "I like you and I want you to be with Zoe. Besides, I know you'll take care of her. She needs that because she's always taking care of everyone else."

As always, Quentin was impressed with Zeke's concern for

his sister. And surprised at how much the young man really comprehended. Most people thought he didn't pay attention or understand the things he did notice.

Zoe's conversation with her grandfather ended. Upton started toward the shed and she followed. She didn't look upset, but something was definitely on her mind.

Quentin glanced at Zeke. "Hold up, son. Your grandfather's coming this way. Cover the extractor and the hive boxes to keep dirt out."

The boy did as instructed as a knock sounded on the door. Quentin pushed the protective netting back on his hat and opened the door, rolling his chair outside. Zeke followed, closing the door.

Quentin removed his hat. "You're leaving, sir?"

"Yes."

"'Bye, Grandfather." Zeke gave the man an awkward hug. "You can come see us anytime you want."

Zoe looked as though she might protest, but all she did was raise a brow.

Upton cleared his throat. "Y'all should come visit me, too. Anytime."

Zeke and Zoe looked startled.

Quentin could tell Burl was sincere. Maybe he had decided he wanted to be closer to his only remaining family. Since neither brother nor sister had responded, Quentin stuck out a hand. "Thank you, Mr. Upton. We just might do that."

The older man looked at Zoe, saying gruffly, "I'd really like it."

Zoe looked perplexed as her grandfather bade them all farewell. As he walked away, Quentin glanced at his wife's face. She looked thoughtful. Almost sad.

He turned his head toward Zeke. "Go ahead and finish up, Zeke. You're doing a fine job."

After a quick smile at his sister, the boy stepped back into the shed.

Quentin waited until the door was closed before wheeling his chair in front of Zoe. "Everything okay?"

"That was strange." Her gaze followed Upton until he disappeared around the corner of the livery. She gave Quentin a polite smile as she looked toward the Fontaine hotel. "Grandfather told me he transferred the money to my account and he took care of Dinah's tuition."

"That's good news. What has you looking so serious?"

She huffed out a breath. "Oh, he started on about me working now that you and I are married. He said you wouldn't want me to. I don't see how he could know what you want."

"Whatever you do is fine with me. If you don't want to work any longer, I can take care of us."

She looked at him then, a slight frown gathering on her forehead. "That's nice, Quentin, but not necessary. Now that I have my inheritance, I can take care of my brother and me. I like working, especially at the hotel." She snorted. "He said I should get busy havin' kids."

Quentin wanted to say he would help with that, but that depended on the outcome of his surgery. "Do you *want* kids?"

He'd never thought to ask. Hell, he'd never thought it a possibility for him.

She shrugged. "I don't know."

"I could ask Annalise about it. We might be able to—"

"No," she said quickly. "Don't."

He couldn't stop a rush of disappointment, but he wasn't surprised. It would take time and patience to change her mind about being intimate with him.

"Before my surgery tomorrow, I plan to talk to Annalise about it."

"No, Quentin."

"Are you embarrassed? I'll speak with her privately."

"I mean, there's no need to talk to her. At least not for me."

"It's something we might need to know in the future."

She was quiet for so long that a drum of apprehension began inside him. "Once you're recovered from surgery," she said, "and Annalise says it's all right for you to do things on your own, I'll be moving out."

"The hell you will!"

Looking startled at his outburst, she drew back.

"We're married, Zoe," he gritted out. "That means forever."

"I told you I don't want that."

"Well, I do."

She shook her head.

A low-grabbing pain knotted his belly. "You can't forgive me for how I treated you years ago."

"It isn't that."

"Then what?"

She looked him square in the eye. "I've forgiven you, but I won't let you hurt me again. I can't."

"Things are different now. I said vows to you and I meant them. Are you saying you didn't mean anything you said to me?"

Her eyes filled with tears. "When Annalise thinks it's all right, Zeke and I will be moving back to our place."

The words slammed into him like a bullet. He reached for her, but she stepped away. He felt so damn helpless sitting here, unable to touch her.

"I have to go or I'll be late for my shift at the Fontaine."

He wanted to hit something. As he watched her hurry away, he decided he wasn't giving up. Not yet. She still had feelings for him and somehow he would get her to admit it.

Now he wasn't working only against a skittish wife, he was also working against time.

The next day, Zoe stood beside her husband's bed and listened as Annalise described the surgery Quentin was about to undergo. The doctor would put him under using chloroform then make a cut on his spine and see if she could determine whether surgery might enable him to walk again.

A knock sounded on the open bedroom door and Zoe looked over to find Cora Wilkes Baldwin. The older woman's smile took in Zoe and her husband, but she spoke to Zoe. "I thought you might want someone to sit with you during the surgery."

As Cora's husband, J.T., had undergone a similar procedure less than a month ago, Zoe welcomed the offer.

"Yes, thank you."

"Good." Cora came into the room, greeting Annalise.

Quentin squeezed Zoe's hand and smiled. She smiled back then moved to help the doctor scoot the bed away from the wall. That would enable Annalise to easily access her patient and her surgical instruments from wherever necessary.

On the small table against the wall, the doctor laid out her instruments then the inhaler she would use to administer anesthetic.

"Ready to get started?" she asked Quentin.

"Yes." Using the strap beside his bed, he levered himself out of the wheelchair and onto the mattress.

Zoe had assured the doctor that she would be able to assist with the surgery, and she watched as Annalise filled the inhaler's reservoir with chloroform. Using a hand-bellows, Zoe would pump air through a tube into the chloroform. A second tube would carry the mixture of air and anesthetic to the patient as a gas, which Annalise would administer.

Zoe was fully prepared to help. She wanted to. But when she reached for the small bellows, her hand shook.

Astonished, she threw a look at the doctor. She hadn't expected the surgery to rattle her this much. "I'm not sure I can do this," she said in a low voice.

With a gentle smile, Cora left her place beside Zeke and walked over to Zoe. "I can do it."

"Thank you. I think that would be best."

Hoping she wasn't letting Quentin down, she passed the hand-bellows to the older woman. When Zoe started around the bed to make room for Cora, Quentin reached for her.

"Zoe?"

She paused, her throat tightening at the worry in his eyes. "I'm not going anywhere. I'll be here when you wake up."

"Okay." Relief settled on his features and he released her hand.

On wobbly legs, she moved several feet away to stand beside her brother. She watched Annalise place a rubber mask over Quentin's nose and mouth then Cora began a slow pumping with the hand-bellows. Before too long, Quentin lost consciousness and the doctor began.

Zoe had never considered herself squeamish, but that was Quentin's blood. She looked away.

Annalise worked meticulously, explaining the procedure as she went. Zoe prayed her husband would have no trouble waking up.

J. T. Baldwin had gone into a coma after his back surgery and the possibility that Quentin might do the same scared Zoe spitless.

Her brother seemed to sense her anxiety. He slid an arm around her shoulders. "He'll be okay, sister."

Blinking back tears, she smiled up at him. Even if Quentin didn't regain his ability to walk, he had to recover from the surgery. He just had to.

After what seemed an eternity, Annalise stitched Quentin up.

Zoe wrapped her arms around her middle. "How long until he wakes?"

"Maybe an hour." The doctor glanced up from placing a bandage over his incision. "It may not even take that long."

Zoe didn't draw a full breath the entire time. When Quentin's eyes finally fluttered open, her relief was so great that her chest ached.

She walked to the bed and put a hand on his shoulder as Annalise spoke quietly to him.

"I removed a bullet fragment from beside your spine. If that was the cause of your paralysis, chances are good you'll regain your ability to walk."

Quentin gave a groggy smile. "Any problems?"

"Not a one." The doctor looked at Zoe. "He needs to rest. We can talk when he's more himself."

"Thank you," Zoe said hoarsely. "Thank you."

"He'll sleep off and on the rest of the day."

After issuing instructions and promising to check in later, Annalise and Cora left. Zoe looked down at her sleeping husband.

Emotion welled inside her. Reaching out a trembling hand, she smoothed a lock of hair away from his forehead.

"Sister?" Zeke came up beside her, his voice sober with concern.

"I'm okay," she said reassuringly. "And Quentin is, too."

"Good." Her brother nodded. "I'll fetch you a chair so you can sit."

"Thank you." Initially, Zoe had thought she would check on Quentin throughout the day following his surgery, but she wanted to stay.

As her brother disappeared into the hall, she recalled what she had said to Quentin about *not* staying.

She knew she'd done the right thing by telling him that she and Zeke would be leaving once Quentin was recovered enough from his operation.

That didn't mean she had liked doing it. In fact, she'd hated it. When those words had come out of her mouth, Quentin had looked destroyed.

She might not want to admit it, but the man had deep feelings for her. She had feelings for him, too, even though she didn't want them.

He'd quickly masked the flash of pain in his eyes, but it had reached right out and clutched at her heart.

She didn't want to hurt him; she couldn't let him hurt her either. Staying with him longer would make her want more with him, make her want the real marriage he'd talked about.

Was such a thing really possible? If what she'd felt from him the night before was any indication, then, yes. He could be her husband in every sense.

But what if the surgery didn't work? Would he be even more bitter than he had been when he had first lost the ability to walk?

She didn't want to think so. His attitude had appeared to really change, certainly concerning her. And he showed a lot of patience with Zeke. Her brother was the one person Quentin had never pushed away.

Of course, Zeke couldn't really be pushed away. The teen never remembered a wrong done to him, never held a grudge. He just didn't have it in him, which was another reason Zoe felt so protective of him. Quentin had shown signs of that same protectiveness, and not just to butter her up. His regard for her brother was sincere and that meant a lot to her.

Quentin's regard for her was sincere, too. And the man was committed to making their marriage work.

For the first time, Zoe questioned her decision to leave.

* * *

Ten days after his surgery, Quentin and Zoe made their way down the side of Main Street. Still in his wheelchair, Quentin liked being outside when he could.

As he rolled down the street, Zoe walked alongside him. They had made one turn around Whirlwind and stopped at the Pearl for a glass of lemonade. Just as they crossed the street to head home, a short, wizened man walked down the ramp in front of the newspaper office. He wore a suit jacket and bowler hat. Zoe thought he had to be hot. Summers weren't gentle in Texas. Even Quentin wore a light cotton white shirt with the sleeves rolled back.

The older man stopped in front of Quentin and Zoe, extending a hand to Quentin. "I'm told you work at the *Prairie Caller.*"

"Yes." Quentin shook the man's hand.

"I'm Egan Weaver, an agent for the Weaver Water Company. I'd like to post a notice in your paper."

Zoe could see the fatigue on Quentin's face. She hoped he wasn't going to start back to work already.

Before she could beg off for him, Quentin did it. "I've recently had surgery and I'm not working at the moment. Hoot Eckert is the man you want to see. He's the editor for the *Caller* and usually returns from lunch around one-thirty."

"I'll see Mr. Eckert, then. Thank you." Weaver tipped his bowler hat to Zoe. "Good day, ma'am."

"Good day."

As the man walked toward the Fontaine, Zoe continued down the street with Quentin. She looked back, seeing the man disappear inside Whirlwind's newest hotel. "Why do you think he's here?"

"Maybe to determine if Whirlwind needs water."

"Which we do."

"His company might want to drill a water well," Quentin

said. "I've heard about companies that do the drilling. We would all have to contribute, maybe by buying into the venture. Or by buying bonds that would pay back our money when they mature."

"Most people don't have the money to buy bonds right now. It's all they can do to put food on the table."

They reached Quentin's house and went up the ramp. Zoe opened the door. As he wheeled his chair past her, he said, "Things are desperate here, especially for ranchers and farmers who need water for crops and livestock. Some people will find the money to buy into that water well, if that's a possibility."

"Do you think they should?" Zoe had counted pennies for years now. "It sounds risky to me."

"This type of venture has worked in other places across the country, but I don't know this Weaver fella. I'm not sure if he's with a reputable water company or not."

Nodding, she moved to the side of the door. "How are your legs today? Do you still have sensation?"

The question had Quentin grinning. "Yes, and I'm able to move my ankles now as well as my toes. Sensation seems to have finally returned."

"What about the pain?"

"My feet and legs still tingle, but nothing like they did right after the operation."

"You're doing so well, I can move back to my room."

"No." A muscle flexed in his jaw, but his voice was light when he said, "What if I need help during the night?"

"You're just using that as an excuse to get me to stay."

"Is it working?" His eyes twinkled.

Staying in his bedroom probably wasn't a good idea, but she wasn't willing to take the chance that he might hurt himself or otherwise ruin the progress from the surgery so far. "All right."

He smiled, one of those soft, secret smiles he seemed to have for only her that made her weak-headed for about a second.

Zoe walked farther into the front room. "Are you hungry? Do you want some lunch?"

"I'm not hungry, but I'd like to try to stand. Can you help me up?"

She turned. "Do you think you're ready?"

"I have to try it sometime."

Uncertain, she frowned. "Why don't you wait until Zeke returns from Haskell's? Then there will be two of us to support you."

"I want to try it now."

Glancing from him to the table several feet away, she bit her lip. "If you can't get your balance when you stand, you're going right back into that chair."

"Yes, ma'am." He looked amused.

"I'm serious."

"I promise."

She went to him, concerned at the fatigue on his features. "You're not too tired?"

He shook his head.

"All right." She stabilized his chair against the back of the door. Bracing one hand on an armrest, Quentin slid an arm around Zoe's shoulders when she bent to fit her shoulder under his, supporting him to his feet.

Slowly, steadily, he rose.

She straightened as he did. "Are you okay?"

"Yes." His face was creased in concentration.

She drew in his scent, a mix of soap and the outdoors and man. The open placket of his white shirt revealed the hollow at the base of his strong throat, a swath of bronzed skin, a smattering of dark hair on the flat planes of his chest.

She could feel him all the way down her side. He had strong

hands, probably from setting type and pushing himself around in the wheelchair. His thighs weren't as thick or powerful as they had once been, but there was strength there. Strength he hadn't had for a long time.

After a moment, he straightened to his full height, five inches taller than Zoe. He appeared to be steady and she held her breath.

He took a few halting steps then angled his body so that she was pressed against the wall adjacent to the door. He leaned into her.

"Oh, I knew it! You're not ready. Are you in pain?"

He squeezed her waist. "I'm standing, Zoe. For the first time in seven years!"

The sheer excitement, the disbelief in his eyes had her smiling. Maybe the surgery would completely restore his ability to walk, the sensation in his body from the waist down.

"That's wonderful!" Thrilled, she smiled up at him.

His gaze dropped to her lips. Before she could take another breath, he dipped his head and brushed his mouth against hers.

She froze. "Quentin."

"C'mon, Zoe. Kiss me," he said huskily. "Not because you're expected to, like at our wedding, but because you want to."

She didn't try to tell him that wasn't what she wanted. She *did* want to kiss him even though she knew she shouldn't.

But when his mouth settled on hers, her arms went around his neck. He murmured something against her lips, but her heart was beating so loudly she couldn't make out the words.

One of his arms was braced just above her shoulder and the other curled around her waist, bringing her right up against him. She could feel everything happening in his body. And plenty was happening.

He deepened the kiss and she shyly touched her tongue to his. The rumble in his chest made her shudder in response.

Every inch of him was pressed against her. Her arms were around his hard shoulders, her breasts flattened against his muscular chest and she felt the hard ridge of his flesh straining against her stomach.

Heat flushed her entire body. Memories rushed back of their wedding night, when he had helped her out of her dress. His surgery and subsequent care had pushed that to the back of her mind.

She felt herself floating, weightless, her blood moving through her veins like slow warm honey. He held her right against him, chest to breast, thigh to thigh.

The last time she'd been in his arms this way had been the night before he had been shot seven years ago.

The reminder snapped her back to the moment. What was she doing? She didn't make any sudden moves, just pressed her hand against his chest until he stopped.

He lifted his head, eyes glittering hotly. Instead of loosening his hold, he kept her curled into him. "What?" he rasped.

"We shouldn't be doing this," she said in a half whisper. "You're not strong enough."

"When you kiss me like that, I feel plenty strong."

She flushed. "You need to sit."

"Fine." Frustration scored his words.

Her pulse rioted as she helped him slowly into his chair. His features were taut with desire, color high on his cheekbones.

He caught her hand before she could back away. "Zoe, I want—"

"Annalise said not to overdo it."

"I'm being careful."

She pointed a shaking finger at him. "*That* is not what I

call being careful, especially the first time you get on your feet."

"We're going to be together, Zoe Prescott."

The sound of her new name caused a hitch in her breathing. "Don't get ahead of yourself. You don't even know if you can do…if we can be together that way."

"It's going to happen."

An image flashed into her head of them together in his bed. And it sharpened the panic rising inside her. She backed toward the door. "I have to get to the Fontaine. I'll be home in a few hours."

Then she fled. She knew it was cowardly, but she had to get away. She wanted him. The strength of that desire overwhelmed her. She had to move out soon. She had never considered having to deal with this much temptation, not once.

Three hours later, she was cleaning one of the Fontaine's four fancy rooms with indoor plumbing. She had learned this one was occupied by Egan Weaver. Distracted, she pushed aside the curtain that separated the main room from his bathing room and moved inside to clean the bathtub, basin and floor.

She could still feel the press of Quentin's mouth against her and there was still an ache deep inside her. An ache only Quentin had ever put in her.

Gradually, she became aware of voices in the other room. She stepped toward the curtained doorway, intent on announcing herself, but the words of one man stopped her.

"This whole town is ripe for plucking."

She drew back, frowning. The voice was unfamiliar.

"Little Bitter Creek isn't far from here. We can say we'll be drilling the well near there and that it will provide water for Whirlwind and the surrounding ranches."

Leaning closer to hear better, she realized her feet might be showing beneath the curtain.

She eased to the side as Weaver said, "I've already made up bonds for a water company. Knowing how this area has suffered the last year because of the drought, I reckon we'll be able to sell as many bonds as we want."

"We'll tell the people the bond money is for our working capital, to pay for the equipment and labor needed to drill the well. Once they figure out there is no water well, we'll be long gone."

Weaver chuckled.

Zoe was growing more outraged by the second; her brain whirled. What to do? She could confront them, but there were two of them. Weaver was a slight man, but Zoe had no idea what the other lowdown dog looked like. What if they were dangerous?

She would wait quietly until they left then she was going straight to the sheriff.

"I put a notice in Whirlwind's newspaper that there will be a meeting tomorrow night at the church for anyone who wants to come," Weaver said.

The church! The man was going to steal from her friends inside their own church! A red mist hazed her vision.

The man whose voice she didn't recognize said, "I'll stay out of sight until the meeting. When you call me up, I'll present the drawings of the creek and the drilling equipment."

"And the newspaper article about the success of the Portland Water Company with this kind of venture."

Had some real company successfully provided water for a community?

"Yes, the article, too. That will back up our claims."

The door opened, the men's voices fading as Weaver said, "I think everything will work just fine."

The door closed and for a long moment, Zoe stood there, frozen. Furious. How dare those men con the people of Whirlwind! Well, not if she could help it. Intent on going straight to

Davis Lee, she quietly ducked around the curtain and came to a dead stop.

Egan Weaver stood in front of the door, arms folded, his features pinched with irritation.

Zoe's heart kicked hard in her chest.

"Well, well," he sneered. "I thought I heard someone in the bathing room. You were eavesdropping."

"No, I—"

"Shut up! You had to have overheard the discussion about the water bonds."

"Which are fake," she said hotly. "For a fake company and a water well you have no intention of drilling. You won't get away with this."

"No?" He smiled, his mouth a cruel slash that made her instinctively back up a step. "You're married to the newspaperman, aren't you?"

She didn't respond.

"You have a brother, too. Big fella, red hair like yours."

Zoe felt the blood drain from her face.

"If you breathe one word of this to anyone before I've left town, your husband and brother will pay for it."

"You can't steal from these people!" She told herself to be quiet, but the words kept coming. "Everyone in Texas was hit hard by the drought. Ranches, businesses. People need whatever money they have to provide for their families."

"People undoubtedly saw you come in here to clean my room so I can't get rid of you," he said more to himself than her.

Alarm streaked through her.

"A search party would probably be looking for you by daybreak, if not before. But your brother and crippled husband are another matter. I can't guarantee something won't happen to them. Do you understand what I'm saying?"

Would he really hurt them? Looking into the man's cold, flat eyes, Zoe knew he would. Queasy, she nodded. "Yes."

"And?"

She had to force herself to say the words. As it was, she could barely grit them out. "I won't tell anyone."

"I'll be keeping an eye on all of you to make sure of that."

Cold sweat slicked her palms, trickled down her spine. She nodded again.

He stepped away from the door and opened it slightly. "Get out of here and keep your mouth shut or you'll be sorry."

Her legs shaking so badly that she could scarcely walk, she made it to the door and out. She ran down the stairs as fast as she could. Once at the bottom, she looked up.

Weaver stood on the second-floor landing, his icy gaze fixed on her.

Swallowing hard, she walked to the big oak desk that welcomed people to the Fontaine. She glanced right toward the office which had been Russ Baldwin's living quarters before he and Lydia had married and moved to the third floor. From here, she could tell Russ wasn't inside. No one was.

Edgy and apprehensive, she didn't want to finish her job. She wanted to go home, but there was still the lobby to clean and the front porch to sweep. If she worked her full shift, she could watch Weaver, too. See if he left the hotel.

Mind racing, she moved the registration book and Russ's fancy writing pen to dust the desk. Her muscles tensed at every movement she caught from the corner of her eye.

There was no doubt in her mind that Weaver would hurt her family if she warned anyone about his cold-blooded, calculating scheme.

She couldn't—wouldn't—let anything happen to Quentin or Zeke. They had both already lost too much.

Chapter Four

Several hours later in the kitchen, Quentin watched Zoe cut out biscuits and put them in a pan. He was still reliving the kiss. And the way she had torn out of the house as though trying to escape a twister.

That kiss had spurred more than physical desire for him. It had strengthened his determination to walk. In the time since she had helped him to his feet, he had done it again by himself—and just barely managed to avoid crashing to the floor by catching himself on the desk in the next room that served as a parlor and his office.

His muscles were weak and aching, but he could feel them! If he could make himself stand on his own at least once a day, he might be able to surprise Zoe by walking soon. Besides changing his bandages, she helped him with exercises suggested by Annalise. He wouldn't have gotten this far without his wife.

If she moved out, as she had announced days ago that she would, Quentin was afraid he would see her only around town. Just like before. He wanted more than that.

Disappointed and frustrated with her decision to leave once his doctor agreed, he'd been thinking about her words for the past ten days. And trying to come up with a way to convince her to stay.

As she fixed supper, Zeke sat at the dining table with Quentin, working laboriously over a ledger where he recorded the money he received from the odd jobs he did around Whirlwind.

The front door was open to let some of the heat from the burning stove escape out the screened door. Outside, red and gold rays of the setting sun slanted across the side of the Fontaine. The town was quiet.

Quentin's attention was more on Zoe than her brother. He tried not to be too obvious as he admired her sleek curves. The sleeves of her peach-and-white-striped day-dress ended at her elbow. His gaze took in the line of her jaw, her straight nose, the delicate bones of her forearm. She gripped a sharp knife, her slender hands moving gracefully as she began to cut up a chicken for frying.

"I have thirty-six dollars," Zeke announced proudly.

The smile Zoe threw over her shoulder was tight and didn't reach her eyes. Since returning from the hotel, she'd seemed… agitated. A low-thrumming tension vibrated from her.

"What should I do with it?"

Quentin pulled his attention back to Zeke.

Gesturing to the small glass jar on the table that held his savings, the boy gave his sister an exasperated look. "I offered to give it to Zoe 'cuz she always takes care of me, but she wouldn't take it."

"There's no need for that," she said quietly.

"He just wants to help," Quentin pointed out.

"I know." With a soft smile, she glanced at her brother.

He turned to Zeke. "Maybe you could invest your savings."

"In what?"

"I'll give it some thought." Feeling Zoe's attention on him, Quentin looked over.

She watched him soberly. There was nothing of that kiss or desire in her blue eyes. Instead, worry clouded her features.

Had something happened at the hotel? "Did you have a good afternoon?" he asked.

"Yes."

Before she turned away, he thought he glimpsed fear in her face. What could she possibly have to fear?

Quentin frowned. "Anything special going on at the Fontaine?"

She stiffened. "Like what?"

"I don't know." He cocked his head, studying her. Her hair was pulled back in a braid and his gaze caught on a tender patch of skin just below her ear. "Anything out of the ordinary."

"No."

"You seem—"

"I'm fine."

Zeke looked from Quentin to Zoe then back again, a question in his eyes. Quentin wasn't imagining things. Even the teenager knew something was wrong.

Hands on her hips, she turned with a frown. Her skirts swirled around her legs as she looked over at the table then around the front room.

"What is it?" Quentin asked.

"I can't find the skillet."

His gaze went past her to the counter where she'd been working. "The skillet that's sitting next to the dry sink?"

"Yes." She looked back. "Oh, forevermore, it was right where I put it."

Taking down the crockery jar on the shelf above the

dry sink, she dipped lard into the skillet then returned the container to its place.

She stared hard at the counter for a moment before picking up a peeled potato. Taking the knife, she sliced the vegetable. She reached for another potato and fumbled it. Twice.

Muttering under her breath, she managed to stop the vegetable before it rolled off the counter.

Quentin couldn't make out the words, but she was obviously vexed. He'd never seen her scattered. Or clumsy. Another time, he might have found her unfamiliar actions amusing, but something was going on. She was pale and had been so since returning from the hotel.

He moved away from the table and across the few feet separating them. "May I help you do something?"

She started so violently that the knife slipped and she barely missed cutting herself.

"Sorry." Quentin put a hand over hers to steady her.

After a moment, she slid her hand from his and moved a step away. "No, thanks. I'm about to fry the chicken and potatoes."

"Is there something wrong?" he asked in a low voice.

"What would be wrong?"

That's what he wanted to know! But she clearly didn't intend to tell him. Maybe because Zeke was in the room?

Just as Quentin turned back to the table, he heard a dull thud on the wood floor. Before he could look to see what had fallen, Zoe rushed past him and out the front door.

He exchanged a look with Zeke. The boy seemed as perplexed as Quentin felt.

"I'll check on her," he said.

Zeke rose. "I'll pick up the chicken and wash it off."

Glancing at the meat Zoe had dropped, Quentin wheeled around the dining table and out the front door.

She stood at the end of the porch, looking out at the prairie that stretched west past Whirlwind. Golden light from the setting sun streaked her hair, making the fiery braid even more vibrant.

"Zoe."

Though she faced away from him, he saw her run her hands over her face. Was she crying?

He went past the ramp that Jake had built him several years ago to allow him to reach the porch from the street.

Coming to a stop behind her, Quentin cupped her elbow. "What is it?"

She turned, pulling gently from his hold at the same time. Now she looked mad rather than worried. "I'm just clumsy."

"And you usually aren't," he prompted quietly. "Something's bothering you."

"No, it's nothing."

"Sweetheart." He tugged her toward him until she stood against his footrests. Her skirts brushed the tops of his boots and he caught a whisper of her clean scent. "Tell me."

"It's nothing." She gave him a tremulous smile. "I promise. All day, I've been dropping things, misplacing others. I feel like I haven't done anything right all afternoon."

Disappointed that she wouldn't confide in him, he said gently, "You can tell me."

"There's nothing to tell. Dropping the chicken was the last straw and it made me mad, but I'm fine now."

He searched her eyes. She was hiding something. "It's more than that."

She shook her head.

"Are you sure?"

"Yes."

She was lying and Quentin thought he knew why. She didn't trust him enough to confide in him. It was all he could do to hold his tongue.

Though tempted to badger her for answers, he didn't. He wanted her to tell him because she wanted to.

"I'd better finish supper." She started to brush past him.

He snagged her hand. "I wanted to talk to you about something."

Looking wary, she nodded. "All right."

"You said you planned to leave when I'm fit enough. I want you to stay. I want you and Zeke both to stay."

"I don't think it's a good idea."

"Why?" Irritation burned through him. "Because you feel something for me and you don't want to?"

"Partly."

Taken aback at her bluntness, Quentin paused. At least she hadn't pulled away from him yet. "And the other part?"

"I don't think we can make this marriage work."

They could. That wasn't the problem. "You mean, you're afraid to try."

She was silent for a long moment then nodded. "All right, yes."

"Pushing you away was one of the worst mistakes of my life, Zoe. When I told you I wouldn't do it again, I meant it."

"I'm sure you did."

"But you don't believe me."

"I do."

"Then what?" His free hand tightened on the wheelchair arm. "What do you want, woman?"

"Nothing. You've already done more than enough for me and Zeke. You've helped tremendously and I appreciate it."

"I don't want your damn gratitude," he growled. "I want you. I want us to stay married, be a family."

"I'm not sure I want that."

A hot sharpness tightened his chest. He forced himself to

think past it. "Then staying with me awhile longer can't hurt. In fact, it could help you decide."

Did he sound as desperate as he felt? Probably. He saw her glance toward town, toward the Fontaine. The tension he'd noticed earlier returned.

What now? "Zoe?"

Features taut, she looked at him, blue eyes burning into his. "All right. Once you've recovered, I'll stay for a little longer."

"You will?"

She nodded.

What had made her change her mind? His gaze went past hers, searching for what could've prompted her to agree.

He recognized Russ Baldwin's broad back as the man disappeared into the Fontaine. Egan Weaver, the man from the water company, stood talking to another man Quentin didn't recognize. Naomi Gerard and her husband, Ef, were closing up the smithy for the day.

What had Zoe wound up tighter than an eight-day watch? Quentin had no idea and he knew she wouldn't tell him. Not yet anyway.

Directing his attention back to her, he smiled. "Thank you. You won't be sorry."

She glanced toward town then moved around him. "I'll finish supper."

"I'll help you." Watching the sway of her skirts, he wheeled his chair back inside.

Halting in the doorway, he glanced back at the Fontaine. The townspeople he'd seen earlier were gone now.

He'd convinced her to stay awhile longer. To some extent, he was satisfied. But something didn't sit right. He strongly suspected her agreement to spend more time with him was based on something or someone besides him, but what or who?

* * *

Quentin knew she was hiding something from him. Last night, she'd seen the hurt in his eyes, the same hurt he'd once made her feel, and she got no satisfaction from it. She wanted to tell him everything about what she'd overheard at the hotel, but she was afraid of what Weaver might do.

Anxiety chewed at her. Hiding her apprehension from Quentin promised to be as difficult as shoveling sunshine.

After they'd gone to bed, she had worried about it. Her restlessness had woken Quentin.

She'd felt him stir. "Zoe?"

"Hmm." She had tensed.

"I'm here."

That was all. He hadn't pushed, hadn't said anything else. And she'd been able to sleep after that. Just knowing he was there calmed her. It also made her want to protect him even more.

He had made her all kinds of nervous last night by saying he wanted her to stay. She still wasn't sure that agreeing to do so was the right thing, but regardless, she was staying. Her leaving might protect Quentin, but it wouldn't protect Zeke. However, if she stayed, Quentin and Zeke could watch out for each other when she wasn't around.

Safety wasn't the only reason Zoe had allowed herself to be convinced. Like Quentin, she wondered if things could work between them. More time together would help her determine if she wanted anything more with him.

That evening, she, Quentin and Zeke arrived at the church just before Egan Weaver's meeting was scheduled to begin. It was straight-up six o'clock. Every pew in the church was full. Zoe hadn't seen this many people in here since Jake and Emma Ross's wedding. Though dismayed at the size of the crowd, she understood.

They were desperate. And Weaver was taking advantage.

Eyes narrowing, she watched the lying sack of bones make his way to the front and up to the reverend's podium! He had some nerve.

She, Quentin and Zeke found a place along the wall with Davis Lee, Josie and their baby. Davis Lee's brother, Riley, stood a few feet away next to their neighbor, Jake Ross. His brother, Bram, had only just returned empty-handed from chasing a murdering cattle rustler named Cosgrove.

"Ladies and gentlemen," Weaver said over the low din of the crowd. "Thank you for coming tonight. Let's get started, shall we?"

The room quieted as the man explained that he worked for a company that drilled for water near areas that didn't have a natural supply.

"After I give you a general overview, I'll take questions."

The con man explained that in order to get to the water, the Weaver Water Company needed capital for equipment and labor.

"The citizens of Whirlwind will be given the opportunity to purchase bonds. Money from those sales will be used to drill the well. When the bonds mature, you receive your money back plus interest."

"And when do the bonds mature?" Davis Lee asked, shifting his dark-haired infant daughter to one shoulder.

Weaver smiled. "One year from the date of purchase."

It all sounded so legitimate. And maybe it was when someone else was involved. But Zoe knew what Weaver had planned and it was killing her to keep her mouth shut.

A man stepped up beside Zoe and she automatically eased closer to Quentin to give the newcomer some room.

"Evenin', ma'am."

She froze. She knew that voice. It belonged to the man she'd overheard talking to Weaver yesterday evening in his hotel room. All day, she'd been looking over her shoulder, especially when she had left her job at the Fontaine to have supper with Quentin and Zeke.

The man beside her was her height with a slender build. Neatly combed brown hair, hazel eyes, bland features. There was nothing memorable about him. It probably allowed him to sneak around without much notice.

She flicked a glance at Quentin. His attention was trained on Weaver, who was explaining that his company wanted to drill the water well at Little Bitter Creek near Whirlwind.

The stranger gripped Zoe's wrist, keeping both their hands hidden by the folds of her skirts.

She tried to jerk away. He squeezed hard and she bit back a gasp at the bite of pain.

"You'd best keep your mouth shut," he said in a low, cold voice.

Weaver's gaze locked on hers and her heart kicked hard.

He gestured in her direction. "This is my associate, Cyrus Gordon."

As the collective gazes of the audience members moved to the man beside Zoe, he released her and bowed to the audience.

She wanted to get away from Gordon something fierce, but she barely had room to move her foot, let alone get to another spot.

Quentin raised his hand, waiting until he could be heard before asking, "Have you done this in other places? What kind of experience do you have?"

Cyrus Gordon drifted away as a murmur of appreciation went through the audience. Zoe rubbed her wrist, glaring after the man.

"Good question, Quentin," Jake said quietly beside him.

"Excellent questions," the con man boomed. "Weaver Water Company has been involved with the successful drilling of several water wells in Kansas and Oklahoma Territory. I have some newspaper articles documenting that fact."

He held up a clothbound volume. "I'll pass around the book containing the information. Please return it to me at the end of the meeting. I can answer any questions you have. I realize this is hard-earned money you're thinking of spending."

And he was stealing it!

"Say we bought these bonds," Davis Lee spoke up. "When would the drilling start? How long before we'd be able to get water from the well?"

"Drilling would start within a month, Sheriff. It will take that long to get the equipment to Abilene by train then by wagon to Little Bitter Creek. As far as when the water would be available, that depends on how deep we have to drill. Once we hit the pocket of water, it will be ready to use."

Oooh, Zoe fumed. This made her so mad. Weaver knew exactly what to say to lull these people into trusting him. If she hadn't overheard his atrocious plan, she'd be halfway to believing him herself.

The lying varmint answered a few more questions. During a lull in which no one asked anything further, the meeting was dismissed. People made their way up to the con man, including Zeke.

Zoe caught a glimpse of the Eishens. Glen and Lettie were first in line, poring over a document Weaver handed them. Zoe prayed the couple wouldn't fall prey to the snake's scheme, but she knew they were desperate. Their entire pecan harvest was at risk. The drought had hurt their crop just as it had hurt their neighbors' livelihoods.

She searched the crowd for Zeke and finally saw his broad shoulders and red hair. He was talking to Cyrus Gordon. Zoe's stomach knotted. Did Gordon know Zeke was Zoe's brother, as Weaver did?

Apprehension scraped her already raw nerves. She felt the

same cold fear she'd felt when Weaver had first threatened her brother and husband.

Behind her, Quentin, Davis Lee and Jake were talking in low tones. Should she go and fetch her brother? If Gordon didn't already know the teenager was her brother, that would tell him. But she couldn't just let Zeke stay with Weaver's partner.

"Zoe?"

She became aware that Quentin was talking to her. She dragged her gaze from Zeke to her husband.

"You look upset. What's wrong?"

"Nothing."

Maneuvering his wheelchair so that he faced her, he gave her a flat stare.

She forced a laugh. "I promise. I'm squished flat in here with all these people and it's hot."

His mouth tightened, then he turned back to Jake.

Intending to tell Quentin she was fetching Zeke, she touched his shoulder. He glanced up, covering her hand with his.

Jake's black gaze fell to their hands then he looked at Zoe, speculation in his eyes.

She started to pull away when she saw her brother coming toward her—followed by Cyrus Gordon. Her hand tightened on Quentin's shoulder and he frowned up at her.

What was Gordon doing? Showing her he could get close to her brother whenever he wanted?

As they neared, the older man guided Zeke forward with a hand on his shoulder. Everything inside Zoe wanted to smack the man's hand away. Or shoot him! Her free hand curled into a fist.

The two men came to a stop in front of her. Gordon clapped her brother on the shoulder. "I told Zeke you were probably looking for him so I brought him on over."

"Thank you," she said tightly.

"Certainly." The man tipped his hat, his gaze boring into hers for a moment before he moved to the back door. He answered more questions as people left the church.

Relieved that Zeke was back near once again, she turned to Quentin. "Are you ready to go?"

He was studying Weaver, who was still at the front of the church with a few people.

"I want to interview Weaver for the newspaper," Quentin said. "Find out more about him and this venture."

Just the thought of Quentin being so close to the con man made her break out in a cold sweat. "That's not a good idea."

"Why not?"

She chanced a look at the swindler and found his attention locked on her. Equal parts anger and fear made her voice sharp. "I don't like him."

"We don't even know him. If I ask him a few questions for the newspaper, we'll learn something."

Her first inclination was to protest, but then she realized that her husband's questions might expose the deception. Or at least raise Quentin's suspicions.

But what if Quentin's questions angered Weaver? Or what if he convinced Quentin to purchase bonds? This whole thing burned Zoe up.

Davis Lee and Jake said goodbye, walking out of the church together. Quentin turned toward her just as Zeke moved in front of him.

"Quentin, I found somewhere to invest my money! Mr. Gordon explained that if I buy this bond, I'll be helping Whirlwind get water. That's what I want to do."

"You aren't buying any bonds," Zoe said firmly.

"But Zoe—"

"You aren't, period."

"It's my money." His chin angled at her. "Quentin said I should invest it."

Her brother was rarely stubborn, but Zoe could see he meant to fight her on this. "I'm sure Quentin will help you find somewhere else to invest."

"No. This is what I want to do." He glared at Zoe, who shook her head in exasperation.

Quentin touched her hand. "Your brother's always been careful with his money. And it is *his* money."

All Zoe could see was her brother losing every cent he'd worked so hard for. "No."

"The Eishens did it!" Zeke burst out.

Quentin nodded. "Never known Glen or Lettie to be foolish with their money."

If they knew what Zoe knew, they wouldn't have been this time either.

"No." She took Zeke's arm.

He shook her off, glaring, his freckled face red with anger.

She glared back.

Looking at them both, Quentin said, "I'll go ask Weaver some questions right now. If I'm satisfied with his answers, Zeke can buy a bond."

Then Quentin would also become a dupe. She couldn't tell what she knew and she wouldn't let Zeke throw away his money either.

He was her brother. She had always taken care of him and she always would.

"No," she said to Quentin.

"Zoe, why are you so set against it? I won't let him do anything foolish."

Frustrated and afraid, she snapped, "This is none of your affair. Stay out of it."

Quentin recoiled as if she'd slapped him. His face went

blank in a way she had never seen. It was completely devoid of emotion. The coldness of it made her stomach drop, but she grabbed Zeke's hand and tugged.

She knew what she'd said was unfair, but she couldn't take it back.

Zeke looked confused. And hurt. "Zoe?"

"C'mon," she said. "We're leaving."

He looked helplessly at Quentin.

"Zoe, listen," her husband started.

If she did, Quentin would be able to talk her into whatever he wanted. Just as he had last night.

In a low voice, she said, "I agreed to stay with you for a while longer. I didn't agree to let you take over my life."

Hurt flashed in his eyes, then they hardened. He looked at Zeke. "It's okay, son. I'll see you later at home."

He wheeled his chair around and headed toward Weaver, saying to Zoe over his shoulder, "I'll catch up."

Fighting anger and uncertainty, she watched him go. She hated this! She shouldn't have said those things to Quentin. She knew that she owed him an apology.

But she couldn't offer one. If she did, she would end up telling him everything. He and Zeke would be in danger. And she would be to blame.

Chapter Five

Zoe had to apologize to Quentin. She had fretted about it for the past two days. Even though her words had been motivated by fear, that was no reason to have spoken to him so coldly.

She had avoided the apology and the house because she was close to blurting out the truth about Weaver and his scheme.

Since the town meeting, things had been tense and quiet between her and Quentin. And yet, she never once wondered if he would be home when she returned from work each evening. She knew he would be, despite being angry with her.

Home. That was how Zoe thought of Quentin's house now, she realized as she stepped up on the wide porch that evening.

Through the screened door, she could see her husband and brother in the front room, clearly profiled in the glitter of the setting sun as Zeke helped Quentin into his wheelchair. Had her brother been assisting Quentin with his exercises when Zoe wasn't around?

She reached for the door as her husband settled himself in his chair and glanced at Zeke. "What did Mr. Gordon say to you?"

"He said they still had a few bonds," the teenager replied. "I can buy one if I want."

Bristling, Zoe paused.

"You didn't buy any, did you?" Quentin asked.

"Not yet."

The relief she felt was so strong that it caused an ache in her chest.

"That's good." Quentin moved a few feet closer to the young man. "Your sister wouldn't have been happy."

"I don't care." Zeke's voice vibrated with resentment. "*You* didn't think it was a bad idea."

"I said I wasn't sure if it was or not. I've asked Weaver some questions and I'm still not certain you should buy one of those bonds."

Thank goodness, Quentin was siding with her on this. He might not know what she did about Weaver's scheme, but he wasn't comfortable with the "opportunity."

Zoe was tempted to talk to him about this, but if she started asking questions, he would figure out lickety-split that her anxiety was somehow related to Weaver or the bond issue.

"Remember what we talked about earlier?" Quentin asked her brother.

"Yes." The boy's voice brightened. "Will you still let me do it?"

"If Zoe agrees. You need to talk it over with her."

"I don't want to."

"I know, but she's your sister."

"She was mean to you." Zeke turned, enabling her to see his profile and the angry set of his jaw. "She was mean to both of us."

She should probably apologize to her brother, too, Zoe thought, even though she wasn't changing her mind about letting him spend his money on those bonds. And exactly what was Quentin willing to let Zeke do?

Her husband was quiet for a long moment. "Sometimes

people come across as mean when they're just worried or afraid. Zoe loves you very much and she feels responsible for you. She just doesn't want you to make a mistake with your money."

Tears burned her throat.

"It took you a long time to earn that," Quentin continued. "You want to use it wisely."

His words had Zoe wincing. After the way she'd lit into him, he was defending her to her brother. The urge to tell him everything grew even stronger.

"After supper," Quentin said, "why don't you talk to her?"

"Talk to whom about what?" Zoe asked brightly as she stepped inside.

She glanced at Quentin, but he wasn't looking at her. He nodded encouragingly to Zeke.

Her brother eyed her defiantly. "Quentin said I could invest in his bees."

"You'd buy into the business, Zeke," the man corrected. "You'd be my partner and we would share the profits."

Zeke drew himself up, pride shining in his blue eyes. "Yeah, I'd be his partner."

Zoe's gaze shot to her husband, her chest tightening. "Are you sure? Zeke only has the experience you've given him."

"He's good with the bees, Zoe."

The younger man beamed. She swallowed past the lump in her throat.

Quentin showed a faith in her brother no one else ever had. Did he realize he was giving Zeke a way to take care of himself if something happened to her or to Quentin?

She melted inside. "It's kind of you to offer," she said hoarsely.

"I'm getting a good deal. Zeke has a knack for beekeeping and harvesting the honey."

"So?" Zeke demanded impatiently of her. "Can I do it?"

Zoe's gaze locked with Quentin's. Did the man know what this meant to her? It was plain he knew what it meant to her brother.

"Yes," she said softly. "You can do it."

Zeke whooped and rushed around the dining table to scoop her up in a big hug. She hugged him back, grabbing the back of Quentin's chair for balance when her brother put her down quickly and rushed toward the hall.

She laughed. "Where are you going?"

"To get my money!"

Quentin grinned. "You can do it later."

"I want to do it now!"

As Zeke disappeared into his room, Zoe moved closer to Quentin. "You don't have to let him invest in your apiary, although it's very kind."

"He really is good with the bees." Quentin moved away from her, causing a hollowness in her stomach.

He was still angry. She didn't blame him.

"I'm not offering because I'm trying to smooth the waters between you two."

"I understand," she murmured.

"This is the first chance I've had to speak to you in a couple of days. You've been avoiding me," he said coolly.

She shifted nervously. "Not really."

He gave her a flat stare. "You've been scarce since the town meeting, which was probably good. It gave me a chance to cool down."

She grimaced. "Quentin."

"Are you regretting our marriage? Your agreement to stay?"

"No." She eased closer to him, relieved when he didn't move away. "Not at all."

"What am I supposed to think? I know we have a problem."

"It's not—"

"Don't bother denying it."

It's not what you think! She wanted to cry out, but she couldn't. However, she could try to make amends.

"I'm sorry for the things I said the other night." The words rushed out. "I didn't mean them. I was worried about Zeke. You were right—I was being overprotective. It's hard not to be when I'm all he's had for most of his life."

For a long moment, Quentin said nothing. A muscle jumped as he clenched his jaw.

Didn't he believe her? "I really am sorry."

"I'd like to think so, but I wonder if you're only apologizing so I'll stop asking you what's wrong."

Hurt stabbed at her. "I mean it, Quentin. I've wanted to apologize since I said it. You've only ever tried to help me and Zeke. It's clear that you have my brother's best interests at heart. And mine. I appreciate that. You don't know how much."

"I've told you before. Gratitude isn't what I want from you."

At first, she thought he meant he wanted her physically, but no, she realized as she stared into his somber eyes. He wanted her to confide in him.

After the way she'd behaved, he could've told her things were over. Could've helped Zeke buy the bonds. But Quentin hadn't done any of that.

He'd been patient, steady, true. And she'd hurt him.

She was sorry for that, but she was protecting him and Zeke. Wasn't that the important thing?

A little voice niggled at her. Hadn't Quentin thought the same thing about her when he had pushed her out of his life seven years ago?

He turned toward Zeke's room though he looked at her. "I meant what I said about wanting our marriage to work. I'm not going anywhere."

"I know." She held his gaze. She was completely sure of him. She still loved him, she admitted. In fact, she was more in love with him than she had been in the past. "I know you won't leave."

"When you're ready to talk, to tell me what's going on, I'll be here. But my patience is running out, Zoe. You should be aware of that, too."

She nodded, her chest aching as he moved toward Zeke's room. Only now did she realize that she had been—was—building something with Quentin. *They* were building a future.

And her silence could destroy it.

She was sick to death of Weaver and his partner eyeing her and her brother and husband every time they left the house.

She had to find something incriminating on the con man. Until she did, her marriage was in jeopardy.

Over the next few days, Quentin recognized Zoe's apology as an attempt to put things right.

But they weren't right and wouldn't be as long as she kept secrets. However, she'd made an effort. He couldn't expect everything from her all at once.

It crossed his mind that she might be keeping him in the dark to get back at him for pushing her away years ago, but he'd immediately dismissed the thought. Zoe didn't play games like that. Besides, whatever was bothering her put her on edge, made her jittery. It had nothing to do with retaliation.

She'd said she didn't regret their marriage or her decision to stay. That was good, but it was obvious that if Quentin wanted to know what was wrong with his wife, he was going to have to figure it out on his own.

So, he watched her.

Not spying exactly and not every minute, but he paid very close attention when she went to work at Josie's or Haskell's or the Fontaine. He took note of who she spoke to in town and how she seemed afterward, realizing that she was most agitated after her shifts at the hotel. But why?

Three days after Zoe had apologized, Quentin left Annalise's clinic via the back door as he always did. He wheeled his way up the side of the building then out of the shade into the afternoon sun.

According to Annalise, he could do anything he wanted as long as he was careful. And what he wanted was his wife. How much longer until she was ready?

Red dust swirling beneath his wheels, he headed to the newspaper office to talk to Hoot Eckert about returning to work. He approached Haskell's General Store where Charlie stood on the porch under the wood awning, talking to Davis Lee and Matt Baldwin.

Quentin greeted all of them, pleasantly surprised when Matt came down the steps to shake hands.

"How do you like married life?" the rancher asked.

"Pretty well. When are you going to make an honest woman of Annalise?"

Matt and Annalise had reconciled just before Quentin and Zoe's marriage.

The big man grinned. "As soon as she says the word. Josie's making her a dress."

Quentin was slowly healing the rift he'd created with more than half the town when he'd ambushed his former brother-in-law, Jake Ross, in a hail of bullets. His resentment over his sister's death and his paralysis had consumed him.

Matt had been the first to give Quentin a chance to make amends by trusting him with Annalise's safety during one of the rancher's several out-of-town attempts to catch a band of

murdering rustlers. Quentin considered the big man a friend
and he thought Matt felt the same. Friends were something
Quentin didn't take for granted anymore.

After a brief exchange with Davis Lee and Charlie, Quentin
continued to the newspaper office. From the corner of his eye,
he caught a flash of copper and looked over at the Fontaine.
His wife stepped off the hotel's sandstone porch and started
toward the livery a few yards away. She was likely on some
errand for a hotel guest. She didn't appear to have seen him.

He started to call out when she halted in front of the hotel,
but something stopped him. She looked back, her gaze going
to the second-floor balcony. Or was it the third floor? Quentin
wasn't sure.

Fear crossed her face, fear so stark that protectiveness
surged through him. Then she hurried over to the livery.

As he paused at the foot of the ramp in front of the newspaper office, Quentin's gaze panned the long porch of the
Fontaine and its two balconies. He saw no one. Of the people
walking along Main Street, there were no familiar faces. Egan
Weaver's announced plan to drill a water well nearby had
brought a slew of visitors to Whirlwind, but Quentin saw
no one following Zoe or even paying much attention to her.
Certainly not as much as he was.

Even so, something had frightened his wife and Quentin
wasn't having it. What the hell was going on? Was his handi-
cap the reason she wouldn't tell him? Did she think he couldn't
protect her? Well, he could.

He might have decided—reluctantly—to let her tell him the
problem in her own time, but that didn't mean he was going
to sit idly by while she grew more distressed.

It was well after six that evening when Quentin heard the
tap of Zoe's shoes on the porch. He went to the door of his

small office and levered himself out of his wheelchair, bracing himself with his cane.

She came inside, closing the screened door behind her. Looking tired, she hung her calico bonnet on the peg beside the door. Her gaze met his as she smoothed a few stray wisps of hair away from her face. "Hi," she said softly.

"Hi." The dark circles under her eyes attested to the restless nights she'd been having lately, tossing and turning in their bed. Quentin hadn't asked her about those, figuring they were related to the problem she wouldn't share with him.

Glancing at his wheelchair, she started toward him. "Let me help you."

"No." He held up a hand. "Stay there for a minute. Please."

"Why?"

Rather than tell her, he showed her. Shifting to his right foot, he took a halting step toward her.

She drew in a sharp breath. He took another step. And another, using his cane for support and balance.

"Oh, Quentin!" She pressed a hand to her chest, her eyes filling with tears.

Last evening, before starting his exercises with Zoe, he had gotten out of the wheelchair under his own steam. The surprise and admiration on her face then had filled him with satisfaction. The pure joy and affection he saw in her eyes now was even better.

Slowly, carefully, he made his way to her, finally stopping inches away. Close enough to catch a whiff of her clean soap scent, to see the fine grain of her silky skin.

She smiled through her tears. "You did it!"

The sense of accomplishment was greater than he'd expected. "I've been working every day."

"In addition to the time you exercised with me?"

"Yes."

"This is so wonderful." She wiped away the wetness on her cheeks and raised her arms then lowered them, looking uncertain. "I want to hug you."

"Go ahead."

"Are you sure?"

"Yes." Every cell in his body hummed with the need to feel her.

She slid her arms around his waist and squeezed. "I'm so proud of you."

The smile on her face had his heart pounding. He flattened a palm to her lower back, urging her fully against him. For a long moment, he just held her.

He buried his face in her neck, drawing in her scent, sliding his free hand into her low chignon to lock her to him, even though she showed no sign of pulling away.

Every inch of her was plastered against every inch of him. He savored the press of her body against his, the tickle of her warm breath on his throat. The fact that she stood between his legs, right up against him.

He'd thought he would never again be able to experience something so simple.

Still feeling steady, he drew back and nudged her chin up. "It's been a long time since I was able to hold you this way."

She nodded, her eyes soft on his face.

Quentin felt as if he could do anything. Including make love to his wife. But was she ready? Was *he?*

They had a couple of hours alone because Zeke was working this evening at the Whirlwind Hotel for Penn and Esther Wavers.

Quentin lowered his head, his voice hoarse with need when he said, "Zoe?"

"Yes," she whispered quickly, lifting her face to his and letting him know she was aware of exactly what he was asking.

His mouth settled on hers. Her hands framed his face and she kissed him as greedily as he kissed her. Quentin's world narrowed to the woman in his arms. Her mouth hot on his, the satiny feel of her hair in his fingers. He couldn't get enough of her.

All the need, the driving want he had thought he would never feel again swept over him, throbbed deep and low. His legs felt like sand. He thought his knees might buckle.

She tasted sweet and hot. The soft noise she made had his hold tightening. Her nails raked his nape as her fingers delved into his hair. Wanting more of her, Quentin's lips moved to her neck, the only part of her bared by her white shirtwaist. He wanted the garment off, wanted to feel her satiny naked flesh against his.

She moved against him and the full-blown sensation that shot through him was so keen that it bordered on pain. Hard with need, he swelled against her hip. His breathing turned rough.

"Quentin." Her voice shook. "I can feel you."

He could feel it, too, and it felt damn good. He lifted his head to look at her. "I want you."

Her eyes darkened. "I want you, too, but are you ready?"

"I've been ready for a long time," he said huskily. "I want to make love to my wife."

She lifted a shaking hand to his face. "But what if it undoes the progress you've made?"

"I talked to Annalise about it, and she said as long as we're careful and stop if there's any pain, things should be fine."

She flushed. Impatient to see if she turned that rosy-pink all over, he kissed her again, hard. "Tell me yes, sweetheart."

Her blue eyes searched his. He didn't know what she was looking for, but he hoped she found it. She had to or he might explode.

"Yes," she said softly.

Chapter Six

Quentin was barely aware of getting to the bedroom. He felt no pain. All he could feel was Zoe.

He settled on the bed, easing back against the big pine headboard that had belonged to his parents. Drawing her next to the bed, he said hoarsely, "Take your hair down."

She did and when it fell in a wild tumble of red silk, he reached out to touch the thick waves. One shiny curl wrapped around his finger. Her blue eyes darkened with desire as she watched him curiously.

The scent of clean skin and a sweetness that was all Zoe drifted to him.

Her pulse beat wildly in her throat. He wanted to put his mouth there. Everywhere. Her chest rose and fell beneath her high-necked white bodice.

Keeping his gaze on hers, he undid the top button of her blouse then the second. Unbelievably, his hand shook. Maybe he shouldn't be surprised. It had been a damn long time since he'd been with a woman. Plus, this was Zoe. *His* woman.

As he worked his way down, the fabric parted to reveal

glimpses of her pearly skin dusted with freckles. Full breasts swelled over the top edge of her chemise. He didn't know why she hadn't worn a corset today, but he was glad.

She slid her blouse off and he curved his hand around one warm, lush breast. Her breathing hitched when he brushed a thumb across her taut nipple. Impatient to see the rest of her, he untied the ribbon on her chemise and pushed the loose fabric off her shoulders, baring her to the waist.

Her creamy breasts were full, her nipples rosy and tight.

For a long moment, he just stared, taking in the soft pink hue of arousal on her fair skin.

Looking self-conscious, she shifted. "Quentin."

"I'm just thanking my lucky stars, sweetheart. You're a sight."

She blushed, raising her hands to cover herself.

He stopped her, covering the plump flesh with his hands instead. A breath shuddered out of her. That quickly, his blood heated.

He reached for her, but she drew away.

"I don't want to shuck out of my clothes if you aren't."

He pulled his white shirt over his head and dropped it on the floor. Just as he undid the buttons on his trousers, she touched his chest.

He looked up to find her gaze tracking over his torso. She flexed her fingers in the dark hair there then laid her palm over his heart. She looked completely taken with him, as if she were seeing him for the first time.

"You've seen me without a shirt before," he said gruffly, his entire body going hard. He slept in only his short drawers.

"Yes, but I tried not to look."

He grinned. Much to his consternation, she always kept to her side of the bed and he hadn't tried to coax her closer. Now he didn't have to.

She looked at him with anticipation and awe. Expectation.

It brought him up short. For the first time, Quentin was hit with doubt. What if he couldn't do his part?

Did she sense his uncertainty? If so, it didn't stop her from leaning forward and kissing him. When she pulled the tapes on her drawers and pushed them off, Quentin removed his trousers. He waited until she got rid of her shoes and stockings before pulling her down onto the bed.

She knelt beside him, her eyes full of trust and caring. Thoughts of leaving them both unsatisfied disappeared from his mind. There was only Zoe and she was perfect.

She watched him with a look of wonder on her face. At least she wasn't wary, but she wasn't moving fast enough either. He fought for control. He wanted to make it as good for her as possible, but he was on a hair trigger.

Her gaze traced slowly over him, causing a prickle of heat under his skin. She stared for so long that he started to worry she might call a halt.

She reached out then let her hand drop. "Is there anywhere I shouldn't touch you? Your surgery—"

"You can touch me anywhere, Zoe. I won't break." He caught her hand and closed it around him.

Acute sensation shot through him, the intensity taking him off guard. There was a razor-sharp sting in his lower back.

"Quentin?" Concern clouded her blue eyes.

The pain faded to a warm pulse of pleasure. "I'm all right."

Her hands smoothed up his chest then back over his stomach to his thighs. He drew her to him for a kiss, sliding a palm down her smooth belly and easing a finger into her silky heat.

"Oh!" She arched toward him.

"Too much?"

"No, it's good," she breathed.

The sight of her, naked and flushed with desire, unraveled something inside him. He curled another finger inside her and waited until her body softened for him. When his thumb circled the sensitive knot between her legs, she cried out and gripped his shoulder.

She shifted impatiently, taking him in her hand. As her gaze lifted to his, her fingers stilled. Blushing, she asked, "What's the best way for you?"

"You on top." He grazed her cheekbone with his thumb, loving the sight of all that red hair cascading around her shoulders. "But that might hurt you more and I don't want that for your first time."

"I'll be all right."

"No."

"Yes," she insisted, easing onto his lap and straddling him.

He hesitated, fighting the rush in his blood that urged him to bury himself in her right now. "It's been so long. I hope I haven't forgotten how," he murmured.

"I hope so, too, because I've sure never done this before."

He chuckled.

Her eyes were soft with desire. With caring. "I want it to be good."

He cupped her cheek. "It will be just because it's you and me."

She smiled at that. He wasn't sure how much control he could manage.

She shifted and after long, deliciously excruciating minutes, he guided her down on him, watching for any sign of discomfort.

He thought she winced, and stopped. "You okay?"

"Oh, yes."

But he caught a flash of discomfort on her face. He held her hips until she relaxed. "There's no hurry, honey."

She nodded, but as soon as he loosened his fingers, she pushed down hard, drawing in a sharp breath.

So did he, clamping his hands firmly on her hips. "Slow down, Zoe. Don't rush it."

"I'm okay," she said breathlessly.

The tight clutch of her around him felt good. He slid his fingers into her hair and kissed her, deep and slow.

She was only his, had never been with another man. That filled him with a primitive, fierce satisfaction as he nuzzled her neck then bit down gently on her earlobe.

"Oh!" She sank down fully on him.

He could feel her, not just with just his hands, but with his whole body. It was incredible! And before his surgery, it was something he had almost stopped hoping for. Wanting to relish every sensation, every second, he held her still until she squirmed against him.

"Quentin?"

"Hmm." He kissed his way to her breast, taking her in his mouth.

"Do something." She tightened her muscles on him and he surged inside her. "Yes, that," she breathed.

He wrapped his arms around her and brought her even closer, enjoying the feel of her naked flesh against his. The amber light from the setting sun veiled her hair, bringing out the fiery color, giving her ivory skin a golden glow.

Those sky-blue eyes never left his. He could feel the heat beneath her skin, the pounding of her heart against his.

A ragged moan spilled out of her and it set something off inside him. Something primitive and fierce. Flattening a hand against her lower back, he tilted her slightly and began to move. Hard-edged want moved through him, but there was no pain. Just a spike of sensation all over his body.

She let him guide her, holding his face, her blue eyes liquid with desire. He rocked inside her in a slow steady motion, muscles coiling as he fought to wait for her. Finally, she let go and so did he.

Afterward, she laid her head on his chest. She was finally, really his.

They sat together as their pulses slowed, their skin damp and hot. The headboard was rough against Quentin's back.

Pleasure shone on Zoe's face and a tenderness he'd never felt swept through him.

They lay there, drowsy, watching the end-of-day sunlight slant across the foot of the bed. After a long moment, she said, "I'm sorry I couldn't go to the doctor with you today."

"That's all right. I know how busy you've been because of all these visitors to Whirlwind. Both the Whirlwind Hotel and the Fontaine are full to capacity."

She stiffened and his arms automatically locked around her, but she stayed put.

"Tell me what Annalise said during your visit today."

"She believes I'll regain full sensation and likely the use of my legs."

"Well, we know she was right about the full sensation," she said huskily.

He laughed, skimming his hand up and down her velvety back.

"I want to thank you again for offering to let Zeke invest in your bees." She snuggled into him. "You did something for him that I've never been able to do."

"What's that?"

"You gave him confidence in himself. And a way to make a living if something happens to you or me." She lightly stroked his chest.

It took a moment for her words to work past the desire

clouding his thoughts. Why would she say that? He frowned down at her. "Something like what?"

"Nothing in particular. Just if one or both of us passed away or was hurt."

He thought her hand trembled slightly and the smile she gave him this time was wobbly.

"I don't think you need to worry so much about Zeke, especially in regard to his money." In an effort to reassure Zoe, Quentin said, "He told me earlier that he was no longer interested in Weaver's bonds. He told Weaver the same."

Expecting her to be relieved, Quentin was surprised when she tensed against him. "Are you afraid Zeke will do it anyway?"

"No," she said brusquely. "Are you planning to invest?"

Why was she vexed? Things had been going well until he'd mentioned the bonds. "No, I don't plan to."

"Good." She relaxed slightly, settling against him.

Her anxiety had something to do with the bonds. Or was it because of Weaver or Gordon? Testing his theory, Quentin said, "Plenty of people have bought, though. Weaver and his partner have done a lot of business here."

Twin spots of color flagged her cheeks. Angry color. Any mention of the water-company agent or his partner put Zoe on edge.

He tried to remember when his wife had begun acting spooked. He thought it was around the time Weaver came to town. But why would that upset her?

They were as close now as two people could be. Surely she would confide in him.

"I love you, Zoe."

She looked up at him. She didn't say anything and he couldn't deny that her silence hurt like hell. He had no defenses against this woman. He knew she trusted him not to push her away again. Why couldn't she stop doing it to him?

She raised up on one elbow and kissed him. She might not be speaking the words, but he could read the caring in her soft touch on his face, the increasing intensity of their kiss.

Why wouldn't she just say it? Quentin fought back his frustration and irritation. She appeared to want their marriage to work. She was slowly letting him in, dropping her guard. It wasn't much, but it was something.

Still, he wanted more. He wanted his wife, body, soul and heart.

Tomorrow, he was going to find out what she was keeping from him and he wasn't taking no for an answer.

The next morning, Zoe lay in bed next to Quentin. She slowly came awake. She was tender in places she'd never been tender.

She looked up to find him still asleep. His hair was tousled, whiskers shadowing his jaw.

She was his wife in every way now.

The hard lines of his body fitted against the curved softness of hers. The first pinkish-white light of day flowed through the window and over his naked body. Quentin was as hot as a furnace. The sheet covered her, but his hips were draped with only the edge of the linen.

She admired the lean taper of his torso, the band of muscles across his belly, his solid sun-bronzed arms. He smelled of man and salt and a little bit of her. After another long moment of indulgence, she carefully slipped out of bed to fix breakfast.

Quentin loved her. And she loved him. But Zoe hadn't told him so last night. It didn't feel right to say those words when she was keeping something from him.

And she'd seen the hurt in his eyes. That had caused her pain, too. He'd been patient, more than she deserved. Yesterday, Weaver had led her to believe that he and his partner were leaving Whirlwind today. As soon as the con men made tracks out of town, she was going to tell Quentin everything. She just hoped it wasn't too late.

After about thirty minutes, Zoe heard Quentin stir in the bedroom. Using his cane, he walked into the kitchen and her heart swelled again at the progress he'd made. He wore only dark trousers and the sight of his tautly muscled flesh had her remembering last night and the second time they'd made love.

Her gaze followed the dark hair on his chest down to the well-hewn plane of his stomach. She nearly burned her fingers as she took the biscuits out of the stove.

"Morning." The huskiness of his voice sent a shiver through her.

"Good morning."

He waited until she set the biscuits and ham on the table then he hooked one arm around her waist and pulled her to him for a kiss. Zoe held him tight, kissing him back.

"Yuk!"

Zeke's voice had them pulling apart. A flush heated her neck and Quentin winked at her.

"What's for breakfast?" her brother asked then blinked at Quentin. "Hey, you're walking!"

"Yes."

Zeke beamed as he sat next to his brother-in-law. Zoe joined them. As they ate, Quentin watched her intently. At first, she thought he might be thinking about last night. She'd done her fair share of that. But as the meal progressed, she decided his thoughts had nothing to do with their marriage bed. A couple of times he acted as if he wanted to say something then his gaze flicked to Zeke and he remained silent. It made her stomach knot up.

His gaze met hers. "Good breakfast, sweetheart."

"Thank you." Her fingers tangled in her skirts as she smiled. "Do you plan to help Hoot at the paper today?"

"For a while."

"I'm working at the Fontaine."

"I'm helping at Haskell's," Zeke said around his bite of biscuit.

Zoe checked the pocket watch Quentin had set in the middle of the table. "Oh! I didn't realize how late it was."

She rose, hesitating when she realized that Quentin wasn't finished.

"I'll clear the table," he said.

"Thank you."

"Do you have to rush off?" He snagged her hand. "I wanted to talk to you."

The purpose in his dark eyes plucked at her nerves. Was he going to ask her again what she was keeping from him? He had every right, especially after last night.

"I'm afraid I do need to go." She planned to make sure Weaver had left Whirlwind or was close to doing so then she could tell Quentin everything, including that she loved him.

She laid a hand on his shoulder. "We could meet back here for lunch."

He searched her face. "All right, I'll see you then."

After giving him a quick kiss, she finished dressing, put up her hair and left with her brother. More than ready for this thing with Weaver to be over, Zoe waited at the corner of the livery. From here, she could watch Zeke make his way down the street to the mercantile.

And she'd be able to see if Weaver came out of the Fontaine.

She smiled when her brother mounted the steps to the mercantile and turned to wave at her. Hopeful for the first time in weeks, she started for the hotel.

Yesterday, before coming home to find her husband on his

feet, before they had made love, she had wired her grandfather to ask if he knew anything about Weaver or his partner. Upton had sent back a telegram saying he would get back to her after talking to one of his business associates whom he believed knew Weaver.

After that, Zoe had snooped in the con man's hotel room while she'd cleaned it. She had found nothing to prove the swindler was lying about the water well and the bonds. Even though the man was leaving today, she wanted some evidence. That way, maybe Quentin or Davis Lee might be able to get back some of the money taken from Whirlwind's citizens.

She looked up to see the swindler step out of the hotel. He had on trousers and a shirt, not a suit and hat like he'd worn when he had first arrived in town. There was no valise, no luggage at all that she could see. The only thing in his hand was what appeared to be a wooden sign. He certainly didn't look like someone who was leaving town. In fact, he looked as settled in as he ever had.

No! She marched right up to him, hands clenched into fists at her sides. "Why are you still here? You said you were leaving."

"Good day, Mrs. Prescott."

"Answer me."

"My stay has been extended slightly."

"Your *stay?* Get out of here and leave these people alone."

His pleasant features turned dark. "I'll leave when I want."

Anger boiled inside her and when she saw the words on his sign, she became incensed. It read that there were still bonds available for the water well. For a second, Zoe couldn't breathe. "What do you think you're doing with that?"

"Putting it out near the future well site at Little Bitter Creek."

She lowered her voice, so furious she was shaking. "You are not stealing money from anyone else in Whirlwind."

"No? What do you plan to do about it?"

"Go to the sheriff, that's what!"

"I think not." His eyes narrowed to cold slits. "I figured you might not take too kindly to my staying on so I got a little insurance."

He motioned behind her and she turned. At first, she only saw her brother sweeping Haskell's porch. Then she caught sight of Cyrus Gordon. Weaver's accomplice stood at the corner of the store, hand on the pistol at his hip as he watched Zeke in a calculating, threatening manner. Alarm shot through her.

Weaver lowered his voice. "Cyrus is going to stay close to your brother until I order him to stop."

"Tell him now." She barely kept her voice from cracking. "I said I would keep quiet about you stealing people's hard-earned money and I have."

His eyes turned cold. "As long as you keep your mouth shut, your brother and your husband will be safe."

He stepped past her and angled across the street toward the telegraph office and post office. Dismissing her, just like that.

Nails digging into her palms, Zoe wished for a gun. She was not a crack shot, but she could handle a weapon. Still, she didn't think she could shoot anyone unless they were firing on her or someone else.

If she got Weaver to leave town, Gordon would go with him, but how to do it?

She thought again about the gun. She might not be able to shoot the cheat, but he wouldn't know that.

Leave whenever he wanted? Well, they would see about that.

She was sick of his threats, sick of seeing him prey on her friends.

The boiling molten fury she'd felt earlier changed to a cold determination. Her gaze went back to her brother, who seemed unaware of any trouble, thank goodness. Her attention shifted to Gordon, who gave her a mocking smile as he tapped the butt of the pistol in his holster.

Zoe spun on her heel and headed for home.

She was putting an end to this today.

Zoe hurried away. She didn't have a gun, but she knew where to get one. Thank goodness, Quentin was gone.

Stepping inside the house, she hurried into his office. She remained composed, but she felt as if one more run-in with anyone might make her shatter. In the shallow top drawer of her husband's desk, she found what she had come for. She grabbed the pistol and checked it for bullets, finding the chambers full.

She thought only a second about unloading it. She had no idea how dangerous Weaver could be. Sliding the gun into her skirt pocket, she rushed into the front room.

And stopped cold.

Quentin sat in his wheelchair between her and the door, arms folded, clearly waiting for her.

He couldn't know what she had planned. Had something happened to him or Zeke? Dread knotted her stomach, but she gave him a bright smile. "Hi. I thought you were working today."

"I plan to, but first I stopped to talk to Davis Lee."

She frowned. Why had he been with the sheriff?

Quentin gave her a steady look. "I thought *you* were working today."

"I am." She moved toward the door, praying he wouldn't try to stop her. "And I have to get back."

He wheeled his chair to face her. "Why are you here? Did you forget something?"

She wanted to tell him the truth, but she couldn't. Not yet anyway. "I've got to go."

"You're not leaving until we talk, Zoe." He clenched his jaw so hard she wouldn't have been surprised if he'd snapped off a tooth. There was a flush of anger beneath his bronzed skin. "I want to know what's going on. Are you in trouble? Is Zeke? Has he been stealing again?"

"No! He only did that because he thought he was helping me keep Dinah in school." Last year, her brother had stolen all manner of things from their friends, including corsets, and he'd been discovered by Emma Ross.

The mention of her brother stretched Zoe's nerves to the breaking point. Dallying here, talking to Quentin wasn't helping the situation. The only way to help her brother and husband was to get Weaver out of town.

Urgency pounded at her. Until she got rid of the crook, she couldn't tell her husband anything. "I really have to go."

"Tell me what's going on."

"I...can't." Why couldn't he just let her leave? It was almost over. "Not yet."

"Then when?"

"Later, when I get back."

"Later when? Today? This week? This year?"

"Today." She hoped she could keep her word.

"Now." Quentin rolled his wheelchair over to her, his handsome face unyielding, his eyes blade-sharp. "Zoe, you're my *wife*. You can't keep pushing me away."

She didn't want to. She choked back a sob.

"I've been more than patient."

"I know that and I appreciate it. But I really have to go."

"Then I'll go with you."

Her heart nearly stopped. "No!"

"Why not? If you're going back to work, there's no reason I can't tag along."

There was absolutely no way she was letting Quentin get anywhere near possible gunfire.

Fury burned in his eyes as well as hurt. Zoe hated this, but she couldn't take the chance that Gordon might see him and assume Quentin was helping her.

Fear and anger merged until she couldn't tell them apart. Desperate to leave, she pleaded, "I trust you, Quentin. Why can't you do the same for me? Let me tell you in my own time."

"Because you won't," he ground out in a steely voice.

He deserved to know, but fear for her brother wasn't the only reason she refused to confide in Quentin. Just the possibility that he might get wounded had memories of the past flying at her like arrows.

She remembered how he had looked seven years ago after being shot by Jake. Blood everywhere, the complete loss of his spirit for months afterward, bitter resentment, begrudging acceptance of his paralysis. She'd seen the man she loved wither away and become someone she didn't want to know.

Tears stung her eyes. "Please, Quentin, can't you just trust me?"

"We're past that."

That was true, but if there was any chance she might have to use the gun in her pocket, she didn't want Quentin anywhere near her.

Her already frayed nerves snapped. "I can't stay any longer, Quentin."

"If you walk out that door, we're going to have a bigger problem than we do right now."

Heart aching, she paused. But she felt she had no choice. She hurried outside and down the ramp. Hearing the creak of leather behind her, she glanced back. Quentin reached the top of the ramp, looking intent on following her.

Hating this, hating herself, she yelled, "Stay away from me, Quentin! Stay away!"

He rocked to a stop and stared at her. She would never forget the devastation on his face, the hollowness in his eyes as she walked off.

"Please," she whispered. "Just stay away."

If he didn't, she could lose him, lose everything they had. She choked back a sob. She might already have.

Chapter Seven

There was no chance in hell that Quentin was going to stay away from Zoe. He didn't know what was going on, but he was fixin' to find out.

As he started to wheel down the ramp, he wondered if he might need a weapon. He had no idea where his wife was going, but if it was somewhere in town, he could do without a gun.

Just as he dismissed the thought, he saw Zoe ride a black horse out of the livery and cross to the other side of Main Street. She disappeared behind the smithy, urging the horse into a run as she traveled behind the businesses on that side of the street, including the jail.

He caught a glimpse of red hair and blue calico skirts as she took off across the prairie, riding southeast. He sure as hell wasn't going without a weapon now.

He went back into the house and into his office, intending to get his six-shooter. Zoe had been coming out of there when he had arrived home. He hadn't thought much about it at the time, but now…. Dread flickered as he yanked open the top right drawer and stared. His Peacemaker was gone.

What the hell was going on? If his wife had his gun, she believed there was danger nearby. But where and from whom?

Quentin spun his chair around, grabbed his Winchester rifle and his hat from beside the front door and went out, slamming the door behind him. He went straight for the livery, ignoring the voice in his head that cautioned him against riding a horse. It was something he hadn't attempted or even considered since his surgery, but riding was quicker than a buggy and Quentin needed quick.

Inside the stable, he found Pete Carter, who owned the place as well as the saloon next door. Quentin chose a mount and sent Pete to the jail with a message for Davis Lee, asking the lawman to follow Quentin's trail southeast of town.

He didn't wait for Pete's return. The bay mare he'd chosen stood patiently as he managed to get his foot in the stirrup.

He braced himself for a searing pain. Instead, there was only a sense of pressure.

He managed to drag one leg over the saddle and sit up. This might put him back in the wheelchair for life, but Quentin didn't care. Zoe was more important.

He guided the horse out of the livery and settled his hat more securely on his head. Urging the mare on, he bit back a curse as the animal lunged into motion. He clenched his teeth at the painful jarring and gave the horse its head, finding there was less jouncing at full speed. The pain decreased slightly if he leaned forward and relieved pressure on his lower back.

He rode into the morning sun, sweating, the glare forcing him to slow down at times to check broken grass and make sure he was still on Zoe's trail. A wave of agony rolled up his spine, but he didn't stop.

Because the drought had left everything so dry, the sheriff

wouldn't be able to track him using horse hoofprints, but there would be plenty of sign in the scorched boot-high grass. Davis Lee was a damn good tracker.

As Quentin rode, anger vied with pain and concern. He couldn't imagine what was going on with Zoe. Until he had discovered his gun was missing, he had been only angry. Now he was also worried.

After a few minutes, he realized that Zoe was headed toward Little Bitter Creek—the spot near where Egan Weaver had said the water well would be drilled.

Was that where she was going? He remembered how she had tensed up last night when he'd mentioned Weaver and the bonds—which was why Quentin had discussed the man with Davis Lee earlier. Quentin had sent inquiries to newspapers in Kansas and Oklahoma Territory asking for information about Weaver or the bonds. Davis Lee had agreed to wire the law in the towns where Weaver claimed to have sold bonds and drilled a successful water well.

Several minutes later, Quentin topped a rise and at the bottom of the slope, he saw his wife. Holding a gun on Egan Weaver!

Quentin nearly fell out of the saddle. What the devil! He blinked to be sure he was seeing what he thought he was.

Yes, his wife had the business end of Quentin's six-shooter aimed at Weaver's chest, dead center. The man was on his knees, barefoot. A pair of dusty black shoes and grimy socks were several yards away.

Zoe was facing Quentin and her eyes widened when she saw him. The weapon jerked in her hand.

He slowly guided his horse closer. "What's going on, Zoe?"

"Mr. Prescott!" Weaver started to turn.

With a visibly shaking hand, Zoe jabbed the gun toward him. "You don't move!"

The man stilled, his mouth flattening.

The last thing they needed was for that weapon to discharge. Quentin dismounted, determined not to let Weaver see any weakness.

Pulling his rifle from its scabbard, he remained beside the horse for support in case his legs gave out.

"Well, I'll be," Weaver said. "That surgery worked."

"Yes." Quentin's voice was tight.

Zoe flicked him a concerned look. "Quentin, I told you to stay away."

Her words lacked the bite they'd had earlier. "There's no way I was going to do that. Tell me what's happening here."

"She's crazy, that's what!" Weaver burst out.

Zoe leveled the gun on the man, her hand now as steady as a rock. "Let Quentin see what you've got."

The man turned a wooden sign toward Quentin.

Water Bonds Still Available. Quentin's gaze returned to his wife.

"There are no bonds," she said flatly. "There never have been."

Frowning, he looked at Weaver as Zoe continued, "And there's no water well either."

"He and Cyrus Gordon have been conning the whole town," Quentin deduced. "How did you know?"

And why hadn't he guessed? He'd been uneasy enough with the bond undertaking to discourage Zeke.

"On Weaver's second day in town, I was cleaning his bathing room in the hotel when I overheard him and Gordon discussing the plan to scam everyone in Whirlwind. He caught me and threatened to hurt you and Zeke if I told anyone about it."

Her actions were starting to make sense now to Quentin.

"I wanted to tell you when it first happened, but I was afraid." Her voice thickened and for the first time, her features showed an emotion besides fury. "He made it clear that he or Gordon could get to you and Zeke anytime they wanted."

Quentin's eyes narrowed. He wanted to protest that neither he nor Zoe's brother would've been easy targets, but they would have been. Zeke was too trusting with strangers. And Quentin had been in that damn chair, then in bed for almost two weeks after the surgery. It had taken another six days to get on his feet for longer than a few minutes.

He understood why Zoe believed she had better stay quiet, but he still wished she had confided in him or asked for his help with this. As with everything, she had handled it alone.

"Why did you meet Weaver here?" he asked.

"I *followed* him. I'm not going to let him steal from anyone else. I want him gone."

Concern streaked through him. "Gone? As in dead?"

"Out of town, out of our lives."

Quentin breathed a little easier until Zoe wagged the pistol at the con man. "You're going to return every penny you've stolen."

"There's nothing left," he smirked.

Her mouth tightened. When Quentin heard her thumb down the hammer, his gaze sliced to her. "You're not going to shoot him, are you?"

"He deserves it. Look at everyone he's stolen from. He took money from the Eishens, their last dime! He would've happily taken Zeke's money, too, if you hadn't stepped in."

Quentin didn't think Zoe would really pull the trigger, but the disdain and righteous anger on her face had him wondering.

She glared at Weaver. "You're going to mount up right now and ride out."

"You can't run me out of town, lady."

She took a threatening step closer. "No?"

The man paled.

"Zoe?" Quentin eased next to her.

"He should pay for what he's done."

"Not like this. Don't do it, sweetheart," he urged, dismissing a twinge in his lower back. "You couldn't live with yourself if you shot an unarmed man."

"I think I could." Her gaze stayed steady on Weaver. "This lowdown critter anyway."

Clearly unsure of her, the con man threw a nervous look at Quentin. "Stop her."

Ignoring him, Quentin spoke quietly to Zoe. "Listen to me. When my sister died, I blamed Jake and I thought he should pay, but shooting him was a mistake. Alienating my brother-in-law, who was my only remaining family member, and pushing you away was worse than losing the use of my legs."

"Jake isn't like this lowlifer."

"I know, and thank goodness I didn't kill him, but I could have. I tried to. The regret I've had over that has eaten at me for years."

"It's not the same thing, Quentin."

"Maybe their wrongs aren't the same, but my desire for revenge and yours are the same. Trust me, this is not the way to handle it. This no-account dog will get what's coming to him."

She hesitated and Quentin shifted his weight, relieved that the slight twinge he'd experienced was dulling.

Her mouth set in a mutinous line. "He's going to get away with stealing from our friends."

"Maybe so, but he won't cheat anyone else. He's going to jail. Davis Lee isn't too far behind me."

Zoe glanced at him. "Is Weaver why you went to see Davis Lee this morning?"

"Yes."

Admiration glowed in her eyes as she gestured to the swindler. "So, what do we do with him?"

Quentin patted his rifle. "We keep him here until the sheriff arrives."

Weaver cursed, sending a longing look toward his boots.

Zoe turned to Quentin. "I can't believe you rode that horse out here. What if you just ruined your surgery?"

"If I did, it was worth it."

"How sweet," Weaver spat.

"Shut up," Zoe and Quentin said at the same time.

The sound of thundering hooves had all of them looking toward the rise. Davis Lee appeared and, once his mount joined theirs, he dismounted.

His features grew stony as Zoe explained the situation.

"I'll get him to the jail," he said when she finished. He nodded at Quentin. "I have a feeling we'll both be hearing plenty about this fraud from the people we contacted earlier today."

"I imagine so."

After tying Weaver's hands behind him, Davis Lee hauled the man to his feet and led him over to a boulder so he could mount. The sheriff tossed the man's boots into his saddlebag.

"Davis Lee?" Zoe stepped toward him. "Weaver's partner, Cyrus Gordon, was hovering over Zeke when I left town. Threatening him."

"I'll take care of it." The sheriff swung into the saddle, gripping the reins of the con man's horse. He looked over at Quentin and Zoe. "You two going back to Whirlwind with me?"

"We'll follow," Quentin answered before Zoe could.

Flipping his rifle barrel-down against his leg, he watched as Davis Lee and his prisoner rode out of sight. Sharp relief ached in his chest. Thank goodness Zoe was safe. He looked over to find her eyeing him with dread, pale and trembling.

"Are you really mad at me?"

"Pretty mad." Without another word, he hauled her to him with one arm and held her close, burying his face in her neck.

Zoe held on tight, not wanting to let go. Her husband had stopped her from shooting Weaver, but she still might have lost her marriage.

For a long minute, they stood like that. Zoe's pulse slowed and against her chest, she could feel Quentin's settle into a steady, comforting beat.

He brushed a kiss across her hair. "You scared the devil out of me when I saw you holding a gun on Weaver. I'm so glad you're all right."

She drew away slightly to look up at him. "Are you all right? When you came riding up, my heart nearly stopped. That was so dangerous."

He barked out a laugh. "Look who's talking."

If anything had happened to Quentin… Zoe wiped away a tear.

"Hey." Quentin nudged her chin up. "What's this?"

"If you've undone your progress from the surgery, I'll never forgive myself. I'm sorry you had to come after me."

"I'm not. I'll never be sorry and I'll always come after you."

She searched his eyes. "I couldn't bear it if you resented me for that, but I also couldn't blame you."

"We're in this together, Zoe. If I did some damage to myself, we'll deal with it."

She nodded.

He started to speak, then stopped, looking uncertain.

"What?" she asked.

"I understand that you were afraid. Is that the only reason you felt you couldn't confide in me?"

"What do you mean?"

"I need to know that you trust me. To hear you say you know that I'll never again do to you what I did before."

"I do know that." She clasped his face in her hands, her gaze soft. "I do."

"I'm glad I finally know everything."

"You don't." She bit back a smile. "Not yet."

He stilled, wariness clouding his eyes. "You mean there's more?"

"Yes." Unable to hide her joy any longer, she gripped the front of his shirt. "I love you. That's everything you need to know."

His eyes darkened.

"I wanted to tell you last night, but it seemed wrong to say it when I was keeping this from you." Why didn't he say something? "And…I didn't know if you'd believe me. I thought you might wonder if I was saying it to keep you from pressing me for answers."

"Zoe…"

"You believe me, don't you? I know I hurt you, Quentin," she whispered. "When I told you to stay away from me, it was for your safety."

"I know.

"Can you forgive me?"

"Sweetheart—"

"I remember how much it hurt when you pushed me away seven years ago." Her stomach in knots, she pressed on. "It would be understandable if you couldn't forgive me. If you changed your mind about wanting to stay married."

"Hey." He gave her a little shake. "You aren't getting rid of me. I never thought I'd get another chance with you. I'm not walking away." He grinned. "And I could if I wanted."

She couldn't stop the tears then. "I was so afraid I'd ruined everything between us."

"You make my life better, Zoe. For years, I've regretted shutting you out. I don't want to live with more regret."

She slid her arms around his neck and carefully pressed against him. "Neither do I. I want us and Zeke to be a family."

"We are," Quentin said simply.

After losing her parents then Quentin, Zoe had never dared hope that her family would consist of more than herself and her brother. But now she had Quentin.

No, she corrected. They had each other.

She pressed kisses to his jaw, up to the corner of his mouth.

His hands tightened on her waist. "No more secrets."

"No more secrets," she said softly.

"No more protecting me."

"All right."

"We're together. That's how we handle things."

"Yes."

After a long kiss, he said, "Let's go home."

Home.

Together.

* * * * *

THE MAVERICK
AND MISS PRIM

Lynna Banning

Dear Reader,

I am fascinated by "odd couples," two people who seem entirely unalike, who get to know each other and then bond irrevocably. This speaks to my lifelong belief that (1) appearances matter less than soul-deep connections between people and that (2) if the core of a person is known, respected and then loved, it matters not how outwardly "different" they are.

I am drawn to the Smoke River, Oregon, setting for two reasons. First, because my mother was raised on a ranch in that area and, second, because a small town in the Old West holds hundreds of stories, intriguing characters and potential plots. This story is part of my series of works set in Smoke River. I love writing them, getting to know my characters and working hard on their happily-ever-afters.

Lynna Banning

For David Woolston

Prologue

"Eleanora Stevenson, I can't believe you said that!" The youngest of the three women gathered around Ellie's kitchen table fixed her large brown eyes on Ellie and slowly shook her head.

"I most certainly did say that," Ellie said, her voice calm. "You both have prospects. I, on the other hand, do not."

Darla Weatherby pursed her lips. "But—"

"But every woman wants to get married!" Lucy Nichols protested. Her perfect oval face, framed by an artfully arranged mass of blond corkscrew curls, paled in disbelief. "My Henry and I will be married in June."

Ellie smiled politely at her friends and lifted her grandmother's bone-china teapot. "You are fortunate, Lucy. You have Henry. And Darla has Mr. Bledsoe. I, however, have a schoolroom full of other women's children. More tea?"

The three young women sipped in silence. Lucy wore yellow calico with white lace at the cuffs, diminutive Darla had dressed in pink muslin flounces and Ellie was in in sky-blue. They looked like spring flowers clustered about the round oak table.

"Did you leave a sweetheart back in Boston?" Darla ventured in her soft drawl.

Lucy's brown eyes widened. "Or find a new one out here in Oregon?"

Ellie sighed. "No, and no. No man has ever courted me." She studied the plate of molasses cookies Darla had brought.

"But that's perfectly awful!" Lucy burst out.

Darla munched one of her own cookies. "Why hasn't some man courted you?"

"Well…" Ellie paused. Lucy and Darla were her two closest friends in Smoke River; they deserved honesty.

"Perhaps because I am so tall? My mother always said no man wants to look up to his wife."

"But the three of us have done everything together for the last six months! Lucy and I will be married in June, so…" Darla hesitated, her slim fingers smoothing a pink ruffle "…we want you to join us!"

Ellie had to laugh. "I very much doubt the three of us will spend your wedding nights together. Let's face it, ladies. I am twenty-six years old, an old-maid schoolteacher without a prayer of finding a man who suits me. Even a short one."

Darla looked pained, but Lucy giggled. Then the three women joined hands around the table. "It won't matter," Darla offered. "We'll always be friends."

Once again Ellie studied the cookie plate. The three of them had shared their secrets, even their wedding plans. But she could never, never admit, even to her few friends, how lonely she was deep inside.

Chapter One

"Miss Stevenson," the girl whispered. "May I be excused?"

Ellie straightened and absently patted the child's blond head. "In a second, Manette."

The girl tugged hard at Ellie's blue calico skirt. "Now," she whispered. "Right now. Please."

Ellie surveyed the classroom where her four other students bent over their slates, experimenting with the spelling of the word *elephant*. All was quiet, for the moment anyway. She leaned down to Manette.

"Very well, you may be excused for five minutes." The girl was out the door in a flash of starched white pinafore and in the next second her blond curls bounced past the window on the way to the privy.

Ellie sighed under her breath. She liked her students—four girls, including Manette Nicolet, and a sullen boy of seven. All lived on farms near the small town of Smoke River.

Manette slipped back into the small schoolroom with a fist full of pale purple flowers; she thrust them at Ellie and scampered back to her desk.

"Lilacs!" Ellie buried her nose in the fragrant blooms. "Oh, how lovely." Inexplicably her eyes filled with tears. The scent brought a familiar soul-deep longing that reminded her how alone she felt.

She swallowed hard. "Thank you, Manette."

"De rien," the perky child quipped.

"Aw, why don'tcha speak English like the rest of us!" The dark-haired MacAllister boy leaned forward and jerked Manette's pinafore ruffle. "Frenchie," he taunted.

Manette doubled up her small fist, turned sideways and whacked him on the shoulder. The other three girls—the Ness twins and Mrs. Rose's granddaughter, Sarah—cheered.

"Please," Ellie shouted. "Please," she continued in a normal voice. "Do not fight."

Teddy MacAllister's brown eyes blazed. "She hit me!"

Under her high-necked blouse of blue muslin, Ellie's heartbeat sped up. She did not allow her students to pick on one another.

She had resolved she would be a good teacher. She had attended Mason Teachers' College and she had excelled. But just this morning she had read over her planned spelling lesson with a stifled groan and understood why her students sometimes fidgeted.

She had spent all of her twenty-six years in Boston. She'd stepped off the train in Smoke River excited about being a school-teacher; only a small part of her dreaded the prospect of being "the *old-maid* schoolteacher."

She glanced down at her planned lesson on addition and sub-traction. "If Teddy has five chickens and three rabbits, how many pets can he give to Noralee for her birthday?"

"Eight!" five-year-old Manette squealed. "But Noralee doesn't want chickens, just rabbits. And what about Edith? Isn't it her birthday, too?"

"You are quite correct, Manette. Now, if Teddy splits his pets between the twins, how many would each of them receive?"

"Four!" shouted Noralee. "But I don't want any chickens, just rabbits."

Soon the students were laughing and competing to answer her ridiculous questions. "Suppose the five of you are a herd of elephants in darkest Africa, and one of you refuses to take a bath in the river. How many clean elephants will there be?"

Suddenly she wondered if farm children knew about elephants. Mercy me! She remembered her own schooling: her teachers had praised her; her mother had found her wanting for as long as she could remember. *Straighten up. What a dreadful hat! Smile, daughter. You look as if you'd lost your best friend.* Mama's constant criticism had left a festering wound on her soul.

Ellie sucked in a long, slow breath. The children gazed at her, eyes shining, their expressions rapt. Their teacher might lack experience, but, like her students, she could learn.

"Now, children, how many letters of the alphabet are there in *rhinoceros?*"

Matt lay flat on his stomach in the shallow gully, his eyes narrowed against the sun's harsh glare. He studied the ridge, his loaded Winchester at his side. A buzzard began circling overhead, its wings black against the shimmering cobalt sky. Hell and damn, the scavenger thought he was dead already.

Had Royce seen him?

He'd tracked his quarry all the way from the Texas border, and if Matt died in this godforsaken corner of Oregon it would all have been wasted—the watching, the days on horseback tracking through endless miles of coyote bush and scrub pine—all of it wasted.

He clamped his jaw tight. He felt every single one of his thirty-one years, probably because he'd spent the past four of them busting his spine on the back of a horse. His sole purpose in life had been revenge, to find Royce and kill him.

He'd promised Pa before he'd died.

And Matt Johnson kept his promises. Sometimes he wondered what it would be like to settle down in one place and live a real life. Sometimes he wondered if he'd recognize a "real life" if it bit him in the—

A shadow moved on the ridge above and Matt held his breath. *Come on out, you bastard. Show yourself.* He brought the rifle barrel up to the edge of the gully, sighted down it, then edged it a hair to the right. His mouth was so dry he couldn't spit, but he couldn't risk moving to snag his canteen.

His horse waited a mile back, sheltered in a copse of sun-bleached cottonwoods the color of gunmetal. He was pinned down here, unable to get back to the gelding until either the shadowy figure behind the rangy mesquite scrambled on over the top of the ridge or Matt shot him. *One or the other, mister. I'll wait here and you choose.*

He smelled smoke. Campfire? Drift from town? On the ridge the sunlight glinted off something and the shadowy figure slipped from behind the mesquite. Matt squeezed the trigger and the bullet whined into the brush at his quarry's feet. The bulky figure clambered up over the top of the ridge and disappeared.

Damn. Matt unkinked his long body, crawled out of the gully and snaked on his belly to the shelter of the nearest bush. He hunkered down and watched the ridge. Nothing moved, but after a while a ghost of gray dust puffed into the sky. Horse, most likely.

He'd lost him. Again. Fellow was more slippery than a mountain trout.

Cautiously, Matt stood up and sniffed the air. Gunsmoke. Dust. His own sweat. And from the west, near Smoke River, came the rich scent of frying meat. Indian camp, maybe.

He cracked the barrel, blew out the chamber and slipped another bullet in place. Then he hefted the rifle and headed back across the sage-dotted plain for his horse.

* * *

Ellie had just started the daily lesson from *McGuffey's Second Reader* when the sound of hoofbeats and a jouncing wagon stopped six-year-old Noralee in midsentence. Ellie flew to the window.

Two horses, one pulling a wagon and the other, a familiar strawberry roan, carrying a man. She recognized Rooney Cloudman, Manette's half-Comanche grandfather. He dismounted and headed straight for the schoolhouse.

The door slammed open. "Sorry to bust in, Miz Stevenson, but we got trouble."

Ellie's heart stuttered. "What kind of trouble, Mr. Cloudman?"

"Indian trouble. The town's under attack! Maybe just hungry renegades, but ya never know. You gotta get these kids out of here. Parents want you to drive 'em to Gillette Springs, where they'll be safe."

"But…but that's forty miles away!"

"'Zactly. Now…" He turned to the bug-eyed children. "Get yer things."

"Wait!" Ellie yelled. "Who's going to drive—"

Rooney was shooing students toward the door like a mother hen. "You are."

"I—I don't know how to drive a wagon. Can't you drive it?"

"Nope. I'm the only one in Smoke River can speak any Indian lingo at all. These young 'uns are your responsibility."

"I—I can't—"

"Don't ever say that around me, Missy. Out here, you gotta learn fast. Now, get yer shawl and come on."

The children trooped after the solidly built man and he lifted them into the wagon bed. Just as she reached the door, Ellie checked. "My lilacs!"

She spun back toward her desk, snatched Manette's bouquet

out of the pail of water on her desk and clutched it to her chest. Water from the stems dripped down the front of her blouse but she didn't care. The scent of lilacs made her dream of wonderful, impossible things.

Outside in the school yard, Ellie climbed up onto the splintery wagon seat and Rooney slapped the reins into her hands. "Flap 'em when you want to go, pull on 'em to stop."

"Do I say 'stop' or 'whoa' or something?" Her voice shook. She was petrified, not only of the horse but of driving a wagon full of children whose parents expected her to keep them safe.

"I loaded some supplies and blankets in the back," Rooney barked. "Now, git!" He slapped the rump of the dapple-gray mare and the wagon jerked forward.

"Turn right at the crossroads," he yelled.

Turn right? How did one turn a horse left *or* right? Tentatively she swung the reins to the right. The horse veered and the wagon circled the schoolhouse before she finally twitched the lines in the other direction and set the horse on a straight path.

"The road's that way," Rooney shouted, pointing away from the town.

The crossroads? How far were the crossroads? She'd walked the half mile into town a hundred times and scarcely noticed the crossroads.

The horse slowed, then picked up speed, and Ellie twisted her neck to check her wagonload of students. All sat gripping the edge, Manette and the MacAllister boy on one side, facing the twins, and Sarah Rose clutching the other side. Five sets of eyes stared back at her, all wide with apprehension. Oh, my Lord, their parents would be worried sick!

She flapped the reins. *She* was worried sick. What was she going to do with a wagonload of children in the wilds of Oregon?

Chapter Two

Matt trotted the gelding into the grove of cottonwoods. From here he could see both the mountain ridge and the road, but he was wrung out after spending a broiling day in a dry gulch. His body needed water or whiskey or both. And some rest. He wasn't as young as he used to be. He'd pick up Royce's tracks in the morning.

The early-evening air smelled faintly of smoke, cut by the sharp fragrance of pine needles. He dismounted and knelt where the lazy stream he'd been following widened into a shallow pool. Pushing back his Stetson, he splashed water over his face and halfway down the neck of his unlaced shirt.

The sound of a horse and wagon on the road outside the grove brought his head up. Mighty rattle-boned contraption; sounded as if it needed a good tightening all around. He waited for it to pass, but it didn't.

Heavens, it was headed straight for him! He jolted to his feet just as a dapple-gray mare crashed into the circle of trees. A wagon jounced behind the animal and a young woman cowered on the bench screaming, "Stop! Stop! Whoa!"

The wagon kept coming. Matt jumped to one side, grabbed the harness and managed to pull the animal to a halt. He smoothed his hand down the gray's nose to calm it, then twisted to look up at the driver.

"What the devil do you think you're doing?"

The young woman's face went from the color of chalk to raspberry pink. "Oh, thank you! Thank you! I didn't know how to make it stop!"

Matt stalked toward her, fists clenched. "Then what in hell are you doing driving a wagon?"

She shot to her feet. "I had no choice. Someone had to—the Indians were coming—"

Matt stared at her. She was babbling, making no sense. Then she began waving her arms, pointing behind her, and her face shaded from raspberry into rose-red. He took a second, more appreciative look. Damn fine-looking woman, all six feet of her.

She was tall, all right. Willowy and plenty womanly, and her movements were graceful as a gazelle. Strands of dark hair poked out of a bun at the creamy nape of her neck.

Against his will, he moved a step closer. She had eyes the color of a noon sky and a face a sculptor might have chiseled out of pink-and-cream marble—even features and a lush-looking mouth. A man could imagine uses for those full lips that would make a lady blush.

The sudden flood of desire made him angry. He had no time for a woman, even one as pretty as this one in starched blue ruffles. His mission didn't include dalliance along the way.

"Just who are you, anyway?" He barked the question out of a dry throat.

She straightened her spine and dropped the reins. "My name is Eleanora Stevenson." Her voice was a clear, cold ripple on a dark river; the sound sent the hunger, and the anger, up a notch. "With a *V*," she added. "And just who might *you* be?"

"Name's Matt Johnson," he snapped. "With a *J*. What are you doing out here in the middle of nowhere?"

She climbed down from the wagon with the calm grace of a queen and jumped lightly to the ground, her blue skirt fluttering. "I am traveling to Gillette Springs, Mr. Johnson."

"Alone?"

"Yes. I mean, no." She tipped her head toward the wagon bed. "With these children."

He studied her flushed cheeks, let his gaze drift to the curve of her breasts and the slim waist. "Why?"

"For their safety, of course." She marched to within two arms' lengths of him and he judged she was just a hair shorter than he was, maybe five foot nine or ten.

The blue-blue eyes looked directly into his. "What are you doing out here in the middle of nowhere?"

"Hunting," he said shortly.

"Hunting what?"

"None of your business, Miss Stevenson-with-a-V."

She sent him a look that would fry flapjacks. "There is no reason to be rude, Mr. Johnson-with-a-J."

"It's a private matter."

She surveyed him with narrowing eyes. "Ah. Then you are hunting a man. Or perhaps you are hiding from one, here in this clump of trees?"

"Hell, no, I'm not hiding. *He's* the one who's hiding. All I'm doing is camping here till morning."

Her eyes clouded. "So are we. I can drive this horse no farther, and the children are tired."

"And hungry" came a small voice from the wagon.

"Mr. Johnson, I trust we can share this campsite."

It wasn't a question, and Matt gritted his teeth. She'd want a campfire, and a campfire could be seen from the mountain ridge. "Looks like I don't have a choice," he growled.

"Thank you. Children? Let's unload the wagon."

Children? He detested children. They cried. They whined. They got sick. His heart stuttered. *They got killed.*

Five small figures burst from the wagon, four girls and a boy of about seven. For an instant Matt's eyes burned. The kid was dark-haired, like Luke, and about the same age and size. Matt wondered if this boy was afraid.

Sure he was. But if he was anything like Matt's own younger brother, he was hiding it under a veneer of bravado. Matt's breath stopped. Luke had been brave; but in the end it hadn't mattered.

The old bitterness rose in his throat. He'd catch that bastard Royce and plant a slug in his heart if it was the last thing he ever did on this earth. Maybe two slugs.

The children tossed out the wagon contents and a haphazard pile of blankets and tin cans rose in front of him. Looked like enough food for an army detail on patrol. Now what would a young woman as good-looking as she was be doing with that much food? To say nothing of four—no, five—young children.

"These kids yours?"

"Only in a manner of speaking. I'm their teacher."

"Looks like you're planning to be here awhile," he said, eyeing the tin cans.

"Oh, no, Mr. Johnson. Just overnight. We are only halfway to our destination."

Good. She would be moving on, too; she and her students weren't going to slow him down a single hour. She bent forward, separating the cans into two piles—beans and peaches.

"That's one fine backside," he murmured to himself. But he wouldn't get too excited about it; he'd be riding out at sunup. Probably never see her or her backside again.

The thought of riding out didn't make him as happy as he'd thought it would. He pivoted, putting his back to her, unable to watch the way she moved any longer. Instead, he moved toward his horse, scrabbled in his saddlebag for the bottle of red-eye.

He uncorked it and had just tipped his head back to swig down a gulp when something tugged on his pant leg.

"I'm thirsty," said a small voice. "What are you drinking?"

Matt gazed down into a pair of pale-blue eyes squinting up at him. Oh, hell. "Thirsty, huh?"

The girl nodded. She wore a rumpled white pinafore over a blue gingham dress. Gazing at the bottle in his hand, she licked her lips.

"What you need is water, not whiskey," he grumbled.

The girl grinned up at him. "My name is Manette." She slipped her tiny hand into his, and Matt blinked in surprise.

Ellie looked up from the stack of blankets next to the wagon to see five-year-old Manette Nicolet grasp Mr. Johnson's large hand. She let the quilt clutched in her fingers drop, propped her hands on her hips and watched Manette lead the disreputable stranger to the shallow pond.

All her nerves went on alert. Manette could charm anyone, but was this man safe? What if he were an outlaw? He said he was hunting—*what* was he hunting? *Or whom?*

A shiver crawled up her spine and she started forward. The craggy-faced man and Manette were kneeling side by side at the small spring, out of which bubbled a steady trickle of clear water. Mr. Johnson scooped water up into his cupped palm, swallowed it down and gestured for Manette to do the same.

The amount of water the girl's small hand could hold barely wet her lips. Johnson scooped again and held the water under Manette's chin. She dipped her head and noisily slurped it down, then turned her head and grinned up at him. She grabbed his still-cupped hand and plunged it into the stream again and studied the resulting pocket of drinking water. Next, she tried her own hand again, and voilà! A palm full of water. Now Mr. Johnson was grinning at Manette.

A hiccup of laughter bubbled past Ellie's lips. Little Manette always wanted to know how adults did things.

Johnson was now patiently demonstrating the pond-dipping maneuver once more. The man still looked like an outlaw, his face tanned to the color of hot cocoa and his cheeks and chin darkened with a shadowy growth of whiskers. His features were regular, but his dark hair was overlong and straggled over his eyes. Could he be an outlaw on the run?

Ellie resumed folding the blankets for the children to sleep in, but her thoughts lingered on the stranger. When Johnson and Manette returned, Noralee and Edith were selecting canned food for their supper.

"I know how to make a hand-cup to drink from!" Manette crowed.

The twins dropped the tins of beans and crowded around her. "Show me! Show me!" The three girls tore past Johnson and sprinted for the pond.

Ellie shot another glance at the rough-looking man. He wore a battered black hat, the brim pulled down so far his face was mostly hidden except for his mouth and chin. The glimmer of a smile appeared and then evaporated in an instant. He didn't seem much like an outlaw right now.

"Kids!" he growled.

Ellie stiffened. She must have imagined the smile; now he was grumpy as an old bear. "You do not like children, Mr. Johnson?"

He didn't answer, just stalked away toward his horse. She watched him unsaddle the animal and give it a handful of oats. Then he unhitched her mare and fed her, as well.

Matt retrieved a hunk of hardtack from his saddlebag for his supper, swallowed another mouthful of red-eye and surveyed the area for a level place to spread out his bedroll. Somewhere away from those children and definitely away from the blue-eyed Miss Stevenson.

He rolled out his pallet as far from the wagon as he could get, but before he could even get his boots off, a quilt blossomed on either side of him. The young boy sought his approval with a quick questioning look; Matt groaned, then nodded and was rewarded with a shy, gap-toothed smile.

Manette didn't ask; she just spread out her blanket and flopped down onto it. She rolled her small body up in her quilt and scooched over closer to him. "I—I'm c-cold," she whispered.

Wasn't his problem, he told himself. But before he knew what he was doing, he'd pulled his boots back on, gathered an armload of pine branches and twigs, and started a fire. A thin spiral of blue-gray smoke wound into the surrounding trees.

Whoa! What was he doing? If Royce was anywhere within fifty miles, he'd see the smoke and Matt's cover would be blown before he even saddled up tomorrow.

Miss Stevenson paced a slow circle around the now-crackling blaze. "Oh, good. Now we can have a hot meal."

She was going to cook something? From what he'd observed she scarcely knew her way around a campsite, let alone how to cook over an open fire.

"Have you a pocketknife, Mr. Johnson?"

With a grunt, Matt fished in his pocket and tossed his pearl-handled jackknife to her. When she snaked out her arm and caught the knife with one hand, his eyebrows went up. She looked too back-east-citified to be much use out west but, well, he guessed looks could be deceiving. And when she jimmied open three cans of pinto beans and two of sliced peaches without cutting herself, his surprise quadrupled. Interesting woman.

He watched her settle the cans of beans close to the flames. The paper labels turned brown and curled up, but before the three other girls had finished laying out their blankets, the beans were steaming hot. She reached for the can closest to her, but Matt knocked her hand away.

"It's hot," he warned.

"Well," she huffed. "I know that."

"Then keep your hands off it!"

"I wasn't going to—" Her blue eyes widened and grew shiny.

Oh, hell, was she going to cry?

"Just like a woman," he muttered. "Weeps over every little thing!" He blurted it out without thinking, then braced himself. She'd probably throw the hot beans in his face.

She glared at him good and hard for a full minute. "I weep only over important things." In icy silence she handed back his knife.

"Get some twigs," he ordered. "Use two to make a holder."

While she scrabbled for a few fallen pine branches, the three young girls crept close to the fire, warmed their hands and toasted their backsides, then snuggled into their folded-over quilts. It was obvious how unprepared Miss Blue and her students were for camping out like this. So why were they?

"Lemme see your twigs," he said, his voice rough. She dropped six or eight small branches at his feet and waited, hands on her hips.

Quickly Matt hollowed out the thicker ends and carved three crude spoons.

"Use two small twigs to lift your beans away from the fire," he instructed.

She bent over, a twig in each hand, giving him another view of her nicely rounded bottom. She managed to jockey the first can away from what were now coals and hot ashes. "Like this?"

"Yeah, just like that. Now..." He handed over the spoons. "Dig in."

"Would you care to share our meal, Mr. Johnson?"

"No thanks. Hardtack and red— Hardtack is plenty filling."

She gave a short nod. "Share the spoons, children."

Between the five of them, they polished off all the beans and then attacked the two opened cans of peaches. It was quiet except for the slurping and lip-smacking.

Matt heaved a tired sigh. All he wanted was for his manhunt to be over. Been way too long since he'd seen a pretty woman, at least one as pretty and refined-looking as Miss Blue. And, she had a backside he'd not soon forget.

An evening song sparrow began warbling in the cottonwood overhead. Matt shucked his boots again, laid them beneath his head for a pillow and stretched full-length on his pallet. He closed his eyes, thinking of his little brother as he had every night for the past four years. Had he lived, Luke would have been thirteen come June. He was only nine years old when he was killed.

His throat felt as if it was full of blackberry brambles. He wondered if Luke had a pony up in heaven.

Rustling sounds told him Miss Blue and her students were rolling themselves up into their blankets for the night. He heard a whispered nighttime prayer from Manette, on his left. In Latin, so she must be Catholic. On his right lay the young boy who reminded him of Luke. Under his lids, Matt's eyes burned.

Ellie lay back on the crocheted afghan, watching the firelight flicker and die down into glowing coals. She had waited until the children had selected their blankets, then had taken the one left over and hidden the wilting but still fragrant bunch of lilacs underneath.

Her back ached. Her head pounded as if a hammer were smashing into her temples. But, she thought with an inner smile, they had made it through the day. She had managed to keep the children safe through the roughest, bounciest wagon ride she ever hoped to take. She'd fed them and tucked them all into their blankets. Teddy MacAllister had insisted on removing his boots to use as a pillow like Mr. Johnson did, and dear little Manette had shared the last of her canned peaches with the man.

She wondered why the children seemed to like this sun-bronzed stranger. Why would they trust a rough man who looked like a criminal, with his unruly black hair and those calculating eyes he kept hidden under the brim of his hat?

She glanced around at the bedrolls spread in a semicircle, toes pointing toward the still-glowing fire. Evenings like these, with the air mild and still and the scent of lilacs, made her insides feel odd, flooded with an unnamable longing. The sparrow above them sang and sang. The sound cut into her soul.

Would she ever find someone to love? Would she ever be loved in return? Oh, God, she wanted to belong to someone fine and upstanding. She wanted her life to be connected to another's. She wanted to share everything, great and small.

And a child…she ached to hold a child of her own. But she was twenty-six years old. All her life she had felt sorry for old maids, and now, she guessed she was one of them.

Had Mama been right? Was she too tall, too outspoken, too…?

She couldn't finish the thought.

Chapter Three

A sparrow overhead trilled an earsplitting warble and Matt opened his eyes. Wasn't even sunup yet; what had wakened the bird? He raised his head half an inch and spied the cause.

Miss Blue was trying to back up the dappled mare to hitch it to the wagon; her legs braced, she leaned forward, pushing against the horse's chest. Maybe he shouldn't have unhitched the animal last night, but he never figured she was so green she didn't know that horses don't back up too willingly.

She stuffed an escaped tendril of mahogany-colored hair back into her bun but apparently didn't notice that the gathered knot at the back of her neck was coming undone. As he watched, four or five tortoise-shell hairpins worked themselves free and skittered onto the bed of pine needles, which meant the mass of shiny hair came tumbling past her shoulders.

Matt's mouth went dry. A woman with her hair down did odd things to his insides. Things he didn't have time for. She swiped the shower of dark waves off her face with one hand and kept pushing the horse.

The horse tossed its head and sidestepped away from her.

She stomped her foot, muttered something he couldn't hear and dropped to her knees to scrabble in the pine needles for her missing hairpins.

When she found them, she combed her fingers through the heavy fall of dark hair, lifted her arms to twist a fistful around and around into a knot, poked in the pins and secured the bundle at the base of her neck. With her arms up, her blue dress pulled taut over her breasts.

Matt swallowed back a groan. He hadn't seen hair like that since he'd left Texas, and it sure sent his pulse up a few notches. And then there were her breasts…

Miss Blue brushed off her hands, rolled the sleeves of her ruffly shirtwaist up to her elbows and stalked after the horse.

For a full minute he watched her struggle to push the gray mare backward.

"Lady, I never saw a more citified way of trying to move a horse. Why'd you come out west, anyway?"

"Because," she snapped. "That's what old maids from Boston do!"

He jerked upright. "Is that so?"

"That is so," she blurted. "If I had not escaped my mother's nitpicking criticism I would have shriveled up and died. 'Eleanora, lower your voice, the neighbors will hear. Eleanora, that is the wrong fork for shrimp. Eleanora this. Eleanora that.'"

She snapped her mouth shut. Heavens, what was she thinking, babbling these bottled-up feelings to a complete stranger! And a man, at that.

"Sounds like you've had a double dose of mother-smothering. Man, that would shrivel anybody up."

She stared at him, unable to speak.

"You want me to hitch up your horse?"

"No!" she shot. "I need to learn how to do this."

But before she finished the sentence, Matt was on his feet beside her.

"Stay away from me!" she snapped. "I can figure it out by myself."

He shrugged. "Suit yourself." He padded back to his bedroll and pulled on his boots. The rosy tint of the sky was giving way to golden sunshine. Time to head out.

But he couldn't, not yet. He wanted to see whether the stubborn Miss Blue could get her mare hitched up proper. Making sure she saw him, he strode over to his gelding, slipped the bridle over his muzzle and tightened the cinch on the saddle. Then he spoke to the animal. "Back up, now." With ease, he purposely stepped the horse backward so she could see how it was done.

He mounted, touched his forefinger to his hat brim and slowly walked Devil out of the copse. He couldn't resist sneaking a sideways look at her; she was watching him, her hands propped on her hips and a perplexed look on her face.

Ellie tried not to watch him. His long, lean body moved so gracefully with the horse that she had to admire him. He reached the edge of the campsite, but instead of continuing on to the road, the tall man drew rein and turned his horse back. His face under the worn black hat was shadowed, but when he stepped his mount toward her, for the first time she could see his eyes under the brim.

They were the oddest color, a sort of gray-green, like ferns. But the expression in them was not soft, like ferns; instead he looked at her with a flinty hardness that made her throat close. An inexplicable tingle went all the way up her spine to the back of her neck.

The man was dangerous, and it wasn't just those steady, unblinking eyes that told her that. His dark hair covered his ears and straggled halfway down his stubbled jaw. The careless, loose-boned way he moved hinted at a coiled strength in his thighs and broad shoulders. His mouth slashed across his chin as if a knife had carved it, and his long, straight nose pointed down at her. He was alert and observant. He reminded her of a predatory hawk.

Ellie moved a step back, but he kept coming. When he was so close she could hear his breathing, he slid one hand into the front pocket of his laced-up canvas shirt, then tossed her the pearl-handled pocketknife she'd returned to him after last night's supper.

"You'll need this come suppertime."

She managed to snag it before it hit the ground, and when she looked up he was already moving off.

"Wait! Your knife—how will I return it?"

"You won't." His voice was raspy, as if he didn't use it much. She guessed he was a solitary man, a lone wolf.

"I could mail it to you," she called after him.

He shook his head. "Don't have an address, Miss Stevenson. You keep it. I might be back this way again sometime." The black gelding moved off into the sunlight.

"Thank you, Mr. Johnson," she called.

He raised one hand, then vanished through the cotton-woods.

Ellie slipped the knife into her skirt pocket, carefully grasped the horse's harness, then backed the horse up as she'd seen him do. She lifted the traces into place, surprising herself at how straightforward the maneuver was. She finished hitching up the horse and felt considerably uplifted. Why, she was even getting halfway competent! A satisfied smile tugged at her lips.

All at once she remembered why she was out here in the wilderness. The parents of her students must be worried sick about them. For a moment a prickle of fear poked a hole in her confidence, but she knew she must keep going. She wasn't half as frightened as she'd been yesterday when she'd started out.

"Children, wake up! It's time to load up the wagon and drive on to Gillette Springs."

* * *

Matt kept his horse headed parallel to the road, waiting to see if Miss Blue and the wagon made it out of the trees. Sure enough, there she came bursting out of the woodsy camp like a bat out of— Didn't she know how to slow the horse down?

She didn't, he realized. First she yanked on the reins, then she flapped them across the mare's back. Poor damn horse had no clue what she wanted. He studied her attempts until he couldn't stand what she was putting that animal through.

Spurring hard, he rode back and drew alongside the wagon, then leaned sideways and grabbed the harness. As the mare slowed, he could hear her yelling at him.

"Just what do you think you are doing?" She halfheartedly flapped the reins one final time before the gray jolted to a stop.

Matt eyed her. She was downright beautiful with her cheeks flushed and her blue eyes snapping. Unexpectedly his heart gave a funny lurch. By God, even if she couldn't drive a horse and wagon more than half a yard, she was one helluva woman.

"All right, Miss Stevenson, you've earned yourself a lesson in horse-and-wagon smarts. Get down," he ordered. He dismounted and lifted her down from the wagon bench. He liked the feel of her waist under his fingers—soft skin and warm flesh. She wore no corset, which sure surprised him. He'd expect a woman as starchy as she was, a schoolteacher from Boston, to be trussed up and laced tighter than an Indian drum.

But she wasn't laced up at all, and his hands were enjoying that fact. Sure felt good to touch a woman. Been so long he'd almost forgotten. For a moment he couldn't seem to loosen his fingers and let go of her.

Up close, he could smell her skin and her hair. Something spicy, like lilacs. Again his heart kicked.

Abruptly he released his hold, climbed up onto the wagon bench and patted the seat. She scrambled up beside him, and when she'd primly settled her skirts so no petticoats showed, he lifted the leather reins and placed them in her hands.

"A horse is smart, Miss Stevenson. You ask it to do something and he'll try his damn—er, darnedest. But your directions have to be two things—clear and consistent. You want a Nervous Nellie, just keep on mixing up your signals."

Ellie stared at her hands, then at him. She did want to learn how to control the horse, but sure as God made green apple trees, Mr. Johnson was the most unlikely of teachers. Sitting beside him so close her skirt brushed against his jeans-clad thigh, the warmth of his body permeated all the way to her bottom. She'd never been this close to a man before. Especially not a man who smelled of horse and smoke and sweat and whose green eyes sent goose bumps down her arms. She was sure she would not remember a thing he was saying.

"Lift the lines up," he instructed. She obeyed.

"Mr. Johnson, I am sure you have more important things to do this morning."

"Yeah, I do," he said evenly. "Now, give the reins a little flick, like this." He covered one of her hands with his and demonstrated. A shocking rush of heat pooled in her belly.

"Oh!"

"Somethin' wrong?"

"It's n-nothing. Um…it looks like it's going to be hot today, doesn't it?"

His dark eyebrows drew down until they almost met above his nose. "What?" He glanced up at the sunlight filtering through the tree branches.

"Yeah, probably be hotter than Hades. You've got a long way to go, miss. You'll want to be on your way pretty quick. Might rig up one of your blankets to make a bit of shade for the wagon."

She spoke without looking at him. "Are you traveling in the same direction?"

"Nope. I'm ridin' west, to those cliffs back there." He jerked his thumb over his shoulder.

"Oh."

Abruptly he turned toward her. "You got a hat to shade your face?"

"No. I— We left in such a hurry—"

He blew out a long breath, yanked the hat off his head, and ran his hand through his dark hair. "Well, lady. Better find one. Otherwise you're going to fry your nose."

"But— Oh, dear. I don't know much about traveling unless it's in a railway car."

"From Boston," he observed drily. "Real taxing, I'd guess."

"Would you…I mean, could you not accompany us?"

Shading his eyes, he squinted through the branches at the ridge to the west. "Shoulda thought of that before, maybe."

"Yes, but you see, I had no choice."

"Seems to me like some idiot sent you off in one helluva hurry."

"He had no choice either," Ellie said stiffly. "The town was under attack by Indians."

She'd had enough of this long-haired, short-spoken, smoky-sweaty-smelling, ungentlemanly man. Was he simply going to abandon them?

He leaned over, laid both reins in her hands and shoved his long legs off the wagon bench. "Good luck, Miss Stevenson. Remember what I said about the hat."

He remounted his black gelding, tipped his battered Stetson and cantered away through the trees.

Ellie bit her tongue to keep her angry words inside. Wretch! How could chasing something be more important than protecting five helpless children and a woman alone? Chivalry was certainly dead and buried west of the Mississippi!

Her sleepy students tossed their folded-up blankets into the wagon bed, clambered aboard and waited for her to drive on.

Shade, he'd said. And a hat.

"Miss Stevenson, d'you think my dad is okay? Since Momma died, he's all alone out at the ranch, and..." Teddy MacAllister's voice petered out.

"I am quite sure your father would join the people in town, Teddy. He will be safe there." She needed to be firm and reassuring enough that the other children wouldn't start wondering the same thing.

Now, to create some shade. Ellie climbed down from the bench, selected a pink-and-white quilt and, with Mr. Johnson's pocketknife, poked a hole in each corner. Then she punched one of her hairpins through each opening and stuffed the curved end into the crack in the weathered side-rail. A dry three-pronged branch pushed up into the quilt's center made a crude tent of sorts over the wagon bed.

But, gracious! When she pulled herself back up onto the bench she felt the unpinned bun at her neck loosen and tumble down to her shoulders. There was nothing to do but plait it into a thick braid. While she twisted the strands of hair she pondered the problem of protecting her nose.

Perhaps she could drape one of the blankets over her head and shoulders? But the sun was already scorching. It would be suffocatingly hot under such a heavy wrap.

She lifted the reins, flapped them gently as Mr. Johnson had demonstrated, and the horse moved forward a few steps. At least she had learned to make the animal start and stop; she could figure out something to fashion for a hat as they traveled.

Carefully she maneuvered the mare through a wide opening between two large pine trees and rattled out onto the heat-shimmery road. Far across the plain she spied a lone rider on a dark horse, heading toward the ridge to the west.

What a maddening man! And he was unsettling as well, in ways she didn't want to think about.

"Miss Stevenson?" came a small voice from under the quilt-tent she'd fashioned. "What about my baby sister? She's only six months old, will the Indians capture her?"

Ellie drew in a calming breath and counted to ten so her voice wouldn't shake. "Edith, I am quite sure your baby sister, and your mother and father, are safe at Mr. Ness's mercantile."

Liar! She wasn't sure of any such thing, but she would die before she would admit it to the children. She wasn't sure how she would do what she had to do today—get them to Gillette Springs. She wasn't sure what to do when she got there.

Worst of all, she wasn't sure why she kept thinking about Matt Johnson's unnerving green eyes.

Pressing her lips tightly together, she turned the mare onto the road in the opposite direction from the rider on the dark horse.

Chapter Four

Matt started up the slope to the top of the ridge, then drew rein and scanned the road behind him. Yep, there she was, rolling along as if she knew what she was doing. Funny-looking drape over the wagon bed. He narrowed his eyes at the small heads visible under the makeshift tent, then studied Miss Blue.

She hadn't protected her face from the broiling sun as he had advised her, but at least she'd made that tentlike cover so the children wouldn't fry. She was a sensible woman at heart, even if she was from Boston.

He turned back to the trail leading up the mountain slope and shot a final glance back to the road. Aw, hell, she was going to burn those pretty cream-and-rose cheeks into a shriveled mask.

Why should you care?

He didn't care, exactly. She was obviously a misfit out here in the West, but he did admire that she had an education and could teach school. Reminded him of his mother. Most of the kids in Coleman County had learned their ABCs from Verlina Johnson.

He urged Devil on up the rise, but he couldn't get Miss Blue out of his mind. Spunky woman, taking care of five kids without enough smarts to bring along a pocketknife. Maybe she was a mite crazy, as well. After a day in the direct sun, she'd have a walloping headache.

The trail got steeper, and when he reached the top of the ridge he pulled up. For the next hour he rode in widening circles, trying to pick up Royce's trail. Tracks were maybe fifteen hours old and hard to see, but when he found an upturned rock beside a crushed patch of bunchgrass, he reined in and smiled. For here on it would just be a matter of time.

He followed the faint trail Royce had left until it abruptly veered north. He pulled Devil up short.

North? Wasn't that where Miss Blue was headed, north to Gillette Springs? Dammit, that meant the man he was tracking was on a collision course with that pretty schoolteacher from Boston. He spurred Devil hard. He couldn't let that murdering bastard Royce get anywhere near Miss Blue and her students.

The burning sun overhead was blinding. Ellie kept her eyes narrowed against the merciless glare, feeling the parched skin of her cheeks and her nose begin to sear. The back of her neck felt like one of her mother's boiled lobsters and her hands—oh, Lord. The palms were still white, but the backs were sunburned and painful. Perspiration gathered between her breasts. In another hour she'd smell as sweaty as Mr. Johnson.

She clenched her fists tightly around the leather reins. She disliked that man! He bullied her just as Mama had. But at the moment, she'd give anything to see him again.

Squinting ahead, she saw something that sent her stomach hurtling straight to her toes. A line of brown dust streaked at an angle toward the road before her, drawing closer and closer to a point a mile or so away where the two paths would cross. Every bone in her body wanted to turn around and head in the opposite direction. She hauled on the reins.

Five outraged voices screeched, jolted awake by the rattling wagon. The children climbed out from under the makeshift tent and sat blinking against the harsh sunlight.

Ellie shielded her eyes and waited. When the dust thinned out some, she caught her breath. A tall man on a black horse was moving toward her.

Inside her sweat-damp shirtwaist her heart hammered against her rib cage. What now?

Matt positioned his horse dead center in the road and waited for Miss Blue to slow the wagon to a stop. Then he stepped Devil forward and tipped his hat. "Good morning, again, Miss Stevenson." He nodded at the five curious faces lined up along the side rail, then returned his gaze to the young woman staring at him from the bench.

"Good morning." She sounded hot and tired and cross.

"Good thinking to rig up a quilt for a tent," he remarked casually. "None of the kids look sunburned."

"Thank you," she said stiffly. "God gave us brains. Surely one should use them."

Uh-oh. She was beginning to sound not only hot and tired but preachy, as well. "Should have used yours a bit more, miss. Your nose looks like a fire-grilled sausage."

"Oh!" Frowning, Ellie covered it with one hand. Heat rose under her fingers. Her skin! Her skin would be ruined. Mama would lecture…

No, she would not! Mama, mercifully, was in Boston. Instead she had Mr. Johnson shaking his finger at her.

"Climb down," he ordered.

"What for?"

He pressed his lips together. "You want to save your nose or not?"

She was off the bench in a flash, looking as though she was about to spit nails.

Matt dismounted. "Got any water?"

"Of course we have water," she snapped. "I saved all the tinned-food cans and filled them before we left."

"Get some."

Her hands—sunburned, he noted—again propped themselves on her shapely hips. "Yes, sir!" She saluted smartly, did a perfect military about-face and stomped to the wagonbed. "Teddy, give me your can of water, please."

The MacAllister boy grinned and handed over a peach can half-full of water. Miss Blue ignored the pop-eyed faces of her students and pivoted toward Matt.

"Water," she muttered.

Matt lifted the can out of her hands, walked three paces off the road, kicked together a small pile of dirt and dumped the water on it.

She sent him an outraged look. "Why did you do that? Water is precious!"

"Come over here."

She took a single step and stopped. "What for?"

Matt knelt to stir the slurry with his forefinger. "Full of questions, aren't you? Come on over here." He sounded more brusque than he had intended, but she picked up her pace and in the next instant she stood beside him. A scent rose from her petticoats— soap and some kind of flowery smell. Bath powder? The thought of dusting anything over her naked body made him grow hard.

Dammit. Good thing he was kneeling.

"Bend down," he ordered. "And don't ask what for, just do it."

"Well!" she huffed. But she bent at the knees, dropped to the ground and settled back on her heels. "Now what?" Her tone was chilly, to say the least.

With one hand Matt grabbed the back of her neck and ducked

her head toward him. With the other he slathered a handful of the mud he'd made across her forehead and cheeks.

She let out a screech. He'd known she'd do that, and before she could leap away he grabbed her hands and smeared more mud over the already sun-reddened backs and up one arm as far as her elbow.

"Should have kept your sleeves rolled down, Miss Stevenson."

"It was too hot! I also unbuttoned my—" She clamped her jaw shut.

Matt jerked his attention to the front of her blue shirtwaist. Sure enough, a line of undone buttons marched down her chest, revealing flushed bare skin all the way to where her breasts began to swell. Whoa, Nellie! If he had his druthers, he'd smear some of this mud all the way down to her nipples!

Slowly.

With an effort, he refocused on her hands, then moved his gaze to her mud-smeared face. She scrambled to a standing position, looking mad as a hornet.

Matt stood, as well. Toe to toe, they stared at each other.

"Why are you ordering me around?" she spat at him. "I hate to be ordered around like a child."

"How come you're all fluffed up like a banty chicken? I'm trying to help you!"

Ellie turned her back on him, facing her wagonload of students. At the sight of her mud-streaked face, they burst into laughter. How humiliating! And Mr. Johnson's deep-toned chuckles just added to the insult. She felt hot all over, not from the relentless sun, but from embarrassment. Keeping her head down, she marched to the front of the wagon, swung herself up and plopped her bottom on the bench. She had scarcely drawn a breath before Mr. Johnson settled his long length beside her.

"Stop acting like an old-maid schoolteacher," he intoned. "I'm doing you a favor. The mud will protect your skin from the sun."

"I— It is just that I am a bit self-conscious with it smeared all over me."

"Well, don't be," he growled. "Besides, it's not smeared all over you." He chuckled low in his throat. "I did think about it, though."

Instantly he ducked his head. "I mean, you look beautiful, mud or no— Oh, forget it."

Ellie gasped. Did he really think she was beautiful?

"Listen, Miss Stevenson, there's a good resting place up ahead, a river, plenty of trees. I think we should hole up there for the afternoon. Rest the horses, replenish our water supply."

"My destination is Gillette Springs, Mr. Johnson."

"We're not going to make it to Gillette Springs unless we stop and rest."

"We? Who is 'we'?"

"You, me and those five kids in the wagon. I'm going with you."

"Why?"

Matt groaned. "Damned if I know. I guess because you need help. Now, close your mouth and don't argue."

"You are probably right," Ellie acknowledged. "I am hot and sticky and tired, and my students are the same. You are correct, Mr. Johnson. We do need help. About that, I will not argue."

"Thanks," he murmured drily. He wouldn't tell her the real reason—that Royce was heading straight for Gillette Springs. Matt figured his quarry was out of coffee and tobacco and that's why he'd changed directions. He had to delay Miss Blue long enough for the killer to load up on supplies and move on.

He swung down from the bench and remounted his gelding. Might be best if he didn't get too close to Miss Blue for a while; his jeans still felt too damned tight.

By the time the wagon pulled off the road and into the woodsy area by the river, it was late afternoon and Ellie was so sun-baked and frazzled she felt like screaming. Despite the mud, the skin on her forehead and the backs of her hands burned like fire. Boston, even on her most picked-on-by-Mama days, was never like this. Oregon, she was discovering, was a different kind of hell.

She felt off balance around Mr. Johnson. His eyes missed nothing. In fact, she thought with a flutter of something in her belly, he looked at her with a gaze so penetrating she felt naked. Worse, when her eyes met his, an odd recognition of something zinged between them.

Did she imagine it? She found it hard even to breathe when he was near, not because of the scent of horse and sweat, but because…because the unhurried, catlike way he moved his body made her ache in places she had never ached before. Private places. Places her mother had never, ever mentioned.

The wagon bumped to a stop beside a shallow bend in the river. The water looked so cool and inviting she felt like ripping off her dress and diving in headfirst.

Mr. Johnson sidled his horse close to the wagon bed, where her students lay sprawled in various positions, panting in the heat.

"Listen up! Anybody want to go swimming?"

A chorus of yesses rose into the dusty air. Even Ellie murmured a quiet "Oh, yes, please."

"Okay. Everybody strip off the top layer of your duds and follow me." He started toward the river, dropping his gunbelt and then his denim shirt as he walked.

The children tumbled out of the wagon, tearing off boots and pinafores and aprons with eager fingers. The Ness twins shed their matching pink dresses, leaving their slight forms clad only in thin camisoles and floppy bloomers. Teddy MacAllister flung off his plaid flannel shirt and splashed into the water in Johnson's wake.

Ellie sat on the wagon bench, nervously plucking the sweat-soaked bodice of her dress away from her skin. She was hot and sticky and she longed to splash cool water all over her body, but she couldn't, not in front of Mr. Johnson. She just couldn't.

"You coming?" he yelled.

"No. Y-yes."

"Take off your dress, like the twins did."

"Oh, no, I couldn't possibly."

"Hell, yes, you could possibly," he shouted at her. "Just shuck your skirt and petticoats. Maybe your blouse, too, if you're wearing something underneath."

"Of course I'm wearing something under—"

His rich laughter stopped her. "Scared, huh?"

No, she was not scared! Shy, perhaps. Not scared. She climbed down from the wagon and with trembling fingers stripped off her skirt and petticoat, then unbuttoned her blouse the rest of the way and shrugged it off. Lifting her head high, she marched to a deserted spot farther up the riverbank and waded in.

Did he really think she was beautiful?

The children romped in the water, splashing each other, belly-flopping and screaming with delight. Absorbed as they were, they paid not the slightest attention to her.

But Matt Johnson watched her for a long minute, then twisted away and plunged into the deepest part of the river.

Chapter Five

Matt knew instantly that he should not have teased her. Half-undressed, she was stunning—willowy and gently rounded every place he tried very hard not to look at. He dived underwater and swam until he ran out of air, then surfaced and shook the droplets out of his hair. He was far enough away now that she paid no attention to him. And she had moved upstream, thinking she could not be seen. But she was wrong. He could see just fine.

So he watched. Couldn't help himself. And the wetter she got, the hotter he felt. Her soaked camisole plastered itself to her breasts and he caught his breath. They were luscious as ripe peaches. Her bloomers clung to her bottom and outlined...well—he swallowed hard—they outlined everything, including the enticing triangular patch of dark hair where her thighs joined.

While her students romped in the shallow part of the river, she sank up to her neck in the deeper water, then dunked her head under. When she brought her face up, the thick braid down her back was unraveling into a glorious tumble of thick, mahogany-colored waves.

Oh, man. Oh man oh man oh man. He had to turn away to adjust his wet trousers, and when he twisted around again she was gone. Thank the Lord. He didn't want to see her any more until her wet underthings dried out. He swam a few yards and waded out onto the riverbank. The sooner he got a fire going, the sooner Miss Blue's smallclothes would dry.

Within ten minutes he had a blaze going that threatened the low-hanging branches of the nearest sugar pine tree. He turned his backside to the flames and watched steam rise from his trousers.

One by one, the children gathered around the fire, shivering and grinning. He wondered where Miss Blue was. He stalked over to his discarded gunbelt, buckled it around his hips and bent to retrieve his denim shirt. Loosening the leather laces at the neck, he worked it over his head onto his dripping torso. When he opened his eyes, there she was!

Fully dressed in her blue shirtwaist and skirt. But… His belly tightened. If her underwear was drying on a huckleberry bush somewhere, that meant *she had nothing on underneath!* Her skirt clung to her long, slim legs, and—his mouth went dry—he could see her nipples clearly through the fabric of her blouse.

Matt groaned. Even when he shut his eyes he could see them, her perfect, small rose-tipped breasts. He forced himself to look away. It was going to be a long, uncomfortable evening.

The MacAllister boy turned from the fire and cocked his head. "Mr. Johnson?"

"Yeah, son?"

"You're making groany noises. Does your belly hurt?"

"Nope." But another one of his organs sure did. He was swollen and hard and sitting down right now in these tight jeans would be downright painful.

The brown-eyed seven-year-old edged closer. "Mr. Johnson? How come you're smiling?"

Matt jerked as if he'd been nipped by a scorpion. "Just thinking about, uh, something."

All at once he realized he hadn't thought about that bastard Royce for a full seven hours. Half a day. Felt kinda good not being angry and churned-up inside. Being able to draw a breath that didn't make his chest hurt with that eaten-up feeling he got in his gut whenever he thought about Royce.

"I'm hungry," said a small voice at his elbow.

Matt knelt down to the girl's level. Manette, he remembered. "Me, too, Manette. What should we do about that?"

"I think we should cook some supper and eat it. There's some more cans of food in the wagon." She slipped her warm hand into his.

"Okay, partner, let's go have a look."

Ellie stepped out from behind the sprawling huckleberry bush where her camisole and bloomers lay drying to see Manette and Mr. Johnson pawing through the cans in the back of the wagon. Her fists clenched. What business did that raggedy man have inspecting their meager supplies?

"Mr. Johnson! May I speak with you?"

The tall man raised his head and thumbed his hat off his face. "Sure. What about?"

"In private," she said without smiling.

"Oh. Well, Manette and I were just choosing some supper vittles. Could it wait?"

"No, it could not. As a matter of fact, it concerns our supper."

He bent toward Manette. "Be back in a minute, honey."

"No, you won't," the girl piped. "Miss Stevenson usually talks a long time."

Ellie flinched. Good heavens, did she really? Was she boring her students?

Mr. Johnson jumped down from the wagon bed and moved toward her with his long-legged stride. She tried to look at his face, but again his hat was pulled so low his expression remained hidden. His mouth, however, was curved in a smile.

"What's up, Miss Stevenson?"

Ellie pursed her lips. "We cannot remain here overnight. We haven't enough food to—"

"You can't lose another day, is that it?"

"Precisely. The children's parents will expect—"

"They'll expect their kids to be kept safe and sound," he interrupted. "Whether they're hungry is secondary."

"But I promised to take them to Gillette Springs, not dillydally another night by this river."

"You can't go on to Gillette Springs right now."

She propped her hands on her hips. "Why not?"

"Not safe, that's why. There's, uh, a dangerous man in town."

"I don't believe you. What makes you think so?"

"His name is Randall Royce. He's a killer, and I know he's in Gillette Springs because I followed his trail."

Her voice hardened with disbelief. "And just how do you know he's a killer?"

"I know he's a killer because he shot my little brother. Luke was still a kid. He tried to stop Royce from stealing one of our horses, and Royce shot him. I've been tracking him for the last four years. Started in Texas, but he's been moving north."

"Why you? Why isn't a federal marshal chasing this man?"

He gave her a speculative look. "Well, ma'am, the truth is a federal marshal *is* chasing him." He fished a well-worn silver badge out of his pants pocket and flipped it over so Ellie could read the engraving on the back. Matthew L. Johnson, U.S. Marshal.

Ellie stared at him. This shaggy-haired, disreputable-looking, blunt-spoken man was a U.S. Marshal?

"I don't believe you."

"Doesn't matter if you do or don't, Miss Stevenson. What matters right now is that we—you, me and your students—have to stay put for tonight, and we might want to eat something while we do it. Now, I've got flour and bacon fat in my saddlebag and I make real fine biscuits. What do you say?"

Ellie said nothing, just peered up under his hat brim to catch a glimpse of his eyes. A glint of amusement shone in his gaze, but when he saw her watching him, it faded into two calm, calculating gray-green chips of marble.

That look sent a tremor through her chest. It wasn't fear; it was fascination. The man might be halfway good-looking with a haircut and a shave. And a smile.

What on earth was she thinking! He might be a marshal, as he claimed, but even if he was, she didn't trust him one smidgen. Maybe he was just a bounty hunter? Or a killer himself, looking to even up a score? Maybe he'd stolen that badge from a real marshal…except that his name was engraved on the back. Maybe he'd robbed the real marshal and assumed his identity?

She gritted her teeth. All right, maybe he was a marshal, but he was a rough, unkempt know-it-all just the same. She didn't feel safe around him.

Oh, yes, you do! You feel perfectly safe around him. What you feel around him is more like attraction than fear.

What nonsense! She was nothing but a lonely, gullible female whose head was turned by a man's admiring look. "Mr. Johnson—"

"Matt," he interjected.

Ellie raised her chin. "Mr. Johnson, when will it be safe to enter Gillette Springs?"

"Tomorrow morning, I reckon. Royce should have cleared out by then."

"But, if you are chasing him, why don't you ride on into town and capture him tonight?"

He raised his head and pinned her with those hard green eyes. "Because that'd leave you and these children out here alone. Unprotected. And," he continued, holding her gaze, "because I'm not going to capture him. I'm going to kill him."

Ellie's hand flew to her mouth. "But you can't! That's murder!"

Matt looked away. "Yeah, it is. Used to make me feel good

just thinking about it. Doesn't anymore. I just know I have to do it."

"But why?"

"Because I promised my pa."

Speechless, Ellie stared at him. In his eyes she saw determination and anger and the desperate look of a man caught in a trap of his own making.

"Could you not give it up?" she ventured.

He snorted. "You crazy? I've spent years busting my butt in the saddle tracking that bas—tracking Royce. Why should I give it up now?"

"Because," Ellie shot back without thinking. "There might be better things to do with your life."

The strangest look came over his face, a deep hunger of some kind. His gaze softened for an instant, then turned back to stone.

"Yeah, there might be, but I swore to get Royce. Besides my father, I swore it to myself."

Ellie looked straight into the man's eyes. "You are not playing a marshal's role in this," she said evenly. "You are playing God."

He didn't respond at first, just stared at her with eyes like green ice. "Never looked at it like that before," he growled. "But you're wrong."

"How old was your brother Luke?"

"'Bout the age of Teddy MacAllister over there. He'd have been nine come Christ—" His voice went hoarse.

For a long minute Ellie could not think of one sensible thing to say. Or even one comforting thing. At last she drew in a resigned breath.

"Mr. Johnson—Matt—we would be pleased to share your real fine biscuits."

Chapter Six

Teddy MacAllister hung at Matt's elbow, watching him mix up flour and bacon fat until it turned into a pebbly mixture, then adding a dash of saleratus and another of salt. The boy had dogged his every step for the past hour, and somehow it made Matt feel good inside. Teddy was a lot like Luke—quiet and intelligent.

The twins, Noralee and Edith, dressed in their matching pink frocks now that their underclothes were dry, clamored to help as well, carrying tins of water to dampen the biscuit mix in the crockery soup bowl Matt always carried in his saddlebag. Manette and her little friend Sarah perched on a nearby boulder, dipping their bare toes in the river mud and giggling.

"Dumb girls," Teddy muttered under his breath.

Matt had to laugh. "Don't like girls too much, huh?" Matt sent one twin off to find two flat stones.

"Aw, they're okay, I guess. Noralee can hit a tree stump with a cow pie at fifty paces."

"And," the thin-faced girl interjected with a shy smile,

"I can sew and make bread and pick apples. Do you wanna marry me?"

"Heck, no!" Teddy bellowed. "I don't care if you can fly, I ain't marryin' you or any other girl."

"Aren't," said a low, clear voice from the opposite side of the crackling fire. "You *aren't* going to marry her."

The boy screwed up his face. "Well, I'm not! Ever!"

"Nobody's pushing, son, so don't work up a sweat over it."

Miss Blue raised her arm and Matt glimpsed a can of tomatoes in her hand. "Would you want this?" she called.

"Sure." Surreptitiously he studied her chest. Apparently her smallclothes were dry because her nipples no longer showed through her blouse. That meant she had her lacy bloomers on, too. He heaved a sigh of relief.

But when she stepped around the fire and pressed the can of tomatoes into his hand, his pulse kicked up anyway. Way up.

"Thanks," he murmured. Every inch of her except for her face was covered up in chaste blue muslin, but her dark hair was loose and tumbled. Heavens. She was a fine woman, but she made him feel funny inside. Lonely-like.

At that moment, Edith returned lugging two flat river rocks. Ellie planted herself next to Teddy and watched Matt push the sticky biscuit dough into a ball. "How about some canned corn?"

"Sure. We can have succotash."

Teddy stared up at him. "What's sucker-dash?"

Matt feigned astonishment. "Your momma never made you succotash?"

"I ain't got a momma."

"Haven't," came Miss Blue's gentle voice.

Matt froze. Poor kid. He curled his arm around the boy's narrow shoulders. "You want to learn how to cut out biscuits?"

At Teddy's nod, Matt laid one flat rock out and dumped the dough on it. "Now, we need an empty—"

Before he could finish, Miss Blue handed him an empty bean can. Matt shot her a look of thanks. "Then, you sprinkle some more flour over your rolling pin—this can, here—and squash out the dough with it." He handed the can to Teddy, who dipped his fingers into the bag of leftover flour and coated the can until it looked snow-dusted. Matt laid his hands over the boy's and demonstrated how to roll the dough.

Teddy pushed the can back and forth across the sticky ball, pressing it all the way to the edges of the rock. Then Matt showed him how to use the upside-down can to cut out the biscuits. He stepped back from the fire to let the boy do it by himself.

He could feel Miss Blue's eyes on him, and his neck began to burn. Why was she staring at him like that? Instinctively he pulled his hat lower and turned toward the twins.

"Girls, how'd you like to make an oven?" He showed them how to position one flat, smooth stone close to the coals and prop the other against it at right angles. Teddy plopped down the biscuit rounds, and when they were all laid out like white polka dots on the dark stone, he dusted off his hands and looked up at Matt, his brown eyes shining.

Matt turned away. He couldn't look at the boy too long— reminded him too much of Luke. He busied himself dumping cans of beans, corn and tomatoes into his cast-iron frying pan and settling it among the coals. Next, he stalked down to the river and knelt to wash the flour and grease from his hands.

He kept his back to Miss Blue. When she spoke near his ear, he damn near fell in.

"Thank you," she said softly. "You are good with the children. They like you."

Matt inhaled a whiff of that lavendery scent she wore. "How about you, Miss Stevenson?"

A long, long silence fell. Matt focused on the sound of the breeze in the treetops, the children's voices around the fire, his own heartbeat hammering against his ribs. At last she spoke.

"I have been watching you."

"Yeah, I noticed. Makes me nervous. Look, Miss Stevenson, I had no business asking you that."

"And I have no idea why I am answering." Her voice was soft but controlled. "Yes, I do like you. Even if you are—"

"A man-hunting marshal?" he supplied.

She laughed. "I was going to say, even if you are rather, well, raggedy, and your eyes are unfriendly."

"I try to keep my eyes hidden."

She smiled. "So I have noticed. That makes *me* nervous. What is it you wish to hide?"

Matt opened his mouth, then shut it with a snap. He wasn't about to admit he'd been covertly admiring her lithe, graceful body. Her hair. He hadn't admired a woman this much as far back as he could recall, and he feared his hunger showed in his eyes.

"Mr. Johnson?"

"Matt," he corrected.

"Mr. Johnson—"

"Supper's ready!" Teddy banged his mixing spoon against the rolling-pin can. "Come and get it!"

Matt rose. He towered over Miss Blue but she didn't cower, and she didn't step back. All of a sudden he wanted to kiss her.

Dammit, what was he thinking? She wasn't the kind of woman a man played loose with; Miss Blue was the "other" kind. The marrying kind.

But *he* sure wasn't. Yeah, he was lonely. Most of the time he felt so hungry for something—he couldn't say exactly what—he hit the red-eye too often. But admiring a woman and catching Royce sure didn't match up. He'd sworn to catch his brother's killer, and that was that.

Ellie felt better after she donned her dry chemise and bloomers, not only cooler after her brief dip in the river but…safer.

Something about the way Mr. Johnson looked at her made breathing difficult. It wasn't dislike she saw in his gaze; more like a gleam of—could she even say it?—desire. Or what she had always imagined desire looked like in a man's eyes. No man had ever looked at her that way. It made her feel, well, valued. Wanted. Or at the very least, noticed. She didn't dare wonder what he read in *her* eyes.

She liked the way he dealt with the children, especially the easy way he included Teddy MacAllister in his activities. The man would make a wonderful father.

Oh, no, he would not! This man was a lone wolf, set on his vengeful mission. However, by delaying her entry into Gillette Springs, he was sacrificing his chance to corner the killer in town. He could just as easily have left them here and ridden off to capture the man.

But he had not. She stepped into the fire circle, watching him patiently show Teddy how to keep the biscuits from scorching. The man was unusual. Possibly even worthy of respect. But he certainly did not look like most men.

She did wish he would trim his hair and shave off the bristly shadow that covered his cheeks and chin.

On the other hand, remembering how she herself had felt being teased and ignored because of her unusual height, maybe what the man looked like was neither here nor there.

After supper the children rinsed out the tin cans and Matt showed them how to scrub the flat "oven" rock and his frying pan with a handful of sand. Dusk faded into darkness except for a sliver of rising moon, and the children rolled themselves up in their blankets, forming a semicircle around the glowing coals. One by one they nodded off to sleep.

Mr. Johnson, Matt, spread his bedroll between the smoldering fire and the river, and Teddy immediately settled himself next to him. Ellie positioned herself on the opposite side of the fire, as far away from Mr. Johnson as she could get. He made her uneasy. Almost angry. He made her feel odd inside when she was near him.

An hour passed. She breathed in the pungent smell of the pine branches he'd cut to lay under their bedrolls and looked up at the stars winking through the trees. An owl tu-whooed somewhere above her head. Finally her eyelids drifted closed, and then she felt someone—a large someone—settle quietly beside her.

Ellie jerked to a sitting position. "What do you think you are doing?" she whispered.

"Getting comfortable," he said quietly. "Teddy snores."

She bit back a laugh. "I didn't know that. It doesn't seem to bother his 'intended,' Noralee," she joked.

"If a girl's smart, she pretends to be deaf and blind at times. That boy needs a friend."

"He lost his mother a year ago, when Indians attacked the train she was on. Ever since then his father has been distant and withdrawn. I think Teddy is feeling lost."

"Bet you never saw an Indian till you came out west. Do they scare you?"

"Some scare me, yes. But I think most are just people like us, trying to feed their families and raise their children."

"Yeah," he grunted into the quiet. "I guess."

"What are *you* afraid of, Mr. Johnson?"

He gave her a long look. "Shirking my duty," he said in a monotone. "Turning out to be a man who doesn't do what he says he will."

"Oh?"

"And maybe," he said even more quietly, "spilling my guts to a stranger."

"I have never understood the code that men out here seem to live by."

"What about you, Miss Stevenson? You afraid of anything besides Indians?"

She settled back onto the ground and wrapped herself in the

pink quilt that had been left over after the children had selected their blankets. "Sometimes I am afraid that my mother was right. That I really am inadequate." There was a subtle wobble in her voice.

"Your mother thought you were inadequate? Inadequate how?"

"Oh, my. Mama had a long list. Inadequate as a person, I guess. As a teacher." She hesitated. "As a woman."

Matt lapsed into silence. He wanted to reach out and touch her shoulder. In his book, this woman was just fine. More than fine.

"Miss Stevenson, why—"

"Oh, call me Ellie, why don't you?"

"Ellie, why did you come out west? What do you want from life out here?"

"Honestly?"

"Yes. Honestly."

"Well, it's hard to explain." Again, her voice was unsteady. "I want to—to feel connected to people. I want to feel that I matter."

"You mean connected to a man?"

"I feel quite silly saying this, especially to a man, but I—I want to love someone. I'd like to have a child. Have a family of my own."

She sat up straight, as if something startled her. "I want you to know, Mr. Johnson, that I have never spoken such words to a living soul."

Matt said nothing, just listened to the whoosh of the wind in the trees. "I want to catch Royce," he said. "See him hang."

"Is that all?"

"I—dammit, I don't know anymore. I thought catching Royce would be it. Now I'm feeling…aw, hell, I don't know what I'm feeling."

Except that it felt good to be honest, to say things he had not consciously thought out before. And it sure felt good—very, very good—to lie beside Ellie, so close he could touch her.

"What," he murmured after a long moment, "will you wish for on your birthday?"

She sighed. "I will be twenty-seven in November." Her voice was sounding drowsy. "On this birthday, I will wish to grow no older!"

He chuckled. "Anything else?"

She stifled a yawn, and her voice was muzzy. "Yes, there is one other thing. I would like to know what a man's kiss feels like."

Matt lay rigid, not moving a single muscle. He'd like to know what kissing *her* would feel like.

Nah. It was the wrong time. The wrong place. He glanced sideways at her. Anyway, she didn't really want a kiss right now. It wasn't her birthday, and besides that, she was sound asleep and snoring a bit herself.

Chapter Seven

Ellie opened her eyes the next morning to see Matt sitting cross-legged on the ground beside her.

"Sit up," he ordered.

Instantly she was wary. Her glance around the campfire showed five quilt-wrapped lumps; the dapple-gray horse was already hitched up to the wagon and stood patiently next to a thick pine tree. What could be wrong?

Reluctantly she rose up onto one elbow. He bent toward her and tipped her chin up with his thumb. Her heart stopped. *Is he going to kiss me?*

She leaned toward him and closed her eyes. But instead of his lips, she felt his fingers smearing something sticky across her cheek. She snapped her lids open.

Matt grinned at her and held up a tin can.

"Oh, no," she moaned. "Not more mud."

He dipped his first two fingers into the can and smoothed the dark contents over her forehead and down her nose, then sat back and surveyed his handiwork with a half smile.

"You look kinda cute, all muddied up like that."

"And pigs flew over the moon last night," she shot back.

His smile faded, but that odd light was back in the depths of his eyes. "No, but something did happen last night." He caught her gaze and held it. "Never met a woman I could really talk to before."

Ellie felt her throat close. She knew if she spoke, she would start to cry, so she remained silent while he smeared the last of the mud on her cheeks and the backs of her hands. She had said things to him last night that she had never shared with anyone before. And, she suspected, the same was true for Matt.

It had changed her somehow. Made her feel close to a man she'd known only twenty-four hours. And if that wasn't strange, even worrisome, she didn't know what was.

"Now," he announced when he'd used up the last of the mud slurry. "Let me see the bottom of your petticoat."

"What? I most certainly will not!"

"Rather broil under the sun, like yesterday?"

"N-no, but—"

Don't argue. Pull your skirt up a few inches."

She peeled back the quilt and inched the blue muslin up to midcalf. He studied the petticoat flounces so intently she began to wonder if he'd never seen a proper lady's undergarments. Most likely a man like Matt had seen dozens of scantily clad floozies who wore no underwear at all.

She did wonder about this man. Had he been close to a woman before? Had he ever been in love? And why did he carry his U.S. Marshal's badge in his pocket instead of wearing it on his shirt? So many things about him were a mystery, including the way he was looking at her petticoat.

He poked a finger at the hem. "Tear off about two feet of that bottom ruffle."

She opened her mouth to protest, then caught sight of the determined look on his face. So she bit through a thread, unraveled a few stitches and tore off a length. The ripping sound made her wince.

Matt produced a three-pronged willow branch, sharpened the ends to a point and poked them through the white muslin. In two minutes he had fashioned a parasol of sorts.

"Isn't fancy," he said, handing it to her. "But it should shade your face."

Ellie experimentally twirled it over her head. "Very clever," she quipped. "This should be all the rage back in Boston." Then she looked straight into his eyes and smiled.

"Thank you, Matt."

Matt felt his face grow warm. He got to his feet and stalked off to load up his saddlebag and tie his bedroll on his horse. He couldn't look at her any more. Noticing that hair of hers, the tangled dark waves touching her shoulders, a yearning such as he'd never felt before tugged inside. He guessed somehow she was carving a little hollow in his heart.

But, hell, he was going to leave her today, get on his horse and pick up Royce's trail where he'd left off. If he was lucky. Royce could be heading to Montana or the Yukon territory. But wherever it was, Matt knew he wouldn't be here, anywhere near Ellie.

"Wake up the younguns, Ellie," he said over his shoulder. "Got to get moving before it gets too hot."

He heard the sleepy noises the children made as Ellie moved among them. Nice, peaceful noises that somehow made his heart ache.

He wasn't getting any younger. How many more years was chasing Royce going to take out of his life? *Why are you asking this? You got something else to do?*

The truth was he'd never thought beyond catching his brother's killer. Until now.

But he couldn't walk away in the middle of a job he'd sworn to do. Besides, he told himself, there would be other women.

But it sure was hard to leave this one.

* * *

From a mile away, Gillette Springs looked peaceful enough, but Matt didn't want to risk it. Putting Ellie and her students within fifty miles of Royce would be a big mistake. The man had a reputation for assaulting women, especially pretty ones.

An even bigger mistake might be letting his feelings about her and the kids make his decision for him. Still, he should ride in first and check the saloons, the sheriff's office, the hotel registry to make sure his quarry had cleared out of town.

He signaled Ellie to pull up and stepped Devil close to the wagon.

"Why are we stopping?" she asked. "We're almost there."

Matt sighed. Ellie was logical to a fault. Trouble was, she had no idea what Royce was capable of. Matt did. He'd learned a lot about the man just following in his shadowy footsteps for so many years. Royce liked whiskey, easy money and women. Matt suspected Royce had robbed a dozen banks between Texas and Oregon. Funny he'd never run into an angry sheriff or a posse; from the look of it, Royce could strike and disappear like the rattlesnake he was.

"I'm going on into town alone, Ellie."

Her face changed.

"Don't worry, I'll be back for you."

"That isn't what I am worried about," she said quietly.

He leaned in toward her. "What is it, then? You've got a frown across your forehead big as my hand."

Ellie swallowed and stared down at her own mud-covered hands. "I am afraid for you. From what you say, this Royce sounds more like an animal than a man."

"He's a man, but he's mean. I don't want you in town just yet—let me check it out first."

"That is thoughtful of you, Matt. Thank you."

"Not thoughtful so much as sensible. Now, climb down from that bench, Ellie. I've got something to say to you."

He dismounted to hand her down, and when she stood before him, her dark hair loose about her shoulders, her sky-blue eyes wide, her mud-smeared face expectantly looking up at him, his mouth went dry.

"Stay there and keep quiet," he growled to the children. Then he walked Ellie around the back of the wagon behind a thick clump of vine maples.

"Here will do," he said.

"Do for what?"

He ignored her question. Slowly he brought his hands up to her shoulders and pulled her toward him. He hadn't planned this. He'd wanted to warn her to be careful, but suddenly something else was more important. He bent his head and pressed his mouth over hers.

Kissing her was like flying on a magic carpet, with swoops and dips that flooded him with hunger. He folded her tight, tighter against his body, and she slid her arms about his neck.

A jolt of scorching heat ran up Ellie's spine and settled below her belly. His mouth moved gently, purposefully over hers, and with each passing second the pleasure of their lips touching grew more exquisite. He tasted of something smoky and rich, and she couldn't get enough.

When he lifted his mouth from hers she was breathing hard and she could feel his body trembling.

"Damnation," he muttered. He kissed her again. This time when he released her she couldn't breathe at all. His eyes looked both puzzled and hungry and they held hers for a long, long minute. Ellie's insides felt as if they were bursting into flower.

Her heartbeat shivered under her prim shirtwaist and all at once she wanted to unbutton it. What was happening to her? Something delicious and unnameable had most definitely occurred, but what?

He brought his mouth to her ear. "Happy birthday," he whispered.

Suddenly she wanted to cry. Tears burned under her lids, but she blinked them back.

Without speaking, he walked her back to the wagon. Matt helped her up onto the bench, then remounted his black gelding and touched his hat brim. "Stay here. I'll be back."

He rode away toward the town.

Matt did not return. She waited hours until the distant mountains flamed gold and purple with the sunset. What now?

The children were bored with the word games she had thought up and tired of running relay races and playing hopscotch on the grid she'd drawn in the sandy earth. And they were growing hungry. Ellie herself was wind-burned and jumpy.

Should she wait, as Matt had instructed? Or should she assume he was not coming back and proceed on her own?

When dusk fell, shadowing the road, Ellie made a decision. She gave the gray mare some water in her cupped hands and a handful of oats from the bag in the wagon bed, loaded up her fretful students and climbed onto the driver's bench. With a gentle flap of the reins she started toward the town's lights winking a mile ahead.

Gillette Springs looked much like Smoke River except that some of the building fronts needed a coat of paint and there were two saloons instead of one. The wagon clattered past a bank, a barbershop and the sheriff's office, but Ellie noted the board walkway on both sides of the main street was completely empty. Strange for a town this size. She reined up at the Gillette Hotel.

"I will need two rooms with two beds in each room."

The bony clerk stared at her through horn-rimmed spectacles, then eyed the children. "Sure thing, ma'am." He handed her a pen and indicated the hotel register. "Are all these children yours, ma'am?"

"Certainly not! I am unmarried."

The clerk's eyebrows went up. Ellie scrawled her name in the indicated space and let out a sigh of relief. She'd done it. She'd driven a wagon and five students forty miles across the hot, windblown plain. They were all safe and sound. Sleepy and hungry, but safe. Mama was wrong; Ellie was most certainly not inadequate!

The children lined up behind her began to spread out onto the two leather-covered sofas in the foyer.

"Are there any messages for me? My name is Stevenson." Surely someone from Smoke River would be arriving to retrieve the children?

"Nope. No messages for anybody. Kind of a funny time to show up in town with all the excitement goin' on."

A cold hand gripped her throat. "What excitement?"

"Havin' a big gunfight in town. Fact is they're still trading shots, off and on, and meantime the sheriff's out with a posse chasin' a bank robber. That's why the hotel is full up and nobody's walking around outside."

Ellie's heart thumped. "Who is 'they'?"

"Dunno their names, ma'am. Two men—one of them's a gunfighter. Big red-haired fella with a scar halfway down his face. I'd guess the other one's chasing him. That one's tall and dark-haired and—"

"Oh, no!" she moaned. It was Matt. He must have run into Royce unexpectedly. Oh, dear God, what if he were injured? Or dead? She felt her face freeze into a cold mask.

"Aw, don't worry, ma'am. You'll be safe enough inside the hotel. Ever' so often one of them cracks off a shot. We all hit the floor and maybe twenty minutes later there's another shot from a different direction. Seems like the two of them are movin' around from building to building across the street from each other, playin' cat and mouse."

"I see." She tried hard to keep her voice steady. "Could you send up a bathtub for each room, and towels and some soap?"

"Will do, Miss..." he glanced down at the register "...Stevenson. Dining room's open until nine, if you're hungry."

"Thank you. And could you get someone to take my horse and wagon to the livery stable?"

"Wouldn't risk it, miss. Just leave it in front of the hotel, why don'tcha?"

Suddenly she was encircled by five grimy faces. "We're hungry!"

Looking down at them, she realized her own face was still mud-smeared; no wonder the clerk had looked at her oddly. "Baths first, then supper." Ellie fished in her skirt pocket for the ten-dollar gold piece she always kept for emergencies, laid it on the hotel desk and accepted both keys.

"Up the stairs, end of the hallway," the clerk directed. "Both rooms got a view of the street."

She herded the children up the wooden staircase and down the partially carpeted hallway. If she weren't so frightened, this might be a real adventure!

After baths and squabbles over who got to sleep in which bed, Ellie and the children descended on the dining room. She felt reasonably clean and somewhat refreshed, and she'd managed to wash and braid her hair. But, oh, Lord, her nerves were so jangled it was as if crows were screeching in her head. She had heard no gunshots during the children's baths, but now she found her attention focused on sounds from outside the dining-room window.

The plump young waitress tapped her pencil against her pad of paper. "And what'll you be having, miss?"

"What? Oh, I'm sorry, I wasn't paying attention."

The girl rolled her eyes. "I can see you're a busy mother. So far I've got three orders for fried chicken and two for steak." She waited expectantly.

"Steak," Ellie blurted. She would need strength to survive this night.

All through the meal, she kept one ear tuned to her students and the other cocked for sounds of gunfire. The longer the silence outside stretched, the more irregular her pulse became. It was like waiting for the thunder to crash after a lightning bolt.

By the time she tucked all the children into bed—Manette and Sarah in one bed and the Ness twins in the other in what Teddy MacAllister termed "the girls' room," and Teddy in the extra bed in Ellie's room—she was worn-out.

"Sure is softer than a bunch of pine branches," the boy said in a drowsy voice. He fell asleep almost at once.

Ellie shed her outer garments and crawled between the sheets of her own bed, so exhausted she could not think clearly.

She could hear, though. Somewhere out there Matt and Royce were trying to kill each other. She lay sleepless, waiting for the sound of gunfire, until her eyelids would no longer stay open.

Matt was right—Teddy did snore. The memory brought tears to her eyes.

Chapter Eight

Matt flattened his body against the brick wall of the bank and edged forward along the narrow shadowed alley until he had a clear view of the main street. The boardwalks on both sides were empty and silent; the townspeople had had the good sense to stay indoors while he and Royce had exchanged gunfire throughout the long afternoon.

He scanned the opposite side of the street and what he saw made his entire frame stiffen. What in the—! Ellie's wagon and the dappled mare stood at the hitching rail in front of the hotel. He'd been pinned down by Royce all day; Ellie must have grown tired of waiting and driven on into town. Damn. She and the children were inside the hotel.

A ripple of cold fear crawled up his spine. He didn't know exactly where Royce was at the moment, but he prayed it wasn't anywhere near the Gillette Hotel. The thought of Ellie and Royce in the same building, even on the same side of the street, made his heart seize up.

He swiped sweat off his forehead with his sleeve and tried to think. Ellie and the children were at the hotel, safe for the moment. But that wasn't long enough. Sooner or later a gunshot would smash into that big dining-room window and...

Wait just a minute. He was no more than thirty feet from the man he'd been chasing for the past four years: why was he thinking about anything other than killing the bastard?

Why was he thinking about that slim, blue-eyed woman inside the hotel? Why was he thinking thoughts that made him go weak in the middle? He shook his head to rattle his brains into sticking to business.

But her face, mud-smeared all over, her chin jutted out in a challenge, kept intruding. Hell, he was probably half in love with her.

He closed his eyes and groaned. Maybe more than half.

Another shot blasted a chip out of the brick wall behind him and he jerked into awareness of where he was and what he'd sworn to do. He knew he had to move. More than that, he had to reach Ellie and those kids before one of them got hurt. Or killed.

His blood went cold. He raised his Colt .45 and put two shots into the front window of the barbershop, then pounded down the dark, narrow alley and circled around to the back door of the hotel.

A weight settled beside Ellie on the bed and a warm, smoky-smelling hand covered her mouth. "Don't scream, Ellie," a low voice murmured in her ear. "It's me. Matt."

She jerked upright so fast his hand smacked her forehead. "What are you doing here? How did you get into this room?"

"Picked the lock," he whispered. "Keep your voice down. Teddy is asleep in the other bed. Never thought I'd be grateful that boy snores."

She started to laugh, then clapped her hand over her mouth. In the faint light through the single uncurtained window she could barely make out Matt's angular face. His lips were pressed tight with tension and his eyes—goodness, she had never seen such determination in a man's gaze. Cautiously she reached over and brushed his dark hair off his forehead.

"I'm not pretty," he grumbled. "Not even clean, and I apologize. I had to get to you before..." How much did he dare tell her? Oh, what the hell, tell her all of it. He might be dead before morning.

"Before what?" she prompted. "There has been no word from Smoke River about the children. Their parents must be frantic with worry. They will expect me to keep them safe, Matt, but I admit I am frightened."

"Royce is here, in town."

"Yes, I know. The hotel clerk told me about the gun fighting during the day. I knew immediately it was you and Royce."

"Your horse is out front, Ellie. Still hitched to the wagon. If I kept Royce busy dodging bullets, do you think you could get to the wagon and drive it around to the back of the hotel?"

"How do you mean, 'keep him busy'?"

Matt sighed, and a breath of warm air caressed the shell of her ear. "He's holed up across the street, in the barbershop, I think. I can pin him down by shooting at him until you—"

"Until I can get the wagon off the street," she said in a jerky whisper.

"I hate like anything asking you to do this, Ellie. It's not your fight. But I think it's a risk worth taking. What do you think?"

"I—I'm not brave, Matt, but I don't think we have a choice. Do you?"

"It's the only way I can think of to keep you all alive. It's just a matter of time until Royce crosses the street to the hotel.

All at once Ellie realized something. Matt *did* have a choice. Twenty-four hours ago his goal had been to capture Royce. Now, when he had a chance to do just that, he had changed his priorities: he'd put her and the children first.

"We have to do it," she whispered.

He leaned over and brushed his lips across her cheek. "You may not feel brave, Ellie, but you are one helluva woman."

"Matt," she breathed. "Don't get killed. I—"

His mouth found hers and for a long minute she forgot everything but the gentle insistence of his lips.

Eleanora Stevenson, you have fallen in love with this most disreputable-looking man whom you have known for exactly two days!

It was her mother's voice in her head. She sucked in a breath. *Yes, Mama, I have. Courtship is different out here in the West.*

Matt laid something soft and bulky between them. "I brought you some clothes."

Ellie grasped a fistful of fabric and lifted. A pair of jeans unrolled and out spilled a man's shirt, laced at the neck like the one Matt wore, a pair of small-size leather boots and a worn gray Stetson with a drooping brim.

"I don't want you to look like a woman," he whispered. "Too dangerous. Royce likes women."

"Where did you get these clothes?"

"From my saddlebag. They're mine, except for the boots."

"Whose—?"

"Don't ask," he said. "In another hour it'll be light outside. Then I want you to get dressed and take the children through the kitchen to the back door. Then you go on out to the front of the hotel and drive the wagon around behind."

"But where sh-should we go then?" Apprehension made her voice catch.

"Head for last night's camp by the river. Someone will send word if— Forget that. I'll leave a note for the hotel clerk, tell whoever comes for the kids where to find you."

He stopped, listening to Teddy's steady snores from the other bed. God, he was tired. It was probably three in the morning now, and he found himself struggling to keep his eyes open. The room was quiet; no gunshots had erupted for the past hour. Maybe Royce had sneaked out of town

Ellie lay next to him, not moving. There was no way he could touch her. Her body was underneath the covers and he lay on top of the counterpane. He nuzzled his chin against her ear. Boy, she sure smelled good, like soap and roses and Ellie. This woman was one in a million, beautiful and brave and sweet-scented.

He closed his lids and drew in slow, deep breaths.

"What are you smiling about?" she murmured.

"How do you know I'm smiling?" he replied without opening his eyes.

She gave a soft laugh. "Because I'm watching you."

His lids snapped open. She had shifted to her side and lay with her jaw propped on her stacked fists, her blue eyes fixed on his.

"Maybe I'm smiling because I still can. Lately I've been feeling, well, kinda undecided about things."

She said nothing, just waited.

"I can track a man from Texas to pretty much anywhere. I can outsmart him most of the time, and probably outgun him, but…it's kinda funny, I guess, but I'm not sure I've got the sand to see this all the way through."

"You mean you've lost your courage?"

Matt chuckled low in his throat. "No. I never get scared for myself. But for the past two days I've been wondering if it's worth it to risk getting killed trying to settle an old score. Wondering if somewhere along the line I took the wrong direction."

Her eyes widened. "Wrong dir—? Whatever do you mean?"

"I'm not real sure yet, but…well, there's got to be more in life than just killing this guy."

What he'd just said hit him with a jolt to the pit of his stomach. Someday he wanted to settle down. Have a son like Teddy— smart and curious and responsible. He couldn't do that if he was dead.

He clenched his teeth. Right now he wanted to spend more time with Ellie. Maybe a lot more time. Maybe even all the rest of the time he'd have on this earth. But if…

"Ellie, I'm dead-tired. Can I stay right here for about half an hour and catch some sleep?"

She didn't answer, just snuggled her head against his shoulder and laid her arm across his chest.

* * *

Matt woke when Ellie slid her willowy body out of bed. Pink-tinged gray light showed through the window, but his body felt leaden, his mind fuzzy. Maybe he was getting too old for this.

Teddy was still snoring. He heard Ellie moving around quietly, getting dressed. God forgive him, he cracked open an eyelid to watch.

She'd slept in her underdrawers and camisole, but it was still enticing to watch her dress. She drew on the jeans he'd brought and slipped the shirt over her head. He'd bet she'd never in her life worn such duds, even when she was a little girl.

Ellie rolled each leg of her pants up three turns, then peeked down at herself. Trousers! Never in her twenty-six years had she ever worn a man's trousers. She flexed both knees. She was beginning to understand why men walked the way they did, sort of stiff-legged with their thumbs hooked in their pockets. She tried stuffing her own thumbs into the pockets of these jeans. Yes, she felt like swaggering.

She took a step, then two, strolled over to check on Teddy, then swaggered back to comb her hair and braid it tight so she could hide it under the gray hat.

"Well, hell," Matt said, just loud enough for her to hear.

"What?" she whispered. "Am I walking like a man or not?"

"Honey, don't ever walk like that when you're not with me. Might tempt some randy cowhand to jump—uh, lay a hand on you."

Ellie dismissed the remark with a slashing motion of her hand. She sashayed around the room in the oversize jeans and shirt, but she still moved like a woman. Looked like a woman.

"That's enough," he said. His voice turned hoarse. "Get the children up."

She leaned over the sleeping boy in the next bed. "Teddy." She shook his shoulder and the snoring stopped, then resumed.

"Teddy, wake up! Get dressed."

Matt headed downstairs to the kitchen to snatch whatever he could find to eat. The last thing he heard was Teddy's querulous voice. "What happened to my boots?"

Ellie explained the plan to the children and lined them up at the back kitchen door. Teddy had stopped asking about his boots; apparently he preferred going barefoot anyway. Ellie kept her mouth shut. The boy's boots were a size too small for her, but she'd stuffed her feet down inside anyway and resolved she would not limp, no matter what.

Matt stepped forward. "Teddy, you'll be in charge until Miss Stevenson can bring the wagon around. Then I want you all to pile in the back real quick-like."

Teddy gazed up at Matt with worshipful eyes. "We can stay and help you, Mr. Johnson."

Matt blinked hard. "Son, that's mighty brave of you, but you'd best stick with Miss Stevenson. She'll need protecting until you reach the river and someone from Smoke River comes to take you home."

Over Teddy's head, Ellie and Matt exchanged a long glance. "Guess it's time," Matt said quietly. He reached out and drew Ellie behind a storage bin.

"Now remember, Ellie, walk slow and steady, like a man does. Keep your head down so the hat covers your face. You'll have to back the mare up a few feet to turn the wagon—can you manage that?"

"Yes," Ellie said with a quaver in her voice. "I remember how you showed me. I can do it." Yes, she could! Mama would never believe it, but...Mama would be wrong.

"Give me five minutes to get situated so I can cover you. When you hear a shot, start moving."

"Yes, all right." Her heart was starting to slam against her ribs so hard she knew he could hear it.

"Are you scared?" he murmured.

"N-no. I am terrified."

He chuckled, then reached under the hem of her overlong man's shirt and slipped a revolver into her waistband. "Got six cartridges loaded. If you need to shoot, don't stop, just keep firing."

"Just keep firing," she breathed. "I'll remember."

He turned his back to the wagon and the children lined up behind Teddy, making sure Ellie was screened from view. Then he moved in close, tipped his head down and brushed his mouth over hers. He kissed her again and she wound her arms about his neck.

"Never kissed anyone that looked like a man before," he said with a soft laugh. "Kinda liked it." He wrapped her dress and shoes around the loaf of bread and hunk of cheese he'd lifted from the restaurant kitchen and stuffed the bundle into her arms.

Tears burned into her eyes. He touched her arm. "Count seconds with me, Ellie, so we'll come out together in about five minutes. Start now. One tomato, two tomatoes, three…"

He glided out the door into the alleyway and disappeared. Ellie kept counting. "…four tomatoes, five tomatoes…" When she reached 297, she heard a shot. The signal! She squeezed Teddy's shoulder and edged out the doorway.

It hurt her squeezed-up toes to walk in Teddy's boots, but she did her best, taking slow steps the way Matt did and keeping her head down. When she turned the corner of the building and surveyed the hotel front, her breath choked up inside her throat. *Just keep walking. Breathe in and step forward. Breathe out and step again.*

She focused on the still-harnessed mare and began to move toward it. More gunshots and the tinkle of glass breaking. She felt naked and alone, even with the cold steel gun pressing into her belly. Pulling the hat brim lower, she forced her trembling fingers to untie the reins from the hitching rail. She kept her spine ramrod-straight; otherwise she would fold up like a rag doll.

The mare tossed her head and glared at her with one huge black eye. Ellie tugged the harness backward. "Back up, girl." She pitched her voice low but it shook audibly.

The mare tossed her head again but stepped backward one step, then two. A window across the street shattered and Ellie chose that instant to climb up onto the wagon bench. Her knees shook, and her too-tight boots made her stumble, but she made it.

She lifted the reins. When she felt the wagon move forward she thought she would weep with relief. *Thank you, Matt, for showing me how to drive this thing!*

The moment she reined to a stop at the back kitchen door where the children waited, a white pinafore streaked forward and clambered into the wagon. On her heels dashed another child, and another, until all four girls were hunkered down on the wooden bottom. Teddy brought up the rear. He unfolded a quilt, pushed the girls underneath and crouched down under it himself.

"Go," he whispered.

Ellie flapped the reins, turned the wagon in a circle so they were heading south and walked the horse away from town as casually as she could. Not one word was uttered for a good half hour, and by then they were on the road, heading for the river camp.

They were safe, thanks to Matt. And thanks to her, she acknowledged with pride. In two days she had accomplished things she'd never dreamed possible—and that included kissing Matt Johnson. She let her head droop so the tears washing down her cheeks would not upset her students.

That man. That brave, courageous man had saved all their lives. For as long as she lived, she would never forget him.

Chapter Nine

Between spurts of gunfire, Matt listened for the sound of a horse and wagon on the road out of town.

He could keep Royce pinned down for only so long; each time he stopped to reload his revolver, gunshots nicked the wooden wall behind him.

Matt held his fire, listening hard for the clop-clop of a single horse's hooves telling him Ellie and the children were on their way. And, there it was! He put three quick shots through the dressmaker's front window to cover the sound of the rumbling wagon, then listened until he could no longer hear it.

Matt squeezed off another round, hoping for some return fire so he could keep track of his quarry's location. Royce did not return fire.

The silence stretched too long. Had Royce caught a bullet?

Matt crouched, waiting in the narrow alley between the feed store and the mercantile. The sun rose like a big yellow ball behind the hotel, flooding his once-dim hiding place with light. He'd have to take better cover.

Cautiously he backed down the alley and circled around behind the newspaper office. Still no movement from across the street. Not more than ten yards separated the two men.

Matt crept cautiously over to the dressmaker's back entrance. Still no sound from Royce. Could he have taken a bullet?

Very slowly Matt stood up. Still nothing. Dammit, he had to know, but he sure as hell wasn't going to cross the street to find out.

"Royce?"

No answer.

"You in there?" Matt cracked the door open.

A lean black cat arched its back and glared up at him with indignant yellow eyes.

"Royce?"

The shop was deserted. Shards of window glass peppered the pine floorboards, but there was no sign of Royce. Somehow the man had again slipped through Matt's fingers. He swore under his breath. The man was slippery as a—

He stopped short, staring down at the floor. Glistening spots of dark blood dotted a path that led out the front door.

Matt bolted through the entrance onto the boardwalk, revolver cocked and ready.

The street was empty. Royce was wounded, but he'd gotten away. Then he heard the fading clatter of a galloping horse.

Matt swore aloud. He'd have to track the man all over again, but it should be easy this time, since Royce was bleeding. He strode down to the livery stable for his horse, mounted and began to pick up signs of Royce's trail. Fresh horse tracks. And blood.

All at once he went cold all over. Royce's trail led straight south, toward the river camp where Ellie and the children would be.

He kicked the gelding hard and began to pray.

The wagon rattled off the road and into the stand of cotton-wood trees bordering the river. Ellie reined the dappled gray to a stop and sat motionless, her head bowed. She'd done what she thought she could never manage: she had climbed up onto the driver's bench under the nose of a murderer and driven the children out of town to safety.

Now she found she could not stop shaking.

Teddy crawled out from under the quilt and sucked in a lungful of air. "It's hot under there," he complained. "And it smells like girls."

Ellie choked back a laugh. "Tell me, Teddy," she asked, trying to keep her face straight, "what do girls smell like?"

"Soap 'n' stuff," he grumbled. "It's hard to get the smell outta my nose."

"You don't have a sister, do you, Teddy?"

The boy's forehead wrinkled. "Not me. Don't want one, neither."

"Either," she corrected automatically.

"Well, I sure don't."

The girls began to emerge from their hiding places under the quilt, Sarah first, then the Ness twins, holding each other's hands. Last came Manette, gripping the loaf of bread under her arm. She presented the block of cheese, still wrapped in a dish towel, to Ellie and slapped the bread onto the bench beside her.

Ellie had never been so grateful for a simple loaf of bread. "Let's eat something, shall we? How about sandwiches?"

She dug Matt's pocketknife out of her trouser pocket and set about cutting thick rounds of bread and folding them over slices of cheese. Manette wolfed hers down and reached out her hand for another. The twins and Sarah nibbled daintily at their food while Teddy waited patiently at the end of the line.

She had just started to slice the cheese for herself when she heard a rough male voice from across the river.

"Might make one o' those for me, too, kid."

Ellie went numb with terror.

A stocky red-bearded man splashed across the river on a scruffy-looking white horse with a black star on its forehead. He rode up to within a few yards of the wagon and drew rein.

"I beg your pardon?" she said in her iciest tone.

"A polite one, are ya? I said make one of them sandwiches for me."

Ellie stared at him. "Who are you?"

"Name's Royce. Randall Royce. Now, kid, where's my sandwich?"

Royce! Ellie flinched. The man Matt was chasing? It couldn't be…unless Matt was— She clamped her lips together, unable to finish the thought.

"J-just a moment," she said as calmly as she could. "I'll s-slice off some more bread."

"Ain't goin' no place, boy. I'll wait."

Ellie's heart plummeted into her stomach. "Teddy," she said under her breath. She motioned the children back under the quilt. When they were all hidden, Ellie turned her attention to the bread beside her on the wagon bench.

Royce stepped his horse closer. "Hurry it up. I'm 'bout starved."

She jammed the pocketknife into the loaf and began sawing off a ragged chunk, then another. She laid them side by side and slapped a slice of cheese down. When she was about to clap the second slice on top, Teddy's grubby fist poked out of the quilt and opened to reveal a palmful of sand and sawdusty-looking grit. From the bottom of his pants pocket, she guessed.

She almost crowed aloud with delight at the boy's ingenuity. Quickly she glanced at Royce, now busy with his horse trappings, and swept the stuff out of Teddy's hand and into her own. She dumped it over the cheese and folded up the sandwich.

"Here you are, Mr. Royce." She held out her concoction. He snatched it out of her hand and stuffed a corner into his mouth. Trembling, Ellie busied herself making a sandwich for herself. She deliberately kept her motions slow to take as much time as possible.

Royce gobbled down half his sandwich and abruptly spat it out. "What the—?"

"It's the cheese," Ellie said quickly. "I buy it special at the mercantile. It's rolled in…" She racked her brain. "…cracker crumbs. Makes it taste—"

"Tastes like hell," Royce bit out.

At least, Ellie thought with relief, he didn't say it tasted like sand. She bit into her own sandwich, smiled and purposely spoke with her mouth full. "Crunchy."

Royce sent her a black look, then led his horse behind the wagon and tied it to a drooping pine branch. Her throat tight, she chewed slowly and watched every move the man made, screening her face behind her half-eaten sandwich.

What should she do? Act as if everything were normal? Try to escape?

But where should she go? She had no way of knowing if it was safe to return to Smoke River. Back to Gillette Springs, then? No, she couldn't risk it. Royce might follow her. Besides, Matt was there.

For the moment the man was sitting on the riverbank, cleaning a… Oh, good heavens! He was cleaning a revolver. Then he toed off his boots and stuck his huge bare feet into the cold water.

She gulped. She had Matt's gun in her pocket. Could she sneak up on Royce and—? And what? Hold him at gunpoint? For how long, an hour? All day?

All night? She edged her fingers toward her weapon.

Too late. Royce reloaded the revolver and laid it within his reach. Ellie's hand froze. For a split second she wished she was underneath the quilt with the children.

Afraid to move, she sat on the wagon bench and tried to think. She was still there a half hour later when the faint sound of hoofbeats reached her ears. *Matt. It had to be Matt.*

She concentrated on remaining motionless, and when the hoofbeats grew louder, she began kicking her boot heels against the side of the wagon to cover the noise.

Royce heaved his bulky frame to a standing position and stuffed his dripping feet into his boots. Picking up the revolver, he stomped toward the wagon, idly sliding the weapon into the holster buckled around his girth.

Ellie kept kicking her heels against the wagon. The more noise she could make, the less chance Royce would hear the approaching horse. And maybe her loud thumping would warn Matt.

"Got anythin' else to eat?"

She shook her head and kept up the drumming.

"Got any— Hey, kid, stop that noise!"

Ellie stilled her feet and waited. Now there was no sound of a horse, just the moan of the wind through the treetops. Where was the rider she'd heard?

Royce strode closer. "Got any whiskey?"

"Nope," she said, keeping her voice as low as she could.

"How come?"

"Don't take spirits." Ellie prayed he would not notice the lumpy quilt in the wagon bed.

"Oughtta try it sometime, kid. Grows a boy into a man damn fast."

Ellie nodded but said nothing.

"I saw you leave town a while back. Where're you headin'?"

She dropped her chin to her chest and pretended she hadn't heard the question.

Royce bellied up to the wagon bench. "Don't talk much, do ya?"

She had to get him away from the wagon and the children hidden in the back. She climbed down from the bench, pushed past the big man's shoulder and muttered a single word. "Thirsty."

She headed toward the river.

"Yeah, me, too." Royce dogged her steps to a flat rock where she perched on her knees and leaned down to scoop up a palmful of water. Her fingers had just broken the surface of the river when she heard the click of a revolver safety and Matt's voice.

"Don't move, Royce."

Something swished in the trees across the river, and then Matt appeared, his gun barrel leveled on Royce.

"Gawdalmighty," the man behind her muttered.

Matt waded into the river. "Drop your gunbelt and put your hands in the air."

Before she could draw breath, a meaty arm snaked around her shoulders and dragged her upright to shield Royce's body. He shoved the cold muzzle of his revolver under her jaw, forcing her head back. Her hat flew off and her unbound hair tumbled down.

She felt Royce jerk in surprise. "Well, I'll be—"

He repositioned his arm across her waist, pulling her back against his chest so tight she couldn't breathe. Something wet and sticky was seeping into the back of her shirt. Blood! He was wounded!

"I've got me a hostage!" he shouted.

Matt kept coming. "Won't work, Royce."

"Yeah? How come?"

"Because," Matt said, his voice flat and hard. "I'm going to kill you no matter what."

"You come one step closer and I'll shoot her," Royce yelled.

Matt's eyes met hers for an instant, and that was all it took. She knew without a doubt that he'd come for her, not for Royce. Now she had to gather her courage and grasp at the life she wanted.

"You hurt her and I'll shoot you anyway. Right through the heart."

Her life hung by a thread. She had to do something. It took her three full breaths to work up enough courage to speak.

"I...I have something to say."

"Yeah?" Matt said.

"If I were standing in your shoes, I would let this man go."

His jaw sagged open, then snapped shut. "Are you crazy? I've been tracking this killer for four years. Why should I give up now that I've got him right where I want him?"

Ellie looked straight into the gray-green eyes of the man she had come to care about. "Because," she said slowly and quietly, "because living is better than dying. Because nothing comes for free. And…" she balled her hands into fist. "…because maybe you have found something more important than killing this man."

"Hell!" Royce burst out. "Women are sure crazy."

For an endless minute Matt stared at the man he'd sworn to kill. "Not this woman," he said quietly. "Not crazy at all."

"Huh?" Royce's arm about her waist went slack.

Matt sent Ellie a long, long look, and when he spoke to Royce it was her he fastened his gaze on. "I'll make a deal with you, Royce. I know you've taken a bullet. You ride with me to the doctor in town and then to the nearest Federal Marshal's office and I won't put another shot into your gut. A trial should have you hanging at the end of a rope."

"Now, why would I want to do that?" Royce grumbled.

Ellie saw in an instant what she needed to do. She ducked her head, twisted away from Royce's grip and dived for the river.

Royce fired at her, but the bullet ricocheted off a flat rock and lodged in a tree trunk. He then swung his revolver toward Matt, but another shot ploughed into the fleshy part of Royce's upper arm. His gun hand went slack.

Matt charged him, knocked his weapon away and wrestled him to the ground. Royce groaned like a branded steer.

"Get up," Matt ordered. "There's a doctor in Gillette Springs and a U.S. Marshal's office in Dakin. That's sixty miles east, so get moving."

He splashed back into the river and hauled Ellie up into his arms. "I'll find you," he breathed into her ear. "Wait for me."

Chapter Ten

The warm June afternoon brought the lazy drone of honeybees and the scent of damask roses through the open window in Ellie's small cabin. She drew in a deep breath, savoring the spicy-sweet scent, and pondered her friend Lucy's question.

Would Ellie be a bridesmaid at Lucy's wedding next Saturday?

"And mine on Sunday?" Darla caught Ellie's hand in hers. "Oh, please?"

Ever since Ellie had returned to Smoke River two weeks ago with all five of her students safe and sound, she'd been invited everywhere—church socials and barn dances, picnics and hayrides. Manette's grandfather, Rooney Cloudman, had told the whole town about her adventure in Gillette Springs while denying his crucial role in talking the renegade Indian braves out of attacking the town. Thad MacAllister, Teddy's father, had enthusiastically embroidered both tales, and now both Rooney and Ellie were treated as if they walked on water.

"Well, will you?" both girls entreated in unison.

"Y-yes, I suppose so." Her heart gave an uncharacteristic

flutter at the thought of the weddings. She swore she hadn't stopped thinking about Matt Johnson for a single minute since her return.

"Oh, good!" Darla released her hand. "Tomorrow let's meet at the dressmaker's and—" She broke off, staring out Ellie's front window. "Oh, my!"

Lucy pushed aside the gingham curtain and gasped. "*Who* is that extraordinary-looking man?" she whispered. Her brown eyes were wider than Ellie had ever seen them.

Darla crowded her aside. "Just look at him!"

Lucy elbowed her way closer. "Why, that's the handsomest man I've ever seen, even including my Henry."

Ellie scooted to the window and peeked over their heads. What she saw made her heart stop.

A man, a tall man on a dark horse, was dismounting in her front yard. She couldn't see his face since his back was to them, but his boots looked shiny; the gray Stetson he wore looked brand-new, the brim stiff and the crown still uncreased. The jeans he wore had extra-long legs and fitted snugly over his...

It couldn't be!

Definitely not. This man looked too well-scrubbed, too close-shaven, his dark hair cut too neatly. But the way he walked, so loose and easy...

"He's coming this way!" Darla squealed.

Ellie pressed her hand against her mouth. It couldn't be him. It couldn't possibly be...

And then he lifted his head and looked directly at her with intent gray-green eyes and a familiar half smile. She bolted out the front door, leaving Lucy and Darla glued to the window.

"Why, just look at that!" Lucy murmured. She watched through the glass as Ellie went flying off the porch and into the man's arms.

"Well!" Darla huffed. "She never said a word about any man. Who is he? Oh!"

She withdrew from the window and closed the curtains. "Lucy," she announced in a voice tinged with disbelief. "You don't suppose—"

"Oh, yes, I do," Lucy blurted. She yanked the curtains aside for a better view. "Oh! She's kissing him!"

"No, silly, he's kissing her."

The two young women watched in rapt silence. After a long minute, Lucy pressed the ruffled shoulder of her dress against Darla's puffed muslin sleeve.

"I wonder if she'll ask us to be bridesmaids."

With reluctance Matt lifted his mouth from Ellie's, then kissed her again before she could open her eyes. She tasted of chocolate. "Delicious," he muttered when he could draw breath.

He rested his cheek against her forehead and inhaled the scent of her hair and the spicy odor of her skin that had haunted his dreams for the past two weeks.

"Delicious," he said again. "I'm in love with you, Ellie. Don't know how it happened, it just did." He pressed his lips just behind her earlobe, let his tongue follow the shell of her ear. "You taste so damn good. Better tell me to stop, or—"

She made a small sound. "I don't want you to stop, Matt. Don't ever stop."

"Marry me," he murmured. "Today. Or tomorrow if today's too soon."

Ellie gulped. "Today is…"

"Tuesday," he said, his voice hoarse. He groaned and sought her mouth again.

"Too soon," she managed against his lips.

"Tomorrow, then." He deepened the kiss until her knees began to tremble.

"Matt, stop. Tell me about Royce?"

"Royce!" He tipped her chin up. "I'm here beggin' you to

marry me and you want to know about Royce? He's in the Deschutes County jail, awaiting trial. Now, kiss me!"

"You didn't kill him, then?"

He tightened his arms around her. "I couldn't, Ellie. I kept thinking about all the things I'd lose if I let myself settle for revenge."

"What things?" His lips were so close to hers that when she whispered the words their mouths touched.

"Mostly you. I couldn't lose you. And then there was something else, maybe a life together, you and me, and also—"

"Tomorrow," she said. Tears sparkled in her eyes. "We will be married tomorrow."

"Let's see, that's…" Matt raised his head and studied the setting sun "…about twelve hours from now. Too long."

"Well, there's nothing we can do about that," Ellie whispered.

"Is that right? Care to sit by my campfire tonight?"

Epilogue

⟨⟨⟨⟨⟨⟨⟨⟨⟨⟨⟨

Everyone said it was the most unusual wedding ever seen in the Smoke River community church. The groom, tall and handsome in a dark suit with his U.S. Marshal's badge pinned on the lapel, paced back and forth in the morning sunlight spilling across the altar, waiting for the bride to appear. Rooney Cloudman, at Matt's side as best man, kept his eye on the restless groom and finally laid a restraining hand on the marshal's arm.

Matt waited. And waited. Had Ellie changed her mind?

At last there was a stir at the back of the small church, but it wasn't Ellie. First came Lucy Nichols in flounced yellow muslin, her tight blond curls bobbing with each step. Then Darla Weatherby moved slowly up the aisle wearing a dress of pink lawn and smiling at everyone along the aisle.

"Where the hell is Ellie?" Matt muttered to the older man beside him.

"Keep yer shirt on, she's comin'," Rooney whispered.

And just then, at the back of the church, appeared a vision in pale blue dimity. Ellie. She was so beautiful Matt's throat ached. Tall and elegant, her face glowing, she paused to take up a bouquet of lilacs and await her escort, Wash Halliday.

"This is taking too damn long," Matt grumbled. Before Rooney could stop him, Matt was striding up the aisle to the back of the church. Without a word he scooped Ellie up into his arms, kissed her thoroughly and carried her up to the altar amid a roar of cheers and whistles.

He set her on her feet, kissed her again and turned to the minister. "Start," he ordered.

Later the bride tossed her bouquet of lilacs into a crowd of unmarried ladies with their arms outstretched. It was caught by Sarah Rose, the boardinghouse owner, who screamed and promptly burst into tears.

* * * * *

Read more about
Sarah Rose and Smoke River in
LADY LAVENDER.
Available at www.Harlequin.com

TEXAS CINDERELLA

Judith Stacy

Dear Reader,

Everyone loves a celebration. Whether it's a birthday, graduation, patriotic occasion or religious holiday, we all enjoy getting into the spirit of the moment. Often, we do this with a party and, for many of us, planning the festivities is wonderful fun. There are decorations to select, a color scheme and tableware to decide on, beverages and food—lots of food—to serve. These special occasions are treasured moments enjoyed with friends and family.

When I came up with the idea for *Texas Cinderella,* I thought it would be fun to make Molly Douglas the Old-West version of our modern-day party planner. And what more exciting event is there to plan than a wedding?

Molly takes on the responsibility of planning the grandest wedding ever seen in Spindler, Texas. But things don't go exactly as she intended—thanks to Adam Crawford, the town's most eligible bachelor. It's a wedding the townsfolk will never forget!

Wishing you many warm, wonderful occasions with loved ones.

Judith Stacy

With love to David, Stacy, Judy, Seth and Brian.
This wouldn't be any fun without you.

Chapter One

Texas, 1887

Something big had happened.

Molly Douglas leaned closer to the window in the dining room of the Cottonwood Hotel and gazed outside. To everyone else seated behind her, or anyone on the street, the town of Spindler looked much as it did every afternoon. Horses drew freight wagons and carriages down the dusty street, men with guns strapped to their hips and women with market baskets strolled the boardwalk. The town was busy—busier than ever these days, thanks to the stagecoach and railroad, or so Molly had been told. She'd only lived in Spindler a short while.

But she knew something had happened. Something big.

Across the street, Grace Maxwell darted out of the general store her parents owned and threaded her way between three men on horseback and an oncoming carriage, waving her arms.

Molly dashed toward the hotel lobby, mumbling a prayer that none of the customers seated in the dining room would ask her for anything. Molly's duties at the Cottonwood Hotel did not include waiting on diners, but she certainly couldn't ignore a paying customer.

"Something's happened," Grace announced, as she rushed into the lobby. Her eyes were wide and her breath came in short little puffs.

"Don't faint before you can tell me," Molly insisted and guided her to the blue circular sofa in the center of the lobby.

Grace had been Molly's first—and was now her dearest—friend in Spindler. At nineteen, Grace was two years younger than Molly. They couldn't have looked more different. Where Grace was short, with golden-blond hair and oddly dark eyes, Molly was tall with deep brown hair and blue eyes.

Molly dropped onto the sofa beside Grace. Her mind raced as she tried to imagine what horrible event could have brought Grace here in such a state.

A train wreck? A robbery? A killing somewhere?

Grace worked at the Maxwell General Store, which housed both the post office and the telegraph office. Grace's family learned the news even before the editor of the *Spindler Weekly Review*.

"What is it?" Molly asked. "What happened?"

Grace pulled in a big breath, as if steadying herself, then whispered, "Adam Crawford."

Molly's heart rate picked up. A warm tingle swept her from head to toe—none of which suited her. But she—along with every other young woman in Spindler—reacted the same way at the mention of the town's most eligible bachelor.

Grace leaned in and lowered her voice. "I just heard Mama tell Mrs. Dempsey that Adam Crawford intended to pay a call on someone," she said.

Molly reeled back as if the words had stung her. Ever since she'd arrived in Spindler she'd heard the gossip that circulated about Adam Crawford. Tall, handsome, he owned a number of businesses in town. It was just a matter of time before he courted a woman. Everybody said so. But who would it be? Now, it seemed, that question would be answered.

An odd sense of disappointment swelled in Molly's chest.

"Don't you want to know who it is?" Grace asked, as if Molly had taken leave of her senses for not asking immediately.

Molly forced her chin up and cleared her throat. "Well, certainly. Of course I want to know."

Grace glanced around, paused for effect, then announced, *"You!"*

"Me?"

Molly jumped from the sofa and pressed her hand to her lips.

Grace got to her feet. "Yes, you. Isn't this exciting?"

Molly shook her head frantically. "No! Why me? Are you sure it's me? It can't be me."

"It's you. I heard Mama say the words myself," Grace told her. "And you know Mama wouldn't make up something like that."

That was certainly true. Emma Maxwell wasn't one for idle gossip, especially when it concerned the one man in town all the women—young and old—had speculated about for months.

"Aren't you happy?" Grace asked.

"No," Molly insisted, trying to ignore her still-racing heart. "I'm not interested in being courted. You know that."

Grace gave her friend a little grin. "Well, you'd better get interested. Adam Crawford is a highly respected, powerful man in this town, and if he's decided to pay a call on you there's nothing you can do about it. Except enjoy it."

Molly cringed as Grace giggled and squeezed her arm.

"Besides," Grace said. "I've seen how you look at him. I know how you feel about him."

Molly couldn't bring herself to deny her friend's words. They were, after all, true.

"I've got to get back to the store. Let me know *everything*," Grace called as she hurried out the door.

With a groan, Molly dropped onto the circular sofa. How could this have happened? How could she have caught the eye of the most eligible bachelor in town?

Unlike all the other young women, she hadn't done a thing to attract his attention. In fact, the attention of Adam Crawford was the very last thing she wanted. They'd never even been properly introduced.

She'd passed Adam on the street a few times and he'd tipped his hat courteously, and he'd eaten in the Cottonwood's dining room often, where he'd smiled pleasantly at her. But that was it. Nothing more had ever passed between them.

Although he did seem to look her way quite often—but that was just because she was new in town, wasn't it?

Molly got to her feet and drifted to the window. She gazed out at the bank building just down the block. Adam owned the Spindler Bank, along with his partner. He lived on the second floor.

Was he there now? In the bank? Making plans to call on her? Plans that would ruin her life?

Molly stilled her runaway thoughts and willed herself to calm down. Since arriving in Spindler to work at the hotel her aunt and uncle owned, she'd spurned the advances of every man in town. She had no intention of being courted by any man because she had no intention of marrying. She couldn't.

Not after what had happened in Philadelphia.

Molly huffed irritably as she entered the dining room. The nerve of that man. Thinking he could simply announce that he intended to pay a call on her and it would have her doing high kicks across the hotel lobby.

She crossed the dining room and let herself into the smaller room through the double doors. This had been a storage area until Molly arrived. After taking one look at the space, she'd suggested to Aunt Libby that the place be cleaned up and used for a private dining room. After conferring with Uncle Roy, who'd been less than enthusiastic about her idea, Molly had been given permission to make the changes—as long as she did the work herself.

She'd done just that. In a matter of days the room was spotless, the windows sparkling in the sunlight. Molly had dug through boxes left by the previous owner in the dusty attic and found curtains and colorful table linens that she'd washed and ironed herself.

When word had gotten out that such a comfortable, quiet space was available at the Cottonwood, so many people had wanted to use it that Molly had begun taking reservations. She oversaw every detail of each event, making sure the occasion was perfect.

Uncle Roy didn't share the town's excitement over the meeting space in his hotel, nor had he complimented Molly on her idea. And he certainly hadn't shared with her one thin dime of the money it brought in.

Molly stood in the doorway looking with pride at the tables set with yellow cloths and floral napkins, in anticipation of the women's luncheon scheduled for later today. She changed the table settings as appropriate. Blue, when a group of businessmen met there. Pink, yellow or pale green for the women and young ladies who gathered to discuss church or civic functions.

With practiced ease, Molly counted out eight plates from the stack on the sideboard for this afternoon's luncheon, pleased that she'd made her mark in town—and improved her uncle's business—so quickly. Hardly a day went by that someone didn't drop by the Cottonwood to inquire about using the room, and each and every one of them complimented her on how lovely it looked.

Molly had learned from the best—her grandmother. As far back as she could remember the older woman had kept Molly at her side as she prepared for guests, instructing her on proper table settings, manners and deportment. Everything had to be perfect. Her grandmother allowed for no less, given her standing in Philadelphia society.

With a gasp, Molly froze and clutched the plates against her. Was that the reason Adam Crawford wanted to call on her? Had he heard about her socially prominent family? Molly, of course, had heard all about Adam's wealthy Charleston family—everything about the man was the talk of the town. Had Adam selected her because he felt she would measure up to his standards? That the two families would be suited for one another?

Bitter anger and dread roiled through Molly, memories so hurtful she could barely stand to recall them. She'd left them behind when Aunt Libby had asked her to move to Spindler, and she rarely thought of them anymore. But now, with the distinct possibility that Adam Crawford would call on her, ask to court her, they all rushed back.

Molly clenched her fist. Darn that man for putting her in this position. She'd left those hurtful recollections behind and that's exactly where she wanted them to stay.

Yet for a moment—just a moment—she imagined what it would be like to have a man like Adam call on her. A man of consequence from a highly regarded, well-thought-of family. How wonderful it would feel to be accepted, wanted.

Especially by a man who already had a special place in her heart.

She drew in a cleansing breath and forced her thoughts into the present. She had a new life here in Spindler, one free of shame and regret, one that she loved. And she wasn't about to let anyone—not even Adam Crawford—change that.

Molly moved about the dining room placing the plates on the tables, feeling the determination build inside her. When Adam called on her, she'd simply refuse. Yes, that's what she'd do.

Although he was awfully handsome.

Molly reined in her thoughts once more. She would tell him she wasn't interested.

And he was quite tall with very wide shoulders.

Not that it mattered, she told herself.

And her heart ached and her stomach fluttered every time she saw him or thought about him, or someone else mentioned him, or—

Molly stilled her thoughts.

She simply would not allow him to call on her. And that would be the end of it.

Adam watched his friend and business partner, Travis Vaughn, sitting across the desk from him as he read the letter Adam had just received. The two of them had been in business together for a few years and had done very well since arriving in Spindler. Now, as they sat in Adam's office in the bank building, he knew they faced one of their biggest challenges ever.

Travis seemed to realize it, too, as he tossed the letter onto the desk and muttered, "Damn."

Silence stretched between them. Adam could see by Travis's frown that he was thinking over the situation, trying to figure how to handle it, or a way to get around it, just as Adam had done before Travis arrived.

"I'm paying a call on Molly Douglas," Adam said.

Travis did a double take at the sudden change in their conversation, then said, "Molly from the Cottonwood? Roy Sumner's niece?"

Adam nodded.

"Forget it," Travis declared.

"It's time," Adam said.

"Forget it," Travis said again. "You've not exactly endeared yourself to that uncle of hers."

Adam couldn't disagree. He was in the middle of a deal to build a hotel in Spindler, a move that would take business away from the Cottonwood. Roy Sumner had made no secret of his feelings about the project.

"She's exactly what I'm looking for," Adam said. "I need her."

Travis kept quiet for a few minutes, then rose from his chair and pointed to the letter on Adam's desk.

"I'm sorry about this," he said. "I feel responsible, somehow."

Adam drew in a quick breath, then let it out slowly trying to shed his irritation with the whole situation. He wanted no part of it, but nothing could be done.

Except pay a call on Molly Douglas. And nothing and nobody would stop him from getting what he wanted.

The clock in the main dining room struck one, jarring Molly out of her reverie. The ladies would arrive any minute for their luncheon and here she stood, still holding the last plate in her hand, daydreaming about Adam Crawford.

Honestly, what had come over her?

She put the plate on the table and stepped back to inspect her work. The reverend's wife and several ladies from the church were coming to discuss the orphanage in Keaton, and Molly had to make sure everything was perfect.

She stared at the table, sure that something was amiss, but couldn't put her finger on exactly what it was. She huffed, annoyed that she'd allowed Adam Crawford to take up so much of her time and thoughts this afternoon.

He sprang into her mind again, and she imagined herself confronting him, telling him that she wasn't interested in being called on or courted. Molly had heard he was a strong-willed man—he hadn't gotten where he was by being otherwise—but she was strong-willed also. She could hold her own against him. Easily. And it wouldn't matter if he—

"Miss Douglas?" a voice called from behind her.

Molly whirled and saw Adam standing in the doorway of the private dining room. Her breath caught and her knees weakened.

Good gracious, he was tall, taller than she remembered. He

had thick black hair and wide, square shoulders. She'd never noticed what beautiful green eyes he had until this moment when they were trained directly on her, seeming to see straight through to her pounding heart.

He wore a dark coat over a white shirt that was open at the collar. He clasped his black Stetson hat in front of him. Handsome. So handsome.

Molly opened her mouth but no words came out. Her hands shook. Thank goodness she'd already put the plates down.

Adam stood in the doorway. His presence filled the room and somehow commanded her attention.

Wild thoughts rushed through Molly's mind. Her dress. It was hardly her best. Why hadn't she worn the blue one today rather than this brown thing? It felt too tight everywhere— her throat, her waist, her bosom. And her hair. She'd twisted it into a quick bun this morning—hours ago. She felt loose tendrils curling at her cheeks. She looked a mess, surely she did.

"I'd like to have a word with you," Adam said.

Molly's heart pumped harder. Oh, heavens, he was going to ask if he could call on her. Here. *Now.*

She lost herself in the warmth of his gaze and said, "Of course."

Of course?

Molly froze. Why had she said that? What had come over her? She'd intended—she'd even practiced—sending him on his way with little more than a curt *No, thank you.* What was the matter with her?

Adam turned his hat over in his hand and took a step into the room. Molly wanted to back away, but she couldn't. Some unseen force held her in place.

"I have a proposal to discuss with you," he said.

Her heart thundered in her chest. "A…a proposal?"

Adam nodded. "I need a wedding, and I want you to plan it for me."

Chapter Two

What the hell was the matter with him?

Adam silently berated himself as he stood in the private dining room, staring at Molly Douglas as if he'd never laid eyes on a woman before in his life.

He'd seen her here in the hotel. He'd passed her on the street a few times. He knew she was pretty. More than pretty, really.

She'd always conducted herself in a prim-and-proper manner, as befitting a well-bred young woman from a respected Philadelphia family. She'd surely suffered through hours of deportment classes learning how to carry herself, how to set a proper table, how to make respectable conversation on most any occasion.

What he hadn't expected was that she'd look so touchable—and that he'd want so badly to do just that.

Brown tendrils of her hair curled against her cheeks, and he was nearly overwhelmed with the desire to wrap them around his fingers, feel their silky softness. Draw her near as well, and breathe in the hint of her sweet scent that floated across the room to him now.

"You're…you're planning a…wedding?" she asked.

The words came out in a breathy little sigh and heightened the pink flush in her cheeks, and made him want to—

Adam gave himself a mental shake. He was here on business, and he'd do well to get on with it and leave before—

He gave himself another shake, a stronger one this time, and walked to her. He pulled a piece of paper from the inside pocket of his coat.

"I need you to handle all the details. The church, flowers, food, music. Everything. It's all written down," Adam said, presenting it to her. "Just do what it says."

Molly stared for a moment at the paper in his outstretched hand, but didn't take it.

He knew she'd helped with weddings in Spindler several times, and since the church frowned on dancing, she'd hosted the wedding celebration here at the Cottonwood Hotel. The list he was trying to hand her called for something more than usual for a town like Spindler, but he knew she could do it. That's why he'd come to her.

"It's two months from now," Adam said, "so you've got plenty of time. Make sure everything is perfect. It has to be perfect."

Molly nodded numbly and repeated, "Perfect."

He stood there for another moment trying to think of something else to say. He couldn't. Yet for some reason, he didn't want to leave.

"Well, thank you," he finally said.

Adam laid the paper on the table beside them and headed for the door, silently cursing himself for his schoolboy behavior. Molly was from an upstanding family. She had certain expectations. She'd probably thought he was a—

"No."

Adam froze, unsure of what he'd heard—or who had said it. Slowly he turned.

Molly stood tall, her shoulders straight, her chin up. Gone was the endearing pink flush of her cheeks. In its place was a blaze of red. Her sweet pouty lips were drawn into a thin line—which made him want her all the more, for some reason.

"No," she said again.

Adam frowned. "What did you say?"

"I said *no,*" she repeated, pushing her chin up even higher. "I won't plan your wedding."

"But—"

"No!" Molly swiped the paper from the table, marched across the room and slapped it against his chest. "I'm—I'm too busy. I have too much work—yes, too much work, as it is. I'm…I'm just *busy!*"

She whirled, head held high, and marched out of the dining room, slamming the door behind her.

Molly pressed her lips together and held her head high as customers in the dining room turned to stare. She ignored them and hurried into the kitchen, past Aunt Libby at the cookstove and into the little room that served as her bedroom.

She closed the door and fell back against it, forcing down her emotions, fighting the urge to cry.

Humiliation roiled through her. What a fool she'd been—an utter fool. Thinking a man like Adam Crawford would call on her. Thinking her past was really behind her, that she would no longer be haunted by things that were beyond her control.

Molly sank onto her bed as the most painful thought of all robbed her strength.

Adam was getting married.

* * *

"Molly? Molly?"

She glanced up from the plate she was drying and saw Aunt Libby, elbow-deep in the dishpan, watching her. Molly wasn't sure how many times her aunt had called her name.

They stood in the kitchen cleaning up from the supper service. The room was big and warm, dominated by a cook-stove and crowded with cupboards, shelves and a sideboard. A small table and four chairs were squeezed into a corner.

The dining room was closed for the night. This was a time Molly usually enjoyed, a time when she, her aunt and Carrie, the serving girl, worked together and caught up on the day's happenings.

"What's wrong?" Aunt Libby asked, giving Molly a kindly smile. Her aunt was a trim woman, with brown hair that showed only a sprinkling of gray.

"Nothing," Molly insisted. She knew she'd been distracted all afternoon and evening, but she wasn't about to tell anyone the reason, not even her aunt.

"Did you see how many slices of pie Jarvis McElroy ate at supper?" Carrie asked, whisking a stack of clean plates from in front of Molly. At sixteen years old, Carrie was pretty and full of life.

"Three!" Carrie declared, not waiting for an answer. "He ate three!"

"I appreciate a man with a good appetite," Aunt Libby said.

"I don't know how he doesn't smother that wife of his," Carrie said, with a quick grin as she stacked the plates on the sideboard.

"Carrie!" Aunt Libby declared, then burst out laughing.

The image of Adam flashed into Molly's mind. Heat rushed to her cheeks.

"I nearly spilled coffee all over that salesman from Keaton

this afternoon. Luckily, I caught myself just in time," Carrie said. She sighed heavily. "How could I be expected to concentrate on my work after Adam Crawford walked into the dining room?"

The plate slipped from Molly's hand. She caught it before it hit the floor.

"Adam Crawford was here?" Aunt Libby asked, giving Molly a sidelong glance.

"Molly talked to him. I wouldn't be able to keep a clear thought in my head if that man spoke to me," Carrie said. She heaved another dreamy sigh. "I still can't decide who's the most handsome. Adam, or that partner of his."

"Travis Vaughn has turned many a head in town," Aunt Libby agreed, scrubbing another plate.

"And he's built himself that big house on the edge of town," Carrie added.

"What did Mr. Crawford want?" Aunt Libby asked Molly, as she set aside another dripping plate.

"He asked about…reserving the dining room," Molly mumbled, careful not to meet her aunt's eye.

"Carrie, why don't you run along home?" Aunt Libby called. "We're about finished here."

Carrie took a quick look around the kitchen, then nodded. "See you in the morning," she called, as she emptied her tip jar into her handbag, grabbed her bonnet and hurried out the back door.

Molly dried the last plate and set it aside, feeling the heat of her aunt's gaze. Since moving to Spindler, she'd grown close with Aunt Libby. She owed her a debt of gratitude for offering her the job that got her out of Philadelphia. Still, some things were hard to discuss.

"So what happened?" Aunt Libby asked, drying her hands on a towel.

Something in her aunt's voice made Molly's heart ache

anew. The woman had never had children of her own, yet she displayed an uncanny ability to understand the thoughts and feelings of younger people.

Molly pulled herself up a little and faced her aunt. "Mr. Crawford asked me to plan his wedding."

"His wedding?" Aunt Libby echoed.

Molly just nodded, unable to say anything.

"Oh, dear…" Aunt Libby's kind face grew more gentle. "I know you've had your eye on him since you came to town."

"No, I haven't," Molly insisted. But when her aunt raised a questioning eyebrow, Molly knew she was right. She'd had feelings for Adam Crawford since the first time she saw him. She'd just been fooling herself, desperate to convince her own mind that she wasn't interested. What else could she do under the circumstances?

"Things are different here," Aunt Libby said softly. "Not like they are back in Philadelphia. That's why your uncle left. That's why I came here with him."

Molly turned away. Despite her aunt's words, Molly knew things really weren't so different.

"None of it was your fault," Aunt Libby said. "You couldn't help what your mother did."

She'd heard those words before, but they brought Molly no comfort.

"Although, you did carry the shame of it," her aunt said. "And suffered the consequences."

Molly had been born out of wedlock. When she was a child growing up in her grandmother's fine home, she'd loved her sometimes-absent mother, Frances. She hadn't understood why her mother never attended Grandmother's parties or luncheons, why she seldom had callers or why people often pointed at Molly and whispered behind their gloved hands.

When she was thirteen, her mother had finally told Molly the truth. How she'd loved Molly's father with all her heart, how desperately they'd wanted to be together. But her father had died in a boating accident before they could marry.

Molly counted herself lucky that she hadn't been given away at birth or sent to an orphanage. Her grandmother wouldn't hear of it. She'd loved Molly too much to let the shame of her birth keep her away from her one and only grandchild.

Her grandmother had never uttered one disparaging remark about Frances, except to concede she had a wild streak in her, something she hoped Molly had not inherited.

But in the end, even her grandmother's wealth and social standing couldn't help Molly. No decent family, no man of consequence wanted her. After years of watching her friends marry and start families of their own, Molly had told Grandmother she wanted to leave Philadelphia. The older woman had agreed. Less than a month later, Molly received an invitation from Roy and Libby Sumner to work for them at the Cottonwood in Spindler.

Molly added the last plate to the stack on the sideboard. "Adam Crawford is getting married."

"You're in love with him, Molly," Aunt Libby said softly.

She forced down her emotions, unable to admit to what she knew was in her heart.

"He's getting married and that's that," Molly said.

Aunt Libby nodded, seeming to accept the situation. "Who's the bride?"

"I don't know." Molly paused. "I didn't ask."

Her aunt's eyebrows shot up. "The biggest piece of news in Spindler since the railroad came through, and you didn't ask? My gracious, gossip will sweep the town quicker than a summer dust storm when word gets out. Everyone will want to know who the lucky bride is."

The back door opened and Uncle Roy walked in. Despite the gray hair at his temples, he looked young, fit and healthy.

He had a good head for business and a strong work ethic that he and Aunt Libby shared.

Uncle Roy hung his hat on the peg by the door. His gaze landed on Molly.

"What's this I hear about you turning down business from Adam Crawford?" he asked.

A flash of anger hit Molly. Had Adam gone to her uncle and told him of her refusal?

"Where did you hear that?" Molly asked.

"Ran into that fella who works for him," Uncle Roy said. "What's that boy's name?"

"Rafe," Aunt Libby. "He told you about it?"

"He did." Uncle Roy eyed Molly sharply. "Is it true?"

"Yes," she said, trying to sound composed and confident. "I'm just too busy. I simply can't accommodate him."

Uncle Roy shook his head. "Whatever kind of shindig he wants, do it. Unbusy yourself. Accommodate him."

Her uncle's stern orders caused Molly's spine to stiffen. She didn't want to displease him, but she most certainly didn't want to plan Adam's wedding.

"He'll want the entire town here," Molly said, trying to sound reasonable. "You know how you feel about that."

He grumbled under this breath. "People racing to Spindler like ants to a picnic since that rail stop went in. Choking the streets, crowding the boardwalks. Can't get a decent pew at church without getting there early. All kinds of businesses opening, trying to force out all of us who got here first."

"And you don't even like Mr. Crawford," Molly pointed out. "His plan to build another hotel in town will only hurt the Cottonwood."

She'd heard the gossip around town—and at their own breakfast table—for weeks. Uncle Roy had made no secret of his feelings on the matter—or on Adam Crawford.

"I can't turn my back on money, plain and simple," he said.

"That boy Rafe said Crawford's got company coming from back east. Investors among them, most likely. We need them here."

"That doesn't make sense," Molly said. She knew she was being too outspoken, but she couldn't stop herself. "Investors in town will likely bring in more and more people, and you don't like—"

"I've got things in the works," Uncle Roy told her. He gave her a hard look. "Tomorrow morning I want you to go over to Crawford's office and tell him you'll do whatever he wants."

"But—"

"I don't want to hear another word about it," Uncle Roy told her. "You just make sure it gets handled."

Molly pressed her lips together, holding back another protest. She couldn't—absolutely could not—plan a wedding for Adam. Somehow, she'd have to figure a way out of it.

Chapter Three

How could a man—one who wasn't even a part of her life—cause so much trouble?

Molly fumed as she slipped out of her bedroom. Aunt Libby wasn't in the kitchen but she'd be down soon. Carrie would arrive shortly to help with the morning meal.

Molly went out the back door of the Cottonwood Hotel. At this early hour here she was, up and heading out to take care of business. And she intended to take care of it, all right, though she doubted Uncle Roy—to say nothing of Adam Crawford—would be pleased.

As she'd hoped, the alley that ran behind the Cottonwood and other businesses that faced Main Street was empty. She didn't want to be seen going to Adam's place above the bank building. Molly figured she could get this dreaded errand over with and get back to the hotel in time to help Aunt Libby with the breakfast service.

At the corner of the hotel, Molly checked the narrow passageway between the Cottonwood and the Palmer Millinery

Shop, saw no one and hurried on to Main Street. She leaned around the corner and looked up and down the street.

Down the block, the doors to every business were still closed, windows shuttered. No merchants out front sweeping the boardwalk, no horses tied at the hitching posts, no wagons rumbling through the street. Molly knew she didn't have much time before the town came awake.

She crossed the street and slipped into the alley beside the Spindler Bank. Her feet silent on the packed dirt, she made her way to the rear of the building.

Across the back alley sat a small barn and paddock and a few outbuildings. Hardly the place a lady—one trying desperately to keep her troubled past a secret—should be, unescorted, especially at this hour of the morning. Molly was thankful that her aunt and uncle never mentioned the unsavory circumstances of her birth or hinted at the wild streak some feared she'd inherited from her mother. Yet she didn't want to press the issue with unacceptable behavior.

Her uncle had left her no choice. He'd told her in no uncertain terms that she was to go to Adam and agree to whatever he wanted. Molly knew Uncle Roy wouldn't change his mind, even if he knew it was a wedding party Adam wanted to hold at the Cottonwood.

Anger, annoyance—something—rose in Molly. She wasn't happy with her uncle for forcing her to do this. In her opinion, the man was shortsighted and stubborn. She disagreed with the way he ran the hotel, even though it was hardly her place to say so. Remembering how Uncle Roy had ignored her well-intentioned suggestions caused Molly's irritation to grow.

Maybe she'd inherited some of her mother's wildness, after all.

She pushed the thought aside and remembered her errand this morning. She'd lain awake for hours last night in her little bedroom off the kitchen of the Cottonwood, deciding how to handle this situation. For a few moments, she'd actually considered doing as her uncle had instructed, allowing Adam to have his wedding at the hotel, spending the next two months planning every detail for him. Molly's heart ached at the thought.

She couldn't do it. She simply could not. For a few moments last night, Molly had allowed herself the thought that she was truly in love with Adam. For those few moments, the joy in her heart nearly took her breath away. Then, just as quickly, the reality of her situation came back to her.

As she lay in the dark, her mind frantically casting about for a solution, one had come to her—a plan so simple she'd sat straight up in the bed. She'd thought it through and planned it carefully, then drifted off to sleep.

Now, all she had to do was pull it off.

Molly straightened her hat, squared her shoulders and headed toward the wooden stairs that zigzagged up to Adam's place on the second floor of the bank building. A smile pulled at her lips.

She was about to make Adam Crawford an offer he absolutely *had* to refuse.

Adam poured himself a cup of coffee. The room where he lived wasn't much to look at. A little stove, a fireplace, a table with two chairs, a bed, a rocker.

One of the ladies who worked at the boardinghouse cleaned the place for him every week. With his permission, she'd fixed it up a little, brought in a couple of rugs and hung some curtains.

He'd had nicer, but it hadn't made him happier.

Adam raised a coffee cup to his lips and sipped, then mumbled a curse. Too hot, too weak.

Same as he felt this morning.

Adam shifted uncomfortably, recalling the night he'd

spent tossing and turning. Thoughts of Molly Douglas had plagued him until all hours of the night. Then, when he'd finally drifted off, she'd come into his dreams. Dreams that had everything to do with *her,* but nothing that involved her refusal to handle the wedding for him.

Adam closed his eyes for a moment recalling yesterday when he'd talked to her at the Cottonwood. He hadn't made the best impression, he knew that. He hadn't even presented his request in the most businesslike of manners.

How could he when she was standing right there in front of him, looking so desirable and smelling so sweet?

An urgency claimed him, as it had yesterday, as it had most of the night. Adam had never felt this way about a woman before—and it couldn't have happened at a worse time.

He needed Molly to plan the wedding. No one else in Spindler could do it. She was from Philadelphia. She knew the proper way things should be handled. He'd been given an extensive list of requirements, and he had to make sure it was followed. And the only way to accomplish that was to turn the whole thing over to the one person in town who could do it. Molly.

Adam took another sip of his coffee, grimaced and set the cup aside. It didn't suit him to be saddled with the wedding preparations. He'd left his home, his family behind in Charleston because he could no longer abide the rigid social standards there.

He'd made that decision the hard way.

But he'd made it and had no regrets. He was happy with his new life in Spindler. Travis was a good business partner. They'd known each other in Charleston. Both had found themselves discontent there—but for entirely different reasons—and decided to try their luck in Spindler. They agreed on most things. Business was good. Life was good.

Except now with all this wedding nonsense.

And his thoughts of Molly.

Grumbling, Adam filled the basin on the washstand in the corner. Better to get his mind on work. He was splashing the cold water on his face—and considering dumping it down his pants—when he heard footsteps outside.

At least Rafe was on time this morning, he thought. Perhaps that meant the day would get better.

Adam yanked the door open.

Molly stood outside.

Naked. He was nearly naked.

Molly's eyes popped wide-open in horror at the sight of Adam towering over her in the doorway, clutching a towel in his hand. He had on trousers—and that was all. One suspender was slung over his shoulder, the top button of his trousers unfastened. His hair hung over his forehead and stuck up in the back. Water ran down his face and dropped from his chin.

She gasped. She knew she should leave, but somehow she couldn't get her feet to move. All she could do was stare at his bare chest. The dark, coarse hair that met in the center of his taut belly and arrowed downward past hard, rippling muscles, then disappeared above his—

Molly's cheeks flamed. Good gracious, what was she doing? She'd never stared so shamelessly at a man before.

Of course, she'd never seen a chest like Adam's before.

The notion jarred her back to reality. Molly dragged her gaze from his chest and belly, and forced it onto his face—which did nothing to help.

His whole body seemed tense, like a coil ready to spring. Color blushed his cheeks. His eyes burned with a heat that somehow shot straight through her.

She gasped. Was he looking at her for the same reason

she was looking at him? Could he possibly have the same thoughts?

Leave! her mind screamed. Yet she couldn't. Molly stood rooted to the spot completely transfixed by the smoldering heat he gave off.

Adam shook his head, sending little droplets of water flying, then dragged the towel down his face.

"Miss Douglas," he said, holding the towel against his chest. "Come…come inside."

She didn't move. Heat swamped her. She knew her cheeks were red.

"No, I'd—I'd better…go," she mumbled.

"It's all right," he said softly, and backed away from her. He turned then and disappeared into his room.

Molly hesitated. What should she do? Run away, as if she were a frightened child? She'd come here to discuss business, after all, at her uncle's insistence.

She drew herself up. She wanted to get this over with. She wanted it to be done with, and the only way to do that was to face it—no matter what Adam Crawford's chest looked like.

Molly stepped through the doorway. Her gaze landed on Adam. In the back. By the bed.

Rumpled pillows. Quilt spilling onto the floor. His back was to her as he stuffed the tail of a white shirt into his trousers and pulled both suspenders into place.

A fresh wave of heat swept her face. She turned away.

"I'm—" Molly's voice failed her. She cleared her throat and tried again. "I'm sorry to intrude so early. I didn't think you'd be—"

Nearly naked?

She pressed her lips together to keep from blurting out the words. Yet more images spread through her mind unbidden.

His chest, strong and muscular. His rippled belly. The dark hair. What would it feel like to comb her fingers through it?

"It's fine," Adam said.

Molly started as his voice sounded from directly behind her. Had she felt his hot breath on her neck? Or was it just her imagination?

She whirled around. Adam stood close enough to touch, and her fingers itched to do just that—even though he had a shirt on now.

"Coffee?" he asked, gesturing to the stove.

Her hands shook so badly she didn't think she could hold the cup.

"No, thank you," she said.

"Probably for the best. I made it myself," he said, and grinned.

Molly's insides quivered.

Adam stepped to the washbasin, leaned down to the mirror and dragged a comb though his hair, slicking it in place.

"To what do I owe the honor of this visit?" he asked, turning to her again.

He seemed composed now, more businesslike, cooling Molly's emotions considerably.

What was she doing looking at him, admiring his chest? He was spoken for. Engaged. Planning to wed.

What better reason to stick to business?

Molly forced her thoughts onto the plan she'd made in her bed last night. It was now or never. She pulled herself up a little and faced him.

"Since I'm unable to accommodate your wedding at the Cottonwood," she said, "I've come to suggest an alternative location."

It wasn't at all what her uncle had told her to do. If he found out about it later—and he probably would, the way gossip ran through Spindler—he'd be furious. Yet she'd decided last night to take the risk. With so much at stake, how could she do otherwise?

"Where?" Adam asked, appearing mildly interested.

"Keaton," she told him and put all the enthusiasm she'd rehearsed in her room last night behind the word. "It's a lovely town, only an hour away by train. They have a beautiful church with a spacious social hall. It will be perfect."

"No, it won't."

Adam didn't even bother to pretend the suggestion suited him, which annoyed Molly a bit.

"The wedding has to be in Spindler," Adam told her. "The party has to be at the Cottonwood."

"As I told you yesterday, I can't accommodate you at the Cottonwood," she said, pleased at the way the lie rolled off her tongue.

"I'll pay you extra," Adam offered.

"I don't need your money," she told him. Another lie.

"It will bring a lot of attention to the Cottonwood," Adam added.

"The Cottonwood doesn't need more attention," she said, and managed not to cringe as the even bigger lie left her lips.

Adam took a step closer. "Look, Miss Douglas, I need this thing done right. That means I need you to do it."

"Nonsense," she declared, tossing aside his assertion with a wave of her hand. "Anyone could do it."

"You," he said, with an authority that sent a hot wave crashing through Molly. "Only you."

"Mr. Crawford," she said, trying to sound reasonable. "Surely there's someone in town—or in Keaton—who can execute this wedding to your satisfaction. I'm convinced of it. If I thought otherwise, then I would be happy to do it myself."

"There's not," Adam insisted. "So, you'll do it?"

Molly's belly tingled. Her knees shook. This was the moment she'd hoped for when she'd made her plan last night. Excitement rose in her. Now, finally, she would end this once and for all.

"Yes, I'll do it," she said. "For a price."

Adam shrugged, unconcerned. "Name it."

Molly folded her hands primly in front of her.

"I want you to build a social hall here in Spindler," she said. "And I want you to make me your partner."

Chapter Four

Adam didn't speak. He didn't move. He seemed to grow larger before Molly's eyes.

His shoulders straightened and his chest expanded. His breath grew heavier. His gaze bored into her.

A wild heat rolled off him that should have sent her running. Instead, Molly stepped closer.

Adam lunged toward her in two quick steps, laid his hands on her shoulders, bent down and kissed her. He covered her lips with his and pulled her against him.

For a stunned moment, Molly couldn't move—couldn't think. His warmth swamped her, robbed her strength. Adam deepened their kiss. Molly rose on her toes. She sighed. He groaned. Then, as quickly as he'd kissed her, he pulled away.

Molly hung there for a moment, her face tilted up to his. His smoldering gaze held her captive for a few seconds longer. He stepped back.

Cool air swirled between them, bringing her back to reality.

Good gracious, what had happened? What had she done? Kissed a man alone in his room? A man who was engaged to be married? What would everyone say if they found out?

Molly drew back her fist and pounded it against his chest, then stomped out of the room.

Heat, anger—something—coursed through Molly as she dashed down the stairs and into the alley behind the bank building.

Adam had kissed her. He'd held her close and kissed her—really kissed her. Not a sweet peck on the cheek, not a tender meeting of lips. The kind of kiss her cousins in Paris had whispered about.

And Molly had let him.

A hotter wave of *something* swept Molly as she walked through the passageway beside the bank and stepped up onto the boardwalk. Another recollection raced through her mind. Not only had she let him kiss her, she'd made it easier for him.

The memory flooded her mind, slowing her steps. Rising on her toes. Leaning in. Lifting her face to his.

Molly's insides boiled. Good gracious, what had come over her?

"We heard what happened!" someone shouted.

"Tell us all about it!"

"Tell us everything!"

Molly froze as footsteps pounded the boardwalk, running toward her. Three young women surrounded her, their eyes wide, all chattering at the same time.

Had they heard how she'd let Adam kiss her? Already? It had happened only moments ago. How could gossip have gotten around Spindler this quickly?

Molly drew back a little, wanting some distance between her and the other girls, though she knew them well. Sarah and

Sally were sisters, pretty girls with sunny yellow hair, both engaged and getting married soon; Molly was handling their party at the Cottonwood. Claire Dempsey was expecting to become engaged soon and had already spoken with Molly about helping with the arrangements.

"Let me talk!" Sarah shouted.

The other girls quieted but didn't take their eyes off Molly.

"Is it true?" Sarah asked. "Is Adam Crawford getting married?"

Relief surged through Molly. Thank goodness she wasn't the talk of the town—for now, anyway.

Molly's mind spun, trying to come up with a graceful way to avoid the question. She'd begun helping with weddings and planning the parties at the Cottonwood shortly after arriving in Spindler. The church, she'd learned, frowned on dancing, so she'd suggested that friends and families of the newlyweds meet at the hotel after the ceremony. She'd overseen two weddings already and they'd both been successes.

Molly kept the wedding preparations of the brides she helped to herself, usually. A marriage ceremony was personal, she thought, and it wasn't right that she spread the details all over town.

But looking at the faces of the three young women surrounding her now, Molly knew she couldn't possibly keep this news to herself.

"Yes, it's true," she said.

All three of the girls gasped. Their eyes widened in shock.

"I don't believe it!" Sally declared.

"How could this have happened?" Claire demanded.

"How could we not have known?" Sarah asked, bewildered.

Then all three of them paused and asked in unison, "Who's the bride?"

"I don't know," Molly admitted.

They all gasped again.

"How could you not know?" Sarah asked.

"Aren't you planning their wedding?" Sally said. "I heard you were."

"It's all over town," Claire added.

Further discussion of Adam was the last thing Molly wanted, yet she knew she had to say something.

"Mr. Crawford and I have discussed it," Molly said, "but we've come to no agreement yet."

"Who could he be marrying?" Sally asked. "He hasn't courted a woman in Spindler."

"I saw him talking to Ruth Pauley outside her boardinghouse the other day," Claire said.

"He wouldn't court her," Sarah insisted. "She's too old. He was probably there because that's where Mr. Vaughn lives."

"Oh, Travis Vaughn is so handsome," Sally said wistfully.

"You hush that kind of talk," Sarah told her sister. "You're engaged to be married."

"I just said he was handsome," Sally snapped. "There's nothing wrong with saying a man's handsome. Besides, Travis doesn't even live at the boardinghouse anymore since he built himself that big home."

"It must be someone outside of town," Claire suggested. "One of the ranchers' daughters, maybe?"

"But which one?" Sally asked.

"I think I know," Sarah declared.

Everyone fell silent and turned to her. She leaned in and lowered her voice.

"I was in the bank last week with Papa and I heard someone say that Adam had gone to Keaton for the day," Sarah said.

Her brows rose. "From what I overheard, it seems Adam goes there quite often."

All the girls gasped.

"That must be it," Claire said. "He must be marrying someone in Keaton."

Sally's eyes widened. "What if he moves there?"

"Stop talking that way," Sarah told her. "You're almost a married woman. You should be thinking about your own husband-to-be."

"I'll think about whomever I want," Sally told her. "Why don't you worry about yourself and keep your nose out of what I'm doing?"

"I'm not going to let you make a fool of yourself and ruin our family name in the process," Sarah shouted.

"How dare you suggest that," Sally shouted back. "Just because you're a year older than me doesn't give you the right to..."

Molly slipped away and dashed across the street. Sarah and Sally argued like—well, like sisters. Molly had listened to them carry on for weeks over their weddings.

Their father had insisted they have a double ceremony to save money, which suited neither of the girls, of course. They couldn't agree on anything. Molly was almost willing to spend what little money she had for two ceremonies just so she wouldn't have to listen to the girls complain and argue.

When Molly opened the back door of the Cottonwood, the delicious smell of baking biscuits wafted out of the kitchen. She hurried inside. Aunt Libby was at the stove tending a pot of oatmeal, a pan of gravy and a skillet of frying eggs. She made it look effortless.

"You're out and about early this morning," Aunt Libby called.

Molly tossed her hat and handbag into her room and grabbed an apron from the peg beside the door.

Aunt Libby gave her a questioning look. Could the older woman somehow tell that Molly was different? That she'd been kissed?

"I wanted to speak with Mr. Crawford," she said, hoping she sounded casual. "Uncle Roy insisted."

"And?" her aunt asked.

Molly was saved from answering when the door to the dining room swung open and Carrie came in.

"The mayor wants to see you, Molly," she said. "He wants to use your private room this morning. He's with Jonas Bradley."

Aunt Libby's brows rose. "The mayor and the owner of the Lucky Strike Saloon are having their morning meal together?"

"Looks serious," Carrie said.

Molly took off her apron and hurried into the dining room. It was almost filled already. Mayor Hawthorne and Jonas waited at the doorway to the hotel lobby, both looking grim.

"Good morning, gentlemen," Molly said with a smile. "Let me check my book and make sure no one is using the room this morning."

She hurried past the men into the lobby, then slipped behind the registration desk and opened the door that led to Uncle Roy's office. The room was small and windowless, barely big enough for a desk, chairs and a cupboard. He'd grudgingly allowed Molly to use one of the drawers.

She pulled out her book, silently cursing herself—and Adam. If he hadn't kissed her she wouldn't still be so flustered she couldn't remember if anyone was using her private dining room this morning. She flipped the pages, saw it wasn't reserved.

"I'll have it ready for you in a minute," Molly promised the men as she breezed past.

"We don't need anything fancy," the mayor told her. "We're talking business this morning."

"Serious business," Jonas added.

Molly made quick work of changing the tablecloths to blue and laying out the table settings. The men, more impatient than hungry, she guessed, walked in just as she was finishing.

"I can't have this," Jonas said, as he sat down.

"I know, I know," the mayor agreed.

"I paid a lot of money to get those girls here for the week, and I can't have this kind of trouble with the church," Jonas said.

Mayor Hawthorne glanced at Molly. "Bring us breakfast—whatever you have this morning. And we need to use this room again later today, us and the reverend. Take care of it, will you, darling?"

Molly ducked into the kitchen. Both Aunt Libby and Carrie turned to her.

"Trouble?" Carrie asked.

Molly nodded. "The mayor wants to use the room again this afternoon—along with Jonas and Reverend Holcomb."

"It's those dancers at the saloon," Carrie declared.

Aunt Libby nodded. "I've heard the talk. The ladies in town aren't happy about Jonas hiring them."

"They dance like those French girls," Carrie said. "I heard they lift up their skirts and show their drawers—onstage."

Molly pulled in a quick breath. "There are cancan dancers at the Lucky Strike?"

"You've heard of them?" Carrie asked. "So it's true? They really dance that way?"

"Molly, weren't you and your grandmother in Paris awhile back?" Aunt Libby asked.

Molly didn't want to talk about Paris.

"The mayor says they'll eat whatever you're cooking this

morning," she said. "I'm going to make sure the room is available for them this afternoon."

She threaded through the dining-room tables and into the little office off the lobby.

He wanted her.

Adam sat behind his desk in his office at the Spindler Bank ignoring the papers spread out in front of him. He couldn't think—about business, anyway. All that occupied his thoughts was Molly.

Her sweet breath. Her tender lips. The taste of her. The feel of her. Her softness against his hard chest. He'd never wanted a woman the way he wanted Molly—even though it made no sense.

No woman had ever meddled in his business before as Molly had. No woman had ever had the nerve to demand a partnership. And sure as hell, no woman had ever punched him in the chest for kissing her.

Somehow, that just made him want her more.

Adam shifted uncomfortably as his desire for her made itself known again. If he didn't get himself under control he wouldn't be fit to walk out of his office.

When she'd shown up on his doorstep this morning, he'd been surprised but pleased to see her. The sight of her in the early hours had taken his breath away, as had her demand that he make her his partner in a social hall, of all things.

Molly Douglas, it seemed, was full of surprises.

Which only made him want her even more.

"Damn…" Adam grumbled.

He sat up and sifted through the papers on his desk. A lot of things needed his attention. He'd received the plans for the hotel he wanted to build from the architect in New York. Travis wanted him to look at a piece of land that was for sale. He had to get this wedding situation settled once and for all.

Plus, he'd need to make another trip to Keaton soon.

A quick rap sounded on his office door and Rafe Watkins walked in. The boy was nearly twenty years old, tall and lanky, with an unruly shock of brown hair. He worked for Adam and Travis, running errands, taking care of things. Rafe was smart and a quick learner.

"This just arrived at the express office," Rafe said, placing an envelope in the center of Adam's desk.

Adam sat back in his chair, uninterested in yet another item he needed to attend to today.

"I think you'd better open it," Rafe said.

"I'll get to it later," Adam said.

Rafe slid the envelope closer. "If you don't mind me saying so, I think you'd better open this one now."

Adam picked it up and mumbled a mild curse. Even Rafe recognized the elegant swirl of the handwriting—and knew what it meant.

Adam ripped open the envelope and drew out the letter. He read it quickly, then shoved out of his chair.

Rafe fell back a couple of steps. "Another problem?"

"You're damn right," Adam said.

He grabbed his coat and hat from the rack in the corner. Seemed he was going to build a social hall after all—with a partner.

Chapter Five

A wave of heat covered Molly like a warm blanket. A scent, familiar yet not, tickled her nose. She looked up from the ledger atop Uncle Roy's desk and her heart lurched.

Adam stood in the doorway.

Her thoughts scattered. Random notions popped into her head. The hard muscles of his chest—she knew what they looked like now. The tenderness of his lips—she'd tasted them herself. His strong fingers—she'd felt them on her shoulders.

Would he kiss her again?

Good gracious, what was she thinking?

Molly slammed the ledger closed. She should have been mad at him. He'd taken a considerable liberty with her. And here she was hoping he'd do the same thing again.

Molly took a deep breath. "What do you want?" she asked.

Adam twisted his lips as if trying to hide a grin. "I'm here to talk business."

Her heart seemed to skip a beat. "You are?"

Adam dropped into the chair on the other side of the desk and laid his hat aside. His presence filled the entire space. His wide shoulders and long legs took up all the room.

"Aren't you happy working here for your uncle?" Adam asked.

His question took Molly by surprise. He looked sincere, concerned.

"I appreciate Uncle Roy allowing me to work here, but—" Molly stopped and glanced at the open door. She certainly didn't want her uncle to overhear their conversation.

Molly stretched across the desk. Adam leaned toward her until their faces were inches apart.

Goodness, he smelled lovely.

Molly pushed the thought away. "I don't agree with the way Uncle Roy runs the hotel," she said softly.

"How so?" Adam whispered.

"Of course, he's had a great deal of experience running a business—far more than me—and I do appreciate how hard he—"

"Stop being nice." Adam made a spinning motion with his hand. "Just tell me what's going on."

His honesty stunned her but brought an odd sense of relief that she could say what she felt, and that he wanted to hear it.

"He refuses to open the restaurant on Sundays to take advantage of after-church diners," Molly said. "I think he should advertise the hotel in newspapers back east. With all the folks coming west these days, it's silly not to. He won't even put up a sign at the train station."

Adam shrugged. "Those seem like good ideas to me."

"Really?" she asked, her spirits lifting.

"What else?" he asked.

Molly glanced at the doorway once more, then strained to lean even closer.

"Uncle Roy doesn't pay me very much," she whispered. "I've brought in quite a bit of extra money since I opened the private dining room, and he doesn't give me a cent of that money either."

Adam sat back a little. "That was your idea?"

Pride rose in Molly. "So was the idea of holding wedding parties here. I've done two already with three more scheduled."

His expression hardened. "What do you know about running a social hall?"

Molly's stomach did an odd little flip. If he was asking this question it could only mean he was taking her demand seriously. He might really take her on as a partner.

Her excitement plummeted. It would also mean that she'd have to arrange his wedding. Work with him—and his bride—on every little detail. Sit in the church and watch them exchange vows, then pretend to rejoice in the celebration of their union at the party she would have worked two months to prepare.

And after it was over, she'd be left to clean up—and think of the two of them on their wedding night.

Despair settled around Molly's heart. She didn't know how she'd manage to do it. Didn't know how she could put herself through it.

But what choice did she have?

She desperately wanted her own business. With it, she'd be free. No more relying on her grandmother's good name. No more worries that her uncle might become angry with her and turn her out without a dime. No sleepless nights wondering what her future would hold.

She would make her own future. And she'd be good at it. She knew she would. Then, if someone learned of her shameful past, it might not hurt so much if she had a business she could be proud of.

Molly gazed across the desk at Adam, still waiting for her answer. With everything she had, she forced away her feelings for him.

If she was going to run her own business, this was what she'd have to do. Business was business. She'd have to learn to separate her personal feelings from her professional commitments. Adam's wedding would certainly do that.

She had two months to prepare for that walk down the aisle. Two long months to harden her heart, distance herself from him emotionally, convince herself that the path she'd chosen was for the best.

Just as well to start now, she decided.

Molly raised her brows. "I'd think, Mr. Crawford, you'd already know the answer to your question, given your own decree that no one within a day's train ride of Spindler could plan this wedding of yours but me."

Adam reared farther back in his chair. He grinned. Then he chuckled. Molly's heart melted. She'd never heard him laugh before. It rumbled in his big chest and filled the room like music, making Molly giggle, too, binding them together somehow.

When he finally settled down, Adam said, "Besides weddings, what did you have in mind for the social hall?"

Molly sat up straighter as all her ideas filled her mind. "Traveling shows are quite popular, as you know. Spindler is growing and the folks here are desperate for entertainment."

Adam didn't say anything, so she hurried on.

"I could have performers come from back east. Poetry and dramatic readings. Dance companies. Actors could present plays," Molly said. "It would be the center of town. I'd have festivals and celebrations. Weddings and parties. All sorts of things."

Adam didn't respond, just looked at her. She couldn't imagine what he was thinking. His expression offered no clue whether he liked her ideas, which irked her.

"Really, Mr. Crawford," she said. "If we're going to be partners, you're going to have to tell me what's on your mind."

"I'll think it over," he said.

Adam pushed out of his chair and headed out the door. Molly scrambled to her feet. She caught his arm.

"Wait," she whispered.

He rounded on her, his gaze knifing straight through to her heart.

For a moment Molly thought he would kiss her. For a moment she wanted him to do just that.

Heat rolled off him, covering Molly. Or maybe it wasn't from him. Maybe it was her. Good gracious, what was happening to her?

"I'll think about it," Adam said. "You think about *this*."

Now she had no trouble reading his expression. Molly braced herself.

"The wedding needs to move up," Adam said. "I need it done right away."

"Molly? Molly!"

She paused near the front door of the Cottonwood, broom in hand. Evening shadows stretched across the street. The town was closing for the night. Reluctantly she pulled her gaze from the Spindler Bank and saw Sally and Claire rushing down the boardwalk toward her. An odd knot coiled inside her. She knew what they wanted.

"Is it true?" Claire asked, her eyes wide.

"Is Adam really hurrying up his wedding?" Sally wanted to know.

"Is it because—" Claire asked, then stopped herself.

Molly had known it was just a matter of time before news of Adam's quick wedding would break. Gossip would be rampant. The scandal would be fierce. After all, there was only one reason to rush a wedding.

"I don't know any more than you," Molly said.

It was true. She hadn't seen Adam in days, not since their meeting in Uncle Roy's office. She wondered if he was still thinking over her idea for the social hall.

Or perhaps he had a bigger problem on his mind.

"We still don't know who the bride is," Sally said. "Except that she lives in Keaton."

"And we're only guessing about that," Claire pointed out.

Was there a woman in Keaton, carrying Adam's baby? An unmarried woman? Molly's heart went out to her.

Adam's baby.

Suddenly Molly's heart ached for herself. Selfish as it was, she knew Adam was lost to her now. Forever. But he was doing the right thing by marrying this woman, whoever she was. Adam had integrity and decency. She'd always known that about him.

"Did you ask Molly?" someone said.

All three of them jumped, jarred back from their thoughts as Sally's sister joined them on the boardwalk.

"No, not yet," Sally told Sarah, annoyed.

"Ask me what?" Molly queried.

"Grandmother Hamilton sent us her wedding dress," Sarah said.

"It's beautiful," Sally said.

"We have to decide which of us gets to wear it," Sarah said. "So we thought you—"

"We thought you could tell us if there's some etiquette rule about who should have it," Sally said.

"I was going to say that," Sarah told her.

"Well, I already said it," Sally barked back.

Sarah ignored her sister and said to Molly, "I say the oldest granddaughter should wear it."

"You only think that because you're the oldest," Sally said.

The last thing Molly wanted was to hear these two arguing yet again about their double wedding ceremony.

"I'll read up on it," Molly promised and hurried into the Cottonwood.

The dining room was empty, closed for the night. She passed into the kitchen. It was quiet there, too. She, Aunt Libby and Carrie had finished their chores for the night.

Molly left the broom beside the stove, then lit the lantern on her bureau when she walked into her bedroom. She'd promised Sarah and Sally she'd read up on their wedding-dress question. She found the book she needed from the small collection she'd brought with her from Philadelphia and stretched out on her bed to read. Several chapters later, she came up with an answer—one neither Sarah nor Sally would like.

Molly sat up. Her room felt confining, stifling. She paced the floor, as much as she could in the tiny space, as a wave of restlessness claimed her. She was used to spending her evenings alone, but tonight she couldn't bear it.

Her belly tingled as a thought came to her. She knew she shouldn't do it. It was wrong—unthinkable, really. She'd been lucky she hadn't gotten caught before. If she did—

Well, she just wouldn't get caught, Molly decided.

Quickly, she changed out of the yellow dress she'd worn all day and slipped into a dark brown one. She found her black lace scarf in her bureau and draped it over her head, pulling it forward to cover her face, opened her bedroom window and climbed out.

What the hell?

Adam squinted into the darkness as he gazed at the rear of the Cottonwood Hotel. He kept to the shadows of the barn across the alley, not sure if he could believe his own eyes.

Was that Molly climbing out her bedroom window?

For the past few days he'd driven himself like a madman, concentrating on business, pushing his employees to do more, spending his evenings in his workroom behind the bank, hammering and sawing on his woodworking projects until he exhausted himself.

None of it helped. He still couldn't sleep at night. He tossed and turned with all sorts of visions in his mind. Finally, he'd taken to walking the back alleys of Spindler trying to clear his head and relieve the tension that kept him wound tight all day.

Seeing Molly's dress creep up past her knees as she slid out of the window didn't help anything.

But this time, worry and concern edged out his other urges.

Where was she going that forced her to sneak out the window? At this time of night? The streets of Spindler were safe enough during the day. But after dark a young woman—especially one as pretty as Molly—had no business being out alone.

He watched as she straightened her skirt, pulled a scarf closer around her face and hurried into the darkness.

Adam followed her.

Chapter Six

She'd be sent back to Philadelphia. Molly knew she would. If anybody—anybody—caught her and realized what she was doing, Uncle Roy would hustle her onto the first eastbound train and send her back to her grandmother without a second thought.

But only if someone saw her, recognized her and told on her.

Molly eased between the barrels and wood crates stacked high at the back corner of the feed store. The darkness closed in around her. She'd been here two nights ago, rearranged things as best she could and made herself a little cove of sorts. She'd even positioned a barrel so she could sit comfortably.

She settled onto the barrel. The half-moon was high overhead, offering little light in the alley. Molly felt safe. Anyone walking by—the sheriff or some drunken cowboy—couldn't see her.

Across the alley, through an open window, Molly peered into the Lucky Strike Saloon. Men stood at the bar, others were seated at the tables. Most had turned their chairs toward the stage Jonas Bradley had built that had caused such a ruckus in town.

Piano music drifted. Men hooted and hollered. On the stage were six cancan dancers.

They formed a chorus line and lifted their long skirts and petticoats in front of them like giant fans. Underneath they wore black stockings. Knees raised, they rotated their lower legs as they swept their skirts back and forth.

Oh, how free they looked. Molly leaned forward, gazing at the dancers through a gap between two wooden crates. Her heart raced. How wonderful, how thrilling it must be to feel that free.

The dancers broke into a series of high kicks, bringing applause and whistles from the men in the audience.

Grandmother had taken her to Paris a year ago to visit cousins. Molly had fallen in love with the city. She'd instantly connected with two of her cousins, girls a few years younger than she. They'd taken Molly to a theater their uncle owned and had sneaked in the back. From the wings they'd watched twenty girls perform the demanding and provocative cancan.

On the stage in the Lucky Strike, one of the dancers kicked the hat off of the head of one of the men sitting nearby, giving him a quick peek at her drawers. Hoots and hollers rose from the crowd.

Molly envied the dancers tonight, as she had in Paris. They weren't worried about their reputations, about what anyone thought of them or what anyone would say. The crowd loved them, and they loved what they were doing.

Molly wished to be that free. If only she could. Watching the dancers through the saloon window she remembered the longing, the yearning she'd experienced that evening in Paris. When she and her cousins had gotten home that night, they'd made their own costumes and danced in their grand bedroom, laughing until they collapsed. The next morning,

Molly had decided she had to leave Philadelphia. She'd never be free there. She'd never have a future there except to live in Grandmother's house, on the fringe of society, and continue to watch her friends marry, have children. She would never have those things. So why not leave, be free like the cancan dancers and find a new life somewhere else?

Inside the Lucky Strike, the dancers formed a line once more, then turned, bent over and threw their skirts over their backs. The crowd went wild.

Molly gasped. One of the girls had a flower embroidered on the seat of her drawers. Good gracious, she'd never seen such a thing. It was—

"What are you doing?" a man's voice boomed.

Molly screamed. A shadow moved through the darkness toward her. It was a man—a huge man. She jumped to her feet atop the barrel, grasped a wooden crate above her and climbed up.

Big hands locked around her waist and pulled her to the ground. Frantic, she batted at her attacker, but he only tightened his grip. She drew in a breath, ready to scream again. A hand closed over her mouth.

It smelled familiar.

"It's me. Adam." He took his hand away.

Her heart raced as she gazed up at him. Relief swamped Molly as she realized that it was Adam, and she was safe. She swayed against him. His arms tightened around her, keeping her on her feet.

"You scared me," she said.

"Good," he barked. "You ought to be scared, out this time of night by yourself. What are you doing?"

Oh, goodness. She couldn't tell him the reason she was here. What would she say?

He didn't give her a chance to answer.

"Don't you know what could happen to you?" he demanded.

"Do you mean some man might come along and grab me?" she asked. "As you're doing now?"

In the dim light she saw his expression soften and his lips twitch with the need to grin.

"Something like that," he said. "Only another man might not be as much of a gentleman as I am."

There wasn't anything "gentlemanly" about the way he held her. His arms were locked around her, holding her tight against him, her softness melting against his hardness.

Molly eased back. He let her, but in the confines of the barrel-and-wooden-crate fortress she couldn't move more than two steps away.

"What are you doing out here?" Adam asked.

"Nothing you need to concern yourself with," Molly told him and tried to sound offended that he'd asked.

"The hell I don't," he said. "From now on I've got a say in everything you do. We're partners, remember?"

Molly's mouth flew open. "We are? You're going to build the social hall? It will really be part mine?"

"Let's get a couple of things straight first," Adam said. "If I agree to this, you'll handle the wedding."

Molly's heart thumped against her chest. "Yes."

"And you'll make sure the wedding is perfect," he said. "You'll do everything you're told."

"No."

He frowned. Molly wasn't sure if he hadn't heard her correctly or simply couldn't believe what she'd said.

"I can't promise the bride will have absolutely everything she wants," Molly told him. "I can't help it if the roof of the baggage car leaks and the candles and flowers she's bringing with her are ruined. Or if the yardmaster throws the wrong switch and everything she owns ends up in Kansas City."

Adam nodded. "But you'll do everything you can to make it as perfect as it can be."

Molly's elation over their business deal dimmed. How wonderful to be engaged to a man who cared this much about the wedding preparations.

She forced aside the ache in her heart and nodded. "I'll do my very best."

"Okay, then," he said. "We're partners in the social hall."

An awkward moment passed. Most business matters were sealed with a handshake, which hardly seemed appropriate, given that Adam had once kissed her.

She was a little disappointed when Adam said, "I'll walk you home."

Molly had wanted him to leave before he figured out what she'd been up to in the alley, but knew he wouldn't leave her here alone.

"Let's hurry," Molly told her.

She ducked around him and struck out toward the Cottonwood. She'd gone only a few paces when she realized Adam wasn't beside her. She turned and found him standing in the alley. He looked at the saloon, then at her hideaway, then at her. Realization dawned on his face.

Humiliation burned through her. She struggled against it but knew her cheeks were bright red.

What would Adam think of her? Would he cancel the partnership he'd just agreed to?

"You were watching the cancan dancers?" Adam asked. His voice was heavy, his expression intense.

"Well, yes," she admitted, then added quickly, "but only because I saw them in Paris."

He looked shocked, as if he expected her to lift her skirt and petticoats, and high-kick her way down the alley toward him.

Which, for some reason, she was tempted to do.

Molly came to her senses. "If—if you tell anyone, my uncle will send me back to Philadelphia. You'll have no one to help with your wedding."

Adam walked closer. He stood in front of her, inches away. Heat rolled off him again.

That wild heat claimed Molly, robbed her thoughts and sapped her strength. He leaned down and covered her lips with his. Molly gasped as his arms encircled her, pulling her against him. His mouth moved across hers. She parted her lips. His warmth filled her.

Adam lifted his head. She gazed up at him and saw the yearning, the desire shining in his eyes. Her heart pounded. How she wished she could be in his arms forever.

He lowered his head once more, but she turned away.

"No," she whispered.

He nuzzled her neck. Her knees weakened. She wanted his kisses, his touch. But should she allow it? This one moment with him was all she'd have.

"We—we can't do this," Molly said, and pushed at him.

He didn't move. His breath was hot against her.

"Please," she said. "This isn't right."

"The hell it isn't," he murmured against her throat.

Molly braced her palms against his chest. "Think of your bride. Think of your unborn child."

Another moment passed before Adam stopped. He raised her head but didn't loosen his grip on her.

"My what?" he asked.

Molly sniffed irritably. Her Paris cousins had explained that at times like this, men didn't always think straight. But, really, how could Adam have forgotten the woman he intended to marry—and their child?

"The wedding, remember? Your bride. The baby you two are expecting," Molly said.

Adam reared back. "What the hell are you talking about? I'm not getting married."

"You're refusing to marry her?" Molly demanded. She stepped out of his arms and swatted at his chest. "I thought you were a decent man—a gentleman. How could you leave the woman you love in a lurch, with a baby on the way?"

"Hold on a minute," he said, waving both arms. "What makes you think I'm getting married? Or that I have a child on the way?"

"You came to me demanding I plan your wedding," Molly explained.

"And you thought I was the one getting married?" Adam asked.

"What else was I supposed to think?" Molly asked. She paused. A little glimmer of hope rose in her heart. "Are you saying you're not the one getting married?"

"I'm not the one getting married," Adam repeated.

"There's not a woman in Keaton who's carrying your child?" she asked.

"Who said anything about Keaton?"

"Everyone knows you go there often," Molly said.

"So the gossips in town assumed I had a lady friend there," Adam concluded. He shook his head. "Look, I'm not getting married, and that's all there is to it."

Molly's spirits soared. A little giggle slipped from her lips. He grinned and took her in his arms again.

"So does that make it all right for me to kiss you again?" he asked softly.

Molly sighed. He leaned down but she put her hand against his cheek.

"Wait," she said. "Who *is* getting married?"

"My partner Travis. He's marrying my sister." Adam shook his head. "I got dragged into the middle of it because Anna and my mama don't trust him to see things are handled the way they want."

"So they asked you to do it?" Molly asked.

"To tell you the truth, I've about had it with all this wedding business. I left Charleston to get away from all the etiquette rules, the social requirements," Adam grumbled. Then he shrugged. "But this is my sister and my mama asking for my help, so what can I do?"

Molly's heart warmed, learning of this new, unexpected side of him. What else about Adam didn't she know?

He didn't give her the chance to ask. Adam kissed her again. He moved his mouth against hers and she let him. His breath grew hotter, his kiss more intense. Finally, he pulled away.

"I like this partnership of ours," he said.

Another moment passed and Molly thought he might kiss her again.

"I'd better get you home," he said.

She looped her arm through his as they crossed Main Street and circled through the alley to the rear of the Cottonwood. Outside her bedroom he lifted her into his arms, then slid her legs through the window and sat her on the sill. She slid inside, then turned and leaned down.

"Good night," she whispered.

Adam touched his palm to her cheek. "Sweet dreams."

Molly smiled as she watched him disappear around the corner.

Chapter Seven

"Molly!"

She stopped on the boardwalk at the sound of her name and turned to find Grace hurrying toward her. The street was crowded with horses and wagons, despite the afternoon heat.

"Is it—is it true?" Grace asked. "Adam isn't getting married?"

Only last night Molly had learned the truth about the pending nuptials, and already word had spread through town. She didn't know who started these rumors since she hadn't told a soul, and could only guess that Rafe wasn't so careful about telling what he overheard from Adam and Travis's conversations.

"It's true," Molly said.

"But what about that woman in Keaton?" Grace asked. "Is Adam still seeing her?"

With a little jolt, Molly realized she didn't know how to answer. Adam had told her he wasn't getting married, but he'd never actually said he wasn't calling on someone in Keaton.

And if he wasn't calling on someone there, why did he vis: so frequently?

"I don't know," Molly admitted.

Grace sighed heavily, as if it were all too much for her. " don't know what's happening to Spindler. The town is gettin so crowded these days, it's almost impossible to keep up o all the news."

"Uncle Roy doesn't like it either," Molly agreed.

Grace glanced down the street. "I'd better get back to th store. Papa will have a fit if I'm not there to help out."

Molly moved along the boardwalk, smiling and speak ing briefly to almost everyone she passed. In her short tim in Spindler, she'd come to know and like so many peopl Though Uncle Roy complained about the growing population Molly enjoyed it.

At Olive Caldwell's dressmaker's shop she grasped th doorknob, ready to go inside. Through the glass displa window she saw Sarah and Sally Hamilton.

Molly stopped. She was almost finished with her list c errands this afternoon and needed to get back to the Cotto wood for the supper crowd. She most certainly didn't hav time to listen to the two sisters arguing again. She was cor sidering coming back later when she saw Olive waving at he from inside the shop.

With no other choice, Molly went inside. The shop wa filled with bolts of colorful fabrics stacked on shelves; bir of buttons and thread were everywhere.

Olive was a neat, tidy woman who kept her composur no matter how demanding her customers were, but today sh looked a little scattered.

The Hamilton sisters had that effect on people.

"You're just in time," Olive declared. She gestured t Sarah and Sally. "We were just talking about their weddin dresses."

"What did you find out?" Sarah asked Molly.

"Which of us should wear our grandmother's wedding ress?" Sally asked.

Olive and the sisters looked at Molly as if she were about o issue a decree that would change the course of history. She vished she could—just to put an end to the girls' bickering.

"I read up on the matter," Molly said, and offered a symathetic smile. "But I couldn't find anything definitive."

"So it's up to them?" Olive blurted out.

"That settles it," Sarah declared. "I'll wear the dress ecause I'm the eldest."

Sally puffed up with anger. "If we don't get this settled oon, I'm calling off the wedding!"

"No, you're not," Sarah told her. "*I'm* calling off the weding!"

The girls glared at each other, then rushed out the door.

"Oh, dear…" Molly muttered. Olive shook her head.

"I'd like to check with you about Constance's dress," Molly said, anxious to move on to a less troubling topic of onversation.

Constance Morgan was engaged to marry a young man vho worked at the Spindler Bank. Molly was especially glad o help with her wedding since Constance was such a pleasure o work with.

"It will be completed in plenty of time," Olive said. "Her inal fitting should be in a day or so."

Molly thanked her and left the shop. The next stop on er list was the Spindler Bank. As she passed the Maxwell jeneral Store she glanced at her reflection in the display vindow. She'd selected an emerald-green dress for today and old herself it was just another dress. But it was one of her avorites. She hoped Adam would like it.

Inside the bank, customers—mostly men—went about their usiness, lined up at the tellers' cages. At the rear, through an open door, Molly spotted Adam. He sat at his desk, head down, writing something. The pen looked too small for his big hand

"Afternoon, Miss Douglas," Rafe said, walking over.

"I'd like to speak with Mr. Crawford," she said, trying to sound as if this were an ordinary business meeting, though she doubted the men standing around her were experiencing a rapid heartbeat, as she was.

Rafe walked into Adam's office and spoke quietly. She saw his head come up. His gaze landed on her and he sprang out of his chair. In an instant, he was at her side. He escorted her into his office. Rafe's gaze bobbed between the two of them before he left the room.

"I hope I'm not interrupting anything," Molly said, as Adam seated her in the chair in front of his desk.

"You are," he said. He smiled and pushed aside the paper he'd been writing on. "And I couldn't be happier."

Molly smiled, too. She glanced back and saw that Rafe had left the office door open. Several men craned their necks, looking inside.

"I'd like to get started on your sister's wedding," she said. "I need the instructions she sent you."

Adam pulled open the center drawer of his desk and drew out the folded papers. He hesitated and said, "Now remember, you promised you'd do this."

"How bad can it be?" Molly plucked the papers from his hand, and just to show how unconcerned she was about the wedding preparations, slipped them into her handbag without so much as a quick glance.

"Would it be all right if I come by your place this evening to discuss the social hall?" Adam asked.

Molly suppressed a smile. "That would be fine."

She rose from her chair. Adam escorted her out of the office and across the bank, all under the close scrutiny of everyone in the building. Once outside, she thought he'd bid her a pleasant afternoon and she'd be on her way. Instead he walked her back to the Cottonwood. Neither spoke, but it was a comfortable silence.

At the entrance to the hotel, Molly gazed up at him, thinking once more how handsome he was. She knew passersby on the boardwalk were staring, watching her every move, but she couldn't seem to take her eyes off him.

Adam didn't seem any more anxious to part company than she was. Finally he said, "Until this evening."

Molly stood in the doorway for a few moments and watched him walk away, his square shoulders, his long back, his—

She flushed and glanced around, hoping no one had noticed how she was ogling him.

At the corner Adam turned back. He waved. She did the same and ducked into the lobby.

A delightful haze enveloped Molly. With the warm thoughts of Adam that filled her head, she wondered if she could float through the rest of the day with her feet never once touching the ground.

Then she caught sight of Carrie standing at the registration desk, her face pale. She hurried over.

"It was awful, Molly, just awful," Carrie said in a hushed voice. "I went into the kitchen to fetch the coffeepot and I heard Libby and Roy outside. They were arguing something terrible. He was shouting—and so was she."

Stunned, Molly could only look at her. In the time she'd lived at the Cottonwood Hotel she'd never once heard her aunt and uncle exchange a cross word, let alone raise their voices at each other.

A frightening thought struck her. Were they arguing about *her?* Had they somehow found out that she'd been spying on the cancan dancers at the saloon and kissing Adam in the alley?

"What were they fighting about?" Molly asked.

"It wasn't right for me to listen, of course," Carrie said, "but I happened to hear something about a problem with the hotel."

Molly heaved a silent sigh of relief. "What's wrong with the hotel?"

Carrie shrugged and hurried back into the dining room. Molly went to the kitchen. Aunt Libby stood at the stove frying chicken. Uncle Roy was nowhere in sight.

"Are you all right?" Molly asked.

Aunt Libby's eyes were red, as if she'd been crying, but she just nodded. "Everything will be fine, Molly. Help Carrie with the diners, will you?"

Molly hesitated for a moment, but when Libby turned back to the stove she knew her aunt didn't want to discuss whatever had happened.

Slipping into her bedroom, Molly unpinned her hat, laid aside her handbag and hurried to the dining room.

"Thinking about Molly Douglas again?" Travis asked.

Adam looked across his desk at his partner. Only a few hours ago, Molly had occupied the same chair. Somehow, the room still smelled of her delicate scent.

"No," he insisted and gestured to the papers strewn between them. "I was thinking about—"

"Stop kidding yourself," Travis told him. "I saw the way you've looked at her since the first day she came to town. And since you started talking to her, you can't keep your mind on business."

Adam waved away Travis's concern. "I've got a lot going on, you know that."

Travis sat back in his chair. "You're in love with her."

Adam opened his mouth to protest, but no words came out.

"Think about it," Travis said. "All this wedding nonsense Anna and your mama want done. You could have handled it yourself. But no. You insisted Molly do it. Why was that?

"I'll tell you why," Travis said, before Adam could answer. "Because it was an excuse. An excuse to spend time with her and get to know her better. And now that you have, you're in love with her."

Travis pushed himself out of his chair. "Think about what I said—but don't think too long. A woman like Molly won't be available forever."

Adam sat at his desk barely aware that Travis had left the office. The room still smelled like Molly, all right, but he didn't need any sort of reminder that she'd been here. Everything the woman did and said was etched into his brain—and his heart?

His pa had always claimed he'd fallen in love with his mama the first time he'd laid eyes on her. He said that's the way the Crawford men did things. They saw what they liked—what they loved—knew it right away, and went after it.

Was that true of himself? Adam wondered. He'd never felt this way about any woman before. Molly had somehow found a special place in his heart. Did that mean he loved her?

And more importantly, did Molly love him?

Adam got out of his chair and paced his office. Her kisses, her touch told him one thing. He'd been so stunned to find her in the alley outside the saloon watching the dancers inside, he could hardly believe it. Obviously there was another side of Molly that nobody knew about, one he'd only glimpsed.

Yet her quiet reserve said something different about her. Was it her Philadelphia upbringing? Or was it something more? What was she holding back? What was she hiding?

He needed to find out. Adam knew he'd never have another decent night's sleep in his life if he let Molly get away from him.

He paced some more, thought some more, then stopped. Despite himself, he smiled.

He loved Molly. Travis was right. He'd probably loved her since the day he'd first seen her, but he'd been too busy, too consumed with business to realize it.

Adam's smile disappeared. Molly was holding something back. She was keeping a secret.

A yearning grew inside him, demanding that he find out exactly what it was. Not that he cared about anything she might have done in her past, though he couldn't imagine what the well-bred daughter of a respected Philadelphia family might have done that she wanted so desperately to keep to herself. He wanted to know because he could help her. Whatever it was, he knew he could take on the load, share it with her, make it easier for her to bear. Somehow, he'd have to find what it was, and to do that he'd have to get her to trust him.

Adam nodded in the silent office. That's exactly what he intended to do.

Chapter Eight

"A theater? With a balcony?" Adam asked.

Molly looked up from the drawing that she'd sketched earlier, lying on the table between them. They sat in the private dining room at the Cottonwood. He'd come over just as the supper service was slowing down. Only a few diners remained in the main dining room.

"Yes, won't that be wonderful?" she said, pleased that he'd figured out her ideas from the rough drawing.

Adam tilted his head and tapped the paper. "This big room in the back? It's a kitchen?"

"It will be heavenly to work in such a large area," Molly agreed.

He nodded thoughtfully. "I guess we'll need a big kitchen for—what is this? Three dining rooms?"

She leaned forward. "A large one for big parties and a medium-size one for smaller events. Of course, we'll need a private room, like this one."

Adam's gaze met hers across the table. They'd made a point

to sit on opposite sides, but Molly felt as if they'd never been closer.

"Babies," Adam said softly.

Molly's stomach did a quick flip and she gasped softly.

"You've thought of them?" he asked.

The low timbre of his voice sent a flash of heat through her before she realized he was pointing to another room on the diagram.

Molly shook off the desire that had unexpectedly claimed her. Good gracious, what was wrong with her? They were supposed to be talking business.

"A large room for babies and small children," she said, glancing away. "Their mothers would appreciate a place for them to play, I'd imagine."

"Wouldn't you?" he asked.

She felt the heat of his gaze on her but didn't look up. The last thing, the very last thing, she wanted to discuss with Adam—or any man—was children.

Molly shrugged. "I'll never marry. Children won't be part of my future."

"That seems like a damn shame to me."

His words stirred something inside her. Molly pushed it away.

"My future lies elsewhere," she said, lifting her chin and putting a little force behind her words. "I want to take responsibility for my success. Running my own business is the only way I can do that. Here in Spindler, I see women doing just that. Olive's dress shop, the boardinghouse that Ruth Pauley runs, the sweet shop and the millinery store the Palmer sisters own. Grandmother would never give me the funds to do something like that, and I'll never be able to do more than scratch out a meager existence as long as I work for Uncle Roy. I want to take charge, do it myself."

"So you can be free?" Adam asked softly. "Like the cancan dancers?"

Molly's cheeks heated, yet she didn't turn away. He knew the truth. She didn't have to pretend with him—not about this. It was a good feeling.

"Can't say that I blame you for feeling the way you do. A long time ago I had my fill of toeing a line drawn by somebody else," Adam told her. His expression hardened. "What I don't understand is why a husband can't be part of that?"

For a moment, the need to explain her past nearly overwhelmed Molly. She wanted to unburden herself, explain about her mother and how her actions had destroyed every chance Molly had to succeed in Philadelphia. But after she told him, what would he say? What *could* he say?

In her heart, Molly knew she couldn't bear to see the look of disappointment on Adam's face. She'd seen it too many times before. The instant when respect dimmed, then disappeared.

Molly turned away. "That's just the way I want things," she said, her voice straining to get the words out.

"You're not telling me something."

Adam's hand closed over hers. It was warm. Soft, yet rough. Both soothing and exciting, somehow. A flash of heat ran up her arm, straight to her heart.

She struggled to tamp down her feelings and pulled her hand from his.

"I could say the same about you," Molly said, managing to put a little challenge in her voice. "Those secretive trips you make to Keaton."

Adam rolled his eyes. "Is the town still gossiping about that? Is that what's bothering you? Come with me."

He shoved out of his chair and clamped his hat on. "We're settling this right now."

Adam circled the table and pulled Molly's chair out,

then caught her elbow and urged her to her feet. "Let's go," he said.

Molly pulled away. "But—"

He leaned down a little. "You want us to be partners, don't you?"

"Well, yes, of course, but—"

"Partners trust each other," he said. "Now, come on."

Adam headed for the door. Molly had no choice but to follow.

He pushed through the swinging door to the kitchen. Aunt Libby and Carrie looked on, wide-eyed as they walked through.

"I'll have her back in a few minutes," Adam said.

Molly grabbed her shawl from the peg by the door and followed him outside. The alley was dark. A cool breeze stirred, hinting at a rain shower.

They walked through the alley and crossed Main Street. Molly was thankful for the darkness and that so few people were out at this hour. Adam looped her arm through his as they walked to the rear of the Spindler Bank.

"Here's my big secret," Adam said, as he pulled a key from his pocket and unlocked the door to one of the outbuildings.

He disappeared into the darkness. A match sparked to life as he lit the lantern beside the door. Molly crossed the threshold as Adam moved around, lighting a half dozen more lamps.

A workroom, she realized. A large bench dominated one wall. An array of tools hung above it. Glass jars were filled with nails. Cans of paint and brushes sat on a wide shelf. Stacks of all sizes of lumber filled every corner. The place smelled of sawdust and turpentine.

"Take a look," Adam called. On the far wall, he opened the door to a big cupboard.

"Toys?" Molly asked, walking over.

The shelves were filled with wooden blocks, wagons, tiny cradles, carved horses and dogs, all manner of toys, gleaming with bright paint.

Molly stared up at him. Did this confirm her worst fear? Did Adam have a baby on the way—or worse, a child in Keaton?

"The only babies or children in Keaton I'm involved with are the orphans," he said. He waved his arm around the door. "I make toys here and take them over from time to time."

Molly's heart melted. She hadn't thought it possible to love Adam more than she already did, but now, seeing this new side of him, she realized how easily that could happen.

"Why don't you tell anybody?" she asked.

"Because it's nobody's business," Adam said.

"But the whole town thinks—"

"The whole town is always going to think *something*," Adam said.

Molly couldn't disagree.

"I like making the toys. It takes my mind off things," Adam said. He angled closer. "Everything but you, that is."

Adam slid his arms around her waist and drew her nearer. He placed a finger under her chin and raised it, then lowered his head and kissed her. The sheer delight of his touch captured Molly. She looped her arms around his neck and kissed him back.

He deepened their kiss. Molly rose on her toes and parted her lips, then gasped when he accepted her invitation. The world seemed to spin and she lost herself in his strength, in the heat he gave off. Adam groaned as he slid his hand up her waist and closed it over her breast. Molly sighed and pressed closer.

Then, just as suddenly, it ended. Adam pulled away. Cold air swirled between them. He held her at arm's length, his breathing heavy, his desire for her obvious.

Molly gulped, bringing herself under control, as well. Good gracious, what had happened? How had she been so quickly caught up in this? What would she have done if Adam hadn't had the strength to stop?

"I'll walk you back home," Adam said, his voice low.

She just nodded. She knew it was the right thing to do but—

Molly refused to allow herself to think further.

The cold breeze blew harder as they walked back to the rear of the Cottonwood. When they got to the door, neither spoke. Molly hurried inside without looking back, glad Aunt Libby and Carrie were nowhere in sight.

In her bedroom Molly lit the lantern on her bureau and gazed at her reflection in the mirror above her washstand.

Did she look any different for what she'd just done? She tilted her head to the left, then the right, and decided that she was the same on the outside.

But on the inside, things were very different.

A tiny glimmer of hope glowed inside her. It was something she'd never felt—not once.

Adam had said he didn't like rigid social standards. He seemed unconcerned about the gossip that swept through town involving him. And after tonight in his workroom, Molly knew he felt something for her.

Could it be love? Could he want to be with her always? And if he did, would he still want that after she told him the truth of her past?

Molly ached with the hope that it could happen. She wrapped her arms around her middle as if to hold in the possibility, squeeze it until it became a reality.

She'd heard the talk around town about Adam's family in Charleston. Wealthy, everyone had said. The closest to royalty or aristocracy possible on this side of the ocean.

If only she knew for sure.

Molly whirled around, realizing there was a way for her to know.

She found her handbag and pulled out the instructions Adam's sister and mother had made for the wedding. Molly hurried to the lantern and held the pages close to the light. A lump rose in her throat as she read, then a single tear slid down her cheek and splashed onto the paper.

The wedding instructions held the demands of a wealthy, well-bred, highly respected bride from a very old, aristocratic family. Everything she'd heard about Adam's family was true. All the rumors were right.

She'd never fit in. They would never want her in their midst.

Adam might accept her—at first—but his family never would. Eventually, he'd regret his decision. He'd resent her. He'd wish he'd never met her. And their children—

A sob tore from Molly's throat. Her room seemed airless, confining. She yanked open the door and rushed into the kitchen, wanting nothing more than to get outside, find a dark corner in the alley and cry until her breaking heart wouldn't give up another tear.

But she spotted Aunt Libby seated at the little table in the corner of the kitchen. A single lantern burned on the wall. She hadn't seen her there when she'd come in earlier.

Molly forced down her tears, unwilling to share her thoughts with her aunt. She couldn't possibly tell anyone, not even Aunt Libby, how foolish she'd been to think that she might have had a future with Adam. A home of her own, a man of consequence who loved and respected her, children whose future would be bright and free from the mistakes her own mother had made.

Odd that Aunt Libby hadn't called out to her, Molly realized. Then she heard soft sniffles and realized her aunt was crying.

Molly hurried over, her own troubles set aside. She'd neve seen Aunt Libby upset—never. Something truly awful mus have happened.

"Aunt Libby?" she asked softly as she approached th table.

Libby looked up as if just realizing Molly was in the room and touched the corners of her eyes with the handkerchief sh clutched.

"What's wrong?" Molly asked, easing into the chair besid her.

A few moments passed in silence. Finally, Aunt Libby dre a big breath. "Your Uncle Roy…"

Molly gasped. "Is he all right?"

She patted Molly's hand. "He's well."

Silence stretched between them again.

"Then what's wrong?" Molly asked.

"Your uncle has made a decision," her aunt said. "I don agree with it, but there's nothing I can do."

Molly recalled how Carrie had overheard them fighting A dozen worrisome thoughts flashed in her head.

"What is it?" Molly asked.

With another heavy sigh, Aunt Libby said, "Roy ha decided to sell the Cottonwood. He doesn't want to live i Spindler anymore."

Molly's eyes widened. "But—how—"

"Don't worry," her aunt said softly. "Your uncle made promise to your grandmother that he would take care of you He's a man of his word, as I'm sure you already know. A soon as a buyer can be found, we're heading for California Molly. And you're coming with us."

Chapter Nine

A beautiful bride. A handsome groom. Friends and family filling the church.

Molly looked on from the back pew as Constance exchanged vows with Harry Burnette. The dress Olive had made for Constance fell in graceful folds of white lace. Harry looked dashing in a black suit. Candles lit the church, casting the congregation, the wedding couple and Reverend Holcomb in warm shadows.

Constance, her mother and her sisters had done most of the wedding preparations. Molly had suggested and ordered the candles and flowers, and had helped with a few other things. The wedding celebration would be held at the home of Constance's parents. Molly was glad for that.

Without wanting to, her gaze swept the congregation. Adam. Was he here?

Annoyed with herself, Molly focused her attention on the bridal couple at the altar. She'd looked for Adam in the church too many times already.

For the past week she'd avoided him. She'd stayed in the

Cottonwood taking care of things that required her attention, including overseeing the details of Adam's sister's wedding to Travis. The family had arrived in town but she hadn't met them yet. When Adam had come to the hotel and asked for her, Aunt Libby had told him Molly wasn't receiving visitors, as she'd asked her aunt to do.

At the front of the church, Reverend Holcomb pronounced Constance and Harry man and wife. The couple looked into each other's eyes with sheer joy. Harry leaned down and gave his bride a chaste kiss on the lips. Then, arm in arm, they walked back down the aisle. Molly didn't remember when she'd seen a more radiant bride—or when she'd felt so miserable at the sight.

The family, then the congregation followed the couple out of the church with gentle laughter and calls of good wishes. Molly remained in the pew as others rose around her. She was supposed to go to the wedding celebration. It was expected. But she didn't know how she could continue to feign happiness, when her own heart was breaking.

The news that Uncle Roy was selling the Cottonwood Hotel had spread through Spindler in less than a day's time. Everyone had understood why he was selling out: her uncle had made no secret of his dislike for the recent changes in the town.

But would Molly go, too?

She remained in the pew watching as friends and neighbors filed past and out of the church. Almost everyone smiled or nodded at her. She'd gotten to know so many people since arriving in Spindler. What a wonderful feeling to be accepted by them. She didn't want to leave them behind.

She didn't want to leave Adam.

Molly pushed to her feet, forbidding herself to think of him again. She'd already spent long days and sleepless night trying to do just that.

True, they were partners now. He'd promised to build the social hall for her to run. It was her best—her only—opportunity to have the future she craved.

But what would it be worth if, one day, she had to stand by and watch him wed some other woman, as he surely would?

Molly dropped onto the pew again, the notion robbing her of her strength. The church was empty now. Reverend Holcomb's wife had extinguished the candles. Miss Marshall had closed the piano lid, gathered her sheet music and left. In the silence, Molly shut her eyes and said a quick prayer that the answer be revealed to her.

She opened her eyes and pulled herself to her feet. Somehow, she'd have to make it through the wedding celebration. Gathering her shawl around her shoulders, she turned and saw Adam leaning against the door frame.

Her heart lurched. It pounded hard in her chest, then rose into her throat and hung there. For an instant she was overwhelmed with the need to rush to him, throw herself into his arms, hold him forever.

But Adam didn't look so happy to see her. His jaw was set, his lips pressed into a thin line and his brows were drawn together. Molly imagined he'd frightened more than one grown man with that look. But she wasn't frightened. Instead, she was drawn to him as never before.

"You owe me an explanation," he told her. Before she could respond, he said, "I've been to the hotel to see you, but your aunt claimed you weren't receiving callers. I'm not a caller, Molly. I'm your partner."

Something about the way he said the words made her heart beat a little faster.

"You owe me an explanation," Adam said again. "And I want it now."

Just then Reverend Holcomb stuck his head inside the church. "I need to lock up," he said.

"We're just leaving," Adam said. He took Molly's arm and led her outside. The wedding guests milled around under the tall trees in the churchyard in the closing darkness as others headed toward the bride's parents' home on the edge of town.

"I'm supposed to go to the party," Molly said.

"You'll be late," Adam told her.

With his arm still hooked through hers, he led the way through town. Businesses were closed for the night; few people were on the streets on a Saturday evening, except for cowboys heading for the Lucky Strike.

They headed down the alley beside the bank. At the stairs leading up to Adam's room, Molly hesitated. It wasn't right for her to go to his place unescorted. It could ruin her reputation. She'd been lucky no one had seen her when she'd gone there before.

"I shouldn't," she said.

"We had a deal," he told her. "I need to know if you intend to hold up your end."

So, it was all business with him. Molly felt foolish, thinking otherwise.

He took her elbow and they climbed the wooden steps to his place. Inside, he took off his hat and closed the door. Molly drew her shawl closer around her, suddenly chilled by the breeze that blew in through the windows.

"I know your mother and sister and all her friends got here two nights ago," Molly said. Even though she'd kept herself isolated at the Cottonwood, the news had reached her no sooner than their trunks were unloaded from the baggage car. "I sent them a note, explaining everything was ready. The wedding decorations they brought with them were beautiful. I'll have them in place in plenty of time for the ceremony on—"

"I don't give a damn about the wedding," Adam told her. He stepped closer, crowding her. "I want to know about *you*."

"You heard about Uncle Roy selling the hotel," Molly said. She drifted away, unable to meet his gaze. "I should have come to you and discussed it. That was wrong of me."

"Are you walking out on our partnership?" Adam asked. "Are you leaving?"

A fresh wave of pain sliced through Molly as visions of Constance and Harry's wedding flashed through her head. She'd seen the love they shared and her heart had ached with envy. How wonderful it would be to marry, to have that someone special to confide in, to turn to, to share her life with. For a few brief moments over the past weeks she'd allowed herself to think she might have that with Adam. But she'd been foolish to imagine that sort of future for herself, considering her past.

"I suppose so," Molly said. The words came out in a strained whisper.

Adam stared down at her. She couldn't read his expression, didn't know if he was angry or disappointed with her.

"I can't stay in Spindler without my aunt and uncle," she told him, reciting all the reasons that had gone through her mind since her aunt had told her of Uncle Roy's decision. As she spoke the words, the ache in her chest grew. "It wouldn't be right. I'd have no place to live. I'd have no money. I'd—"

"Marry me."

His words shocked her. She didn't understand them, couldn't imagine why he'd spoken them.

Then she knew. "You needn't worry about your sister's wedding. Uncle Roy doesn't even have a buyer for the hotel yet, so I'll be here to take care of the ceremony and the party at the Cottonwood."

Adam crossed the room in two long strides. He laid his hands on Molly's shoulders. "I didn't ask because I'm worried about the wedding—or our partnership on the social hall. I asked because I want you to marry me."

Molly's emotions rose, sending a tingle through her. How she'd longed to hear those words from Adam. How she'd wanted to hear them—and to say yes.

But she couldn't. She couldn't marry him.

Tears pooled in her eyes. "No," she said.

Adam tightened his grip on her shoulders. "Why?" he demanded.

She shook her head. "I—I can't."

"Then tell me why," he insisted.

"I—" The pain that stabbed at her heart cut off her words.

"You're keeping something from me, Molly," Adam said. "Tell me what it is. Let me help you."

"No!" The word burst from her lips. Molly dashed for the door. She had to leave, had to get away. The pain was too much.

Adam caught her arm and pulled her into his embrace. She struggled to find words to explain, something that would satisfy his questions so he'd let her leave. But he asked nothing. Instead, he covered her mouth with his and pulled her tight against him.

Molly melted into him. His strength, his warmth held her there, and she knew there was no other place she'd rather be. Adam deepened their kiss. His hands circled her waist and pulled her even closer.

For so long, she'd looked toward a solitary future. She'd known it would be that way. She could never have *this*.

But what sort of life would that be? One without Adam. At that instant, Molly couldn't bear the thought.

Adam spread kisses over her cheek, then down to her neck. His hand rose to caress her breast. He pressed against her and she gasped at the feel of his desire for her.

"I love you. I want to marry you," he breathed against her

neck. He lifted his face and looked into her eyes. "If you don't feel the same, just tell me now."

Molly knew what her future held. She knew, too, what this moment meant. This, surely, would be her only opportunity to know Adam. In a matter of days, she'd likely be gone, off to California with her aunt and uncle, never to see him again.

She wouldn't let this moment pass her by.

Molly draped her arms around Adam's neck and kissed his lips. He groaned, then lifted her into his arms and carried her to his bed in the corner. Adam laid her down and sat next to her. He threaded his fingers through her hair, then lowered his head and placed another kiss on her mouth. His lips trailed down her cheek.

Molly gasped and stroked his hair. She touched his arms, his chest. The heat he gave off warmed her palms. Adam rose from the bed and pulled off his clothes. He tossed them aside and stretched out beside her.

He kissed her as he unbuttoned her dress and slid his hand inside. Molly moaned when his fingers brushed her breast, then gasped with pleasure as his lips followed. He made quick work of her dress, petticoats, corset, shoes and drawers. Molly let him, feeling no shame.

Adam lifted himself above her and slid between her thighs. He kissed her tenderly as he made a place for himself inside her. Slowly he moved with her. She caught his rhythm and moved with him, unable to resist. She wrapped her arms around him and yanked at his hair as pleasure broke within her over and over. Adam called out her name, and he followed her until he was spent.

Molly woke with a start. It was dark, save for a lantern burning low beside the door. Steady breathing broke the silence. She glanced beside her and saw Adam sleeping soundly.

The warm afterglow of their lovemaking enveloped her.

She'd never imagined an act so intimate could exist, could make her feel so wanted and accepted. Adam must really love her. He must really want to marry her.

Tears pooled in Molly's eyes as she clutched the quilt against her bare breasts. She could marry him. She could have a future—a real future with a home and babies, lots of babies—

Babies?

Horrified, Molly sat straight up in bed. Oh, heavens, what had she done? What had she been thinking? To give herself to Adam, to revel in the joy of their union and run the risk of conceiving a child?

Visions of her own life bombarded her thoughts. Out of wedlock. Illegitimate. Unworthy. Unaccepted.

Molly pressed her palm to her lips to keep from crying out. What if, at this very moment, she was pregnant? Had she just condemned another child—her child—to suffer as she had?

She threw off the covers and dashed around the room, pulling on her clothes, praying Adam wouldn't wake. He didn't. As soon as she was decent, she ran from the room all the way to the Cottonwood Hotel. Safe in her bed, Molly cried into her pillow.

Chapter Ten

The first rays of morning light filtered through Molly's bedroom window, rousing her from her bed. She dragged herself to the washstand and looked at her reflection in the mirror. Her eyes were red and puffy from all the tears she'd cried, but she couldn't bear to look any further. Not after what she'd done.

As she stripped off her clothing and washed, the night in Adam's bed played over in her mind. By making love with Adam, giving herself to a man to whom she wasn't married, she'd done the one thing she had always hated about her mother. Now she could possibly be pregnant and might subject her own child to just the sort of life she endured herself.

Molly ran a brush through her hair, pulling out the tangles. Images of her mother flashed in her mind. Now Molly understood her actions. She'd always claimed she loved Molly's father, despite how things turned out.

Molly twisted her hair into a loose bun and thought of how desperately she loved Adam. She knew how wrong she'd been for the sometimes harsh feelings she had toward her mother.

With heavy limbs, Molly dressed. Somehow, she'd have to get through the day—and the next, and the next. Already too much time had passed since Adam's family arrived in Spindler. She should have paid a call on them sooner and assured them all was well with the wedding. Today, she'd also have to—

Heavy footsteps sounded in the kitchen. A fist pounded on her door.

"Molly! Open this door!" Adam shouted.

Her emotions scattered. She didn't want to see him, didn't want to be reminded of what she'd done—and what she was giving up.

Other voices sounded beyond her door, Aunt Libby and Carrie.

"Open it!" Adam shouted as he pounded harder. "I swear I'll break it down!"

Molly jerked it open. Adam filled the doorway looking taller, wider and angrier than she'd ever seen him. Aunt Libby and Carrie stood nearby holding a skillet and a rolling pin, ready to defend her.

"It's all right," Molly said to them.

They both looked troubled, but backed away. Adam strode into her room and slammed the door behind him.

"You owe me an explanation," he told her.

Now he looked more hurt than angry. She could see he'd dressed hurriedly and hadn't taken the time to shave or do more than slick his hair into place with his fingers. It made her want to reach up and smooth it down, but she didn't dare.

"Yes, I suppose I do," Molly said softly.

Yet she couldn't bring herself to speak, couldn't muster the strength to tell Adam her worst secret—even after last night when they'd known each other in the most intimate way imaginable.

Adam drew in a heavy breath as if straining to calm himself. "Whatever it is, Molly, just tell me."

With all her heart Molly wished she didn't have to say these words to Adam, because after she did, things would never be the same. Still, she owed him the truth.

"I was born out of wedlock," Molly said softly.

Molly couldn't bring herself to look at Adam, knowing what she'd see.

"I don't care," Adam said.

Her gaze came up quickly and she saw nothing but sincerity in his face. Still, it brought her little comfort.

"You will," she told him. "One day, you will."

"No, I won't," he insisted. Adam reached out, but she spun away. "Molly, listen to me. You know I left Charleston because I didn't want those strict social mores to rule my life. That kind of thing doesn't matter to me."

"It matters to your family," she insisted.

"You don't know my family."

"But I do," she said. "I know they have the highest expectations of anyone who marries you, as they should. So do their friends. Eventually, my past will come out. Everyone will find out. You'll be ashamed of me."

"The hell I will," Adam told her.

Molly closed her eyes for an instant, wishing it could be true. But she knew differently.

"I won't subject you to that sort of life," Molly said quietly. "Or our children."

"I love you, Molly," Adam said. "I want you to marry me."

Tears filled her eyes as she looked up at him. How desperately she wanted to spend her life with him. But nothing had changed. It never would.

She turned away. "I won't marry you, Adam."

Silence filled the room. Molly kept her back to him and, finally, she heard his heavy footsteps as he left.

She covered her face with her hands and cried.

* * *

"We're closing early tonight," Aunt Libby declared as Molly dried the wet dish her aunt passed her.

"But why?" Molly asked. She couldn't remember a single time the hotel dining room had closed ahead of schedule.

Of course, she'd been distracted these past few days. She'd met Adam's mother and sister and all their friends who'd traveled to Spindler for the wedding. They were warm, genuinely nice people.

She hadn't seen Adam once.

Carrie dashed in from the dining room with her arms full of dirty dishes. "This is the last of them. Everybody's gone," she said.

"Is everything set for the wedding tomorrow?" Aunt Libby asked Molly.

Travis and Anna would wed the next day at the church, then come to the Cottonwood for the celebration. Nearly the whole town had been invited.

"I took Anna and her mother to the church this afternoon," Molly said. "The candles they brought with them are in place, just as they wanted. I'll put the flowers out in the morning."

"Are you sure?" Carrie asked. "Maybe you should have another look. Tonight, maybe?"

Aunt Libby shot her a quelling look and said, "Whose wedding is next? The Hamilton sisters?"

"I thought they'd called everything off," Carrie said, moving a stack of dry plates to the cupboard.

Molly shook her head. "Both Sarah and Sally had been fussing about who would wear their grandmother's wedding gown, but I solved that problem."

"How did you ever convince one of those girls to wear a different gown?" Aunt Libby asked.

"I didn't," Molly said, and couldn't help smiling. "I had

Olive divide the dress in half. Sarah is wearing the top, and Sally the bottom."

All three of them laughed, even Molly. It felt good. She couldn't remember the last time she'd felt lighthearted about anything. The past few days, since Adam had come over and asked her again to marry him, had been the toughest in her life.

He hadn't come back. He hadn't asked a third time. It's what she'd wanted; still, her heart ached for him and for what she could have had.

"Molly, what are you wearing to Travis and Anna's wedding tomorrow?" Aunt Libby asked.

Carrie spoke before Molly had a chance. "That cream-colored dress of yours. You should wear that one, Molly. It's your most beautiful one."

It was Molly's favorite and probably the nicest one she owned.

"Maybe I will," she said.

"Let me see you in it," Carrie said. "Go put it on. "

"Now?" Molly asked.

"It wouldn't hurt," Aunt Libby agreed. "You don't want to be trying to decide what to wear tomorrow morning, with so much going on before the wedding."

"You have to put it on," Carrie told her. "You just have to."

"Well, I suppose it wouldn't hurt," Molly said.

In her room, she changed into the dress. The silk fabric shimmered in the pale light.

"Let's put some of these combs in your hair," Carrie insisted, and spent a few minutes fussing over Molly's hair. "Now, come show your aunt."

Molly walked into the kitchen and did a little spin. Aunt Libby smiled with pride. "You look beautiful," she said softly.

Molly looked down at herself, pleased with the way the gown looked and felt.

"I'll wear this one tomorrow," she said, and headed back into her room.

"Wait!" Carrie cried. She glanced at Aunt Libby and said, "I mean, I'd like to look at the dress awhile longer."

"For heaven's sake, Carrie," Molly said. "You've seen me in this—"

A quick knock sounded on the back door.

"I'll get it!" Carrie exclaimed and rushed over. When she opened the door, Adam walked inside.

Hundreds of memories assailed Molly at the sight of him. His touch, his laugh, his strength. Their lovemaking. His anger and disappointment at her refusal to marry him.

"Evening, ladies," he said, and pulled off his hat.

Tonight he wore a black suit. Beneath it was a crisp white shirt closed at the collar with a string tie. Molly didn't think he'd ever looked more handsome.

"Miss Douglas, I need you to come to the church with me. I have to make sure everything is ready for the wedding tomorrow," Adam said.

His tone was crisp, all business. It hurt Molly a bit, but really, she couldn't blame him.

"I was there earlier with your sister and mother," Molly told him. "Everything is fine."

"I want to check it myself. Now," Adam told her. He took a step closer and lowered his voice. "We had a deal, remember?"

Yes, of course she remembered. How could she forget, after what it had led to?

"Let me change out of this dress," Molly said.

"I don't have all night," Adam told her.

"You'd better run along," Aunt Libby said.

"Yes, just go!" Carrie said.

Everyone certainly seemed on edge tonight, Molly thought,

ut perhaps she deserved it; she'd hardly been herself for ays now.

Adam opened the door and gestured for her to go ahead of im. Molly gathered her skirt and walked outside. The night vas cool. Not a hint of a breeze stirred as they walked to the hurch in silence.

Once inside, Molly gasped in irritation at the sight of the ozens of candles burning, casting the sanctuary in golden hadows. Flowers sat in vases all around the room.

"What's going on?" Molly asked, shaking her head. She ressed her palm to her forehead. "This is awful, just awful. hese candles are for Anna's wedding tomorrow. They can't e used tonight. And these flowers. They aren't supposed to e put out until the morning. Who did this?"

"Don't worry about that now," Adam said.

"Don't worry?" she repeated.

"We'll talk to Reverend Holcomb," Adam said. He held ut his arm and linked hers through it, then guided her to the ain aisle leading to the altar at the front of the church. He topped, drew in a breath and walked forward.

Molly didn't move. "What are you doing?"

"Practicing," he said. "I'm walking Anna down the aisle omorrow, remember?"

"You don't really need practice," Molly told him. "All you ave to do is—"

"I need to practice," Adam told her in no uncertain erms.

"Fine, then," she said. "But I have to find the reverend and et this flower situation handled before—oh, look, there he now."

Reverend Holcomb stepped through the door at the rear f the church and positioned himself in front of the altar. As ey approached, he lifted his Bible and opened it. Adam and Iolly stopped in front of him.

"Reverend," Molly said. "Someone has taken Anna'
flowers and—"

"Shh," Adam said. "First things first. Reverend, go ahead.'

The reverend cleared his voice and lifted his Bibl
higher.

"Dearly beloved, we are gathered here this evening in th
sight of God to bring together this man and this woman i
holy wedlock," the reverend said. "Adam, do you take thi
woman to be your lawfully wedded wife?"

"I do," he said.

Reverend Holcomb turned to Molly. "And do you, Moll
take this man to be your—"

"Wait! What—what's going on?" Molly exclaimed. He
gaze bounced from Adam to the reverend, then back to Ada
again.

Adam dropped to one knee and took her hand. "Moll
would you do me the great honor of becoming my wife?"

Breath went out of her. Her mind spun. She couldn't con
prehend what was happening.

Adam had brought her to the church to *marry* her? He'd l
the candles and placed the flowers for *her?* After everythin
that had gone on between them, after she'd told him the trut
about her past, he still wanted her for his wife?

"No!" Molly jerked her hand from his and raced up th
aisle.

Adam caught her at the church door and whirled her t
face him.

"I love you, Molly. I want you in my life every day," he tol
her, then gestured toward the altar. "This was the only way
could convince you of that."

She shook her head frantically. "I can't marry you. I tol
you why. You have to respect that, Adam. I'm right. My pa
will make you hate me one day."

"No, it won't!"

Adam's voice echoed off the church walls, quieting Molly's tirade. She'd never heard him speak so forcefully before.

"Listen to me," he said. He placed his hands on her shoulders and leaned down until his face was even with hers. "There's something you don't know about me and my family. I don't tell people because it's none of their business. But you're so confounded stubborn I'm going to tell you."

Molly stilled at the serious look on his face. She couldn't imagine what he could tell her that would make a difference in the way she felt.

Adam drew in a breath and said, "A few years ago, back in Charleston, somebody started gossiping about my sister Rebecca. Something happened, something she couldn't help, something that wasn't her fault. But everybody kept repeating the story until the whole city thought ill of her, as if she'd caused the situation. It got so bad that…well, Rebecca couldn't bear it any longer. She tried to take her own life."

"Oh, Adam…" Molly said. She saw the pain etched in the hard lines of his face. She wanted nothing but to comfort him.

"I found her in time, and…she's fine now," Adam said. "She's living in Europe. She got married a few months ago. She's happy now."

Molly touched her palm to his cheek. "What a horrible thing for you—for your whole family—to go through."

His expression hardened again. "All because somebody started gossiping about her. Molly, I don't care what anybody says about you. I don't care now and I never will. Neither will my family. Not after what we've been through."

A small glimmer of hope dawned in Molly. Could he really mean it? Could it be true? Could Adam and his family really accept her now and forever?

"Marry me, Molly," Adam said. "I've asked you three times

now, and some other man might be put off by that, but not me. I love you. You love me, too, don't you?"

"Oh, yes!" Molly threw her arms around his neck and held on tight.

Adam looped his arms around her and pulled her close. After a moment, he leaned back.

"Was that, yes, you love me? Or, yes, you'll marry me?" he asked.

"Both," Molly declared.

Adam leaned down and kissed her.

"Excuse me?" Reverend Holcomb called. "You're supposed to save that for after the ceremony."

Adam and Molly giggled softly. Then Adam took her arm and together they walked down the aisle.

"Are we all in agreement?" the reverend asked.

"We are," Adam said. He glanced down at Molly. "Aren't we?"

"We are," she said.

"All right, then, let's get on with this, shall we?" Reverend Holcomb raised his voice. "Everyone?"

The door at the rear of the church opened and Aunt Libby, Uncle Roy, Carrie, Travis and all of Adam's family filed in.

Molly gasped. "You invited everyone? And you kept it a secret from me?"

Adam smiled with pride. "I'm pretty good at keeping secrets. By the way, I should tell you I bought your uncle's hotel."

"The Cottonwood?" Molly asked.

Adam leaned down and whispered, "You can run it yourself, or we can fill it up with children."

A big smile bloomed on Molly's face. "Now that's the kind of town gossip I can live with."

* * * * *

COMING NEXT MONTH FROM

HARLEQUIN®
HISTORICAL

Available May 31, 2011

- **SAVING GRACE**
  by **Carolyn Davidson**
  (Western)

- **SCANDALOUS INNOCENT**
  by **Juliet Landon**
  (Restoration and Regency)

- **MORE THAN A MISTRESS**
  by **Ann Lethbridge**
  (Regency)
  Second in duet: *Rakes in Disgrace*

- **ONE ILLICIT NIGHT**
  by **Sophia James**
  (Regency)

HHCNM0511

REQUEST YOUR FREE BOOKS!

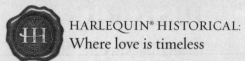

HARLEQUIN® HISTORICAL:
Where love is timeless

2 FREE NOVELS PLUS 2 **FREE GIFTS!**

YES! Please send me 2 FREE Harlequin® Historical novels and my 2 FREE gifts (gifts are worth about $10). After receiving them, if I don't wish to receive any more books, I can return the shipping statement marked "cancel." If I don't cancel, I will receive 6 brand-new novels every month and be billed just $4.94 per book in the U.S. or $5.49 per book in Canada. That's a savings of at least 18% off the cover price! It's quite a bargain! Shipping and handling is just 50¢ per book in the U.S. and 75¢ per book in Canada.* I understand that accepting the 2 free books and gifts places me under no obligation to buy anything. I can always return a shipment and cancel at any time. Even if I never buy another book from the Reader Service, the two free books and gifts are mine to keep forever.

246/349 HDN FC45

Name	(PLEASE PRINT)	

Address		Apt. #

City	State/Prov.	Zip/Postal Code

Signature (if under 18, a parent or guardian must sign)

Mail to the **Reader Service:**
IN U.S.A.: P.O. Box 1867, Buffalo, NY 14240-1867
IN CANADA: P.O. Box 609, Fort Erie, Ontario L2A 5X3

Not valid for current subscribers to Harlequin Historical books.

Want to try two free books from another line?
Call 1-800-873-8635 or visit www.ReaderService.com.

* Terms and prices subject to change without notice. Prices do not include applicable taxes. N.Y. residents add applicable sales tax. Canadian residents will be charged applicable taxes. Offer not valid in Quebec. This offer is limited to one order per household. All orders subject to credit approval. Credit or debit balances in a customer's account(s) may be offset by any other outstanding balance owed by or to the customer. Please allow 4 to 6 weeks for delivery. Offer available while quantities last.

Harlequin® Blaze™ brings you
New York Times *and* USA TODAY *bestselling author*
Vicki Lewis Thompson with three new steamy titles
from the bestselling miniseries SONS OF CHANCE

Chance isn't just the last name of these rugged
Wyoming cowboys—it's their motto, too!

Read on for a sneak peek at the first title,
SHOULD'VE BEEN A COWBOY

Available June 2011 only from Harlequin® Blaze™.

"THANKS FOR NOT TURNING ON THE LIGHTS," Tyler said. "I'm a mess."

"Not in my book." Even in low light, Alex had a good view of her yellow shirt plastered to her body. It was all he could do not to reach for her, mud and all. But the next move needed to be hers, not his.

She slicked her wet hair back and squeezed some water out of the ends as she glanced upward. "I like the sound of the rain on a tin roof."

"Me, too."

She met his gaze briefly and looked away. "Where's the sink?"

"At the far end, beyond the last stall."

Tyler's running shoes squished as she walked down the aisle between the rows of stalls. She glanced sideways at Alex. "So how much of a cowboy are you these days? Do you ride the range and stuff?"

"I ride." He liked being able to say that. "Why?"

"Just wondered. Last summer, you were still a city boy. You even told me you weren't the cowboy type, but you're…different now."

HBEXP0611

He wasn't sure if that was a good thing or a bad thing. Maybe she preferred city boys to cowboys. "How am I different?"

"Well, you dress differently, and your hair's a little longer. Your face seems a little more chiseled, but maybe that's because of your hair. Also, there's something else, something harder to define, an attitude…"

"Are you saying I have an attitude?"

"Not in a bad way. It's more like a quiet confidence."

He was flattered, but still he had to laugh. "I just admitted a while ago that I have all kinds of doubts about this event tomorrow. That doesn't seem like quiet confidence to me."

"This isn't about your job, it's about…your…" She took a deep breath. "It's about your sex appeal, okay? I have no business talking about it, because it will only make me want to do things I shouldn't do." She started toward the end of the barn. "Now, where's that sink? We need to get cleaned up and go back to the house. Dinner is probably ready, and I—"

He spun her around and pulled her into his arms, mud and all. "Let's do those things." Then he kissed her, knowing that she would kiss him back, knowing that this time he would take that kiss where he wanted it to go. And she would let him.

Follow Tyler and Alex's wild adventures in
SHOULD'VE BEEN A COWBOY
Available June 2011 only from Harlequin® Blaze™
wherever books are sold.

Harlequin Presents®

brings you

USA TODAY *bestselling author*

Lucy Monroe

*with her new installment
in the much-loved miniseries*

Royal Brides

Proud, passionate rulers—
marriage is by royal decree!

Meet Zahir and Asad—two powerful, brooding sheikhs
and masters of all they survey. They need brides,
and marriage in their kingdoms is by royal decree!

Capture a slice of royal life in this enthralling sheikh saga!

Coming in June 2011:

FOR DUTY'S SAKE

**Available wherever
Harlequin Presents® books are sold.**

www.eHarlequin.com